DOVER · THRIFT · EDITIONS

Great Short Stories by American Women

EDITED BY
CANDACE WARD

DOVER PUBLICATIONS, INC.
New York

Bibliographical Notes

This Dover edition is a new anthology of works reprinted from standard sources. "The Storm," by Kate Chopin, is reprinted by permission of Louisiana State University Press, from *The Complete Works of Kate Chopin*, edited by Per Seyersted, copyright © 1969 by Louisiana State University Press. A new introductory Note and introductions to the stories have been specially prepared for this edition.

Library of Congress Cataloging-in-Publication Data

Great short stories by American women / edited by Candace Ward. — Dover thrift ed.
    p.   cm.
  ISBN-13: 978-0-486-28776-8 (pbk.)
  ISBN-10: 0-486-28776-9 (pbk.)
  1. Short stories, American—Women authors. 2. Women—United States—Social life and customs—Fiction. I. Ward, Candace.
PS647.W6G74 1996
813'.01089287—dc20
                                        95-47923
                                          CIP

Manufactured in the United States by Courier Corporation
28776910
www.doverpublications.com

Note

TOWARD THE MID-NINETEENTH CENTURY, a new phenomenon appeared before the American public: the professional woman writer. The increasing numbers of female authors coincided with the establishment of publishing as big business and, as publishers quickly found, women's writings — particularly sentimental fiction — sold.

The women writers in this volume, particularly those of the nineteenth century, worked both in and against this sentimental tradition. As Ann Douglas notes in *The Feminization of American Culture*, sentimental literature gave women writers a voice even as it perpetuated stereotypes and locked them (and their characters and readers) into the passive postures associated with the feminine. Thus, while Rebecca Harding Davis' "Life in the Iron-Mills" helped establish American realism, some critics dismissed it as yet another piece of sentimental melodrama; Louisa May Alcott wrote autobiographical fiction that addressed issues such as abolition and women's suffrage yet was heralded as America's foremost children's author.

The local color movement of the late nineteenth and early twentieth centuries played a paradoxical role in the reception of works by other women writers, including Sarah Orne Jewett, Kate Chopin, Mary E. Wilkins Freeman, Willa Cather, Susan Glaspell and Alice Dunbar-Nelson. While an ability to realistically depict scenes from various regional settings earned them critical praise, it also contributed to a limited perception of their work. For these writers, physical detail, dialect and local mannerisms were part of a realism that allowed them to explore the deeper themes of isolation, alienation, female sexuality and racism.

In the twentieth century, the Harlem Renaissance and the modernist movement enabled women writers to address such issues more directly. Building on the foundation of their literary foremothers, Willa Cather, Edith Wharton, Susan Glaspell, Djuna Barnes, Zora Neale Hurston and

Nella Larsen gave fiction new directions. Glaspell and Barnes, particularly, availed themselves of the avant-garde possibilities of fiction that would culminate for Glaspell on the stage of the Provincetown Playhouse and for Barnes in her experimental novel *Nightwood* (1936). Hurston and Larsen drew from and incorporated the traditions of black America in their fiction, raising provocative questions about the individual's responsibilities within and beyond her immediate community.

Since the 1970s, the study of women's fiction has undergone a revolution. Many of the authors represented in this anthology have been rescued from obscurity by writers and critics looking beyond traditional assessments that seemed to echo Hawthorne's dismissal of the "damned mob of scribbling women."

Contents

Rebecca Harding Davis

(1831–1910)

REBECCA HARDING DAVIS was one of five children born to middle-class parents. Five years after her birth in Washington County, Pennsylvania, her family moved to Wheeling (at that time in Virginia). Davis received her early education at home from her mother and became an avid reader like her father. At 14, she was sent to the Washington Female Seminary in Pennsylvania and after graduating with honors in 1848, she returned to Wheeling.

In 1860, the year before the outbreak of the Civil War, Davis submitted a short story about life in an industrial mill town to the *Atlantic Monthly*. While the rest of the country was caught up in questions about slavery and states' rights, Davis had been investigating the conditions and lives of the mill hands — concerns that were as compelling to Davis as those involved in the Civil War. Davis' story caught the interest of James Fielding, then editor of the *Atlantic Monthly*. After anonymous publication in April 1861, it received accolades from Nathaniel Hawthorne, Emily Dickinson, Louisa May Alcott and Ralph Waldo Emerson. Despite these champions and a prolific writing career, Davis' early fame did not last. Her first story had been long forgotten by the time of her death in 1910, and during the later years of her life she was better known as the mother of writer Richard Harding Davis. It was not until 1972, when Tillie Olsen rediscovered "Life in the Iron-Mills," that Davis' literary reputation was revived.

Anticipating Émile Zola's coal-mining novel *Germinal* by 25 years, Davis' stark realism contrasted with the sentimentalism that characterized much fiction of the period. Though later critics complained that Davis' story relied on the kind of melodrama typical of reformist tract writings, "Life in the Iron-Mills" is a landmark of American fiction. As Olsen notes, Davis "extended the realm of fiction" by her effort to render life in the iron mills a "real thing" to her readers.

Life in the Iron-Mills

"Is this the end?
O Life, as futile, then, as frail!
What hope of answer or redress?"[1]

A CLOUDY DAY: do you know what that is in a town of iron-works? The sky sank down before dawn, muddy, flat, immovable. The air is thick, clammy with the breath of crowded human beings. It stifles me. I open the window, and, looking out, can scarcely see through the rain the grocer's shop opposite, where a crowd of drunken Irishmen are puffing Lynchburg tobacco in their pipes. I can detect the scent through all the foul smells ranging loose in the air.

The idiosyncrasy of this town is smoke. It rolls sullenly in slow folds from the great chimneys of the iron-founderies, and settles down in black, slimy pools on the muddy streets. Smoke on the wharves, smoke on the dingy boats, on the yellow river, — clinging in a coating of greasy soot to the house-front, the two faded poplars, the faces of the passers-by. The long train of mules, dragging masses of pig-iron through the narrow street, have a foul vapor hanging to their reeking sides. Here, inside, is a little broken figure of an angel pointing upward from the mantel-shelf; but even its wings are covered with smoke, clotted and black. Smoke everywhere! A dirty canary chirps desolately in a cage beside me. Its dream of green fields and sunshine is a very old dream, — almost worn out, I think.

From the back-window I can see a narrow brick-yard sloping down to the river-side, strewed with rain-butts and tubs. The river, dull and tawny-colored, (*la belle rivière!*) drags itself sluggishly along, tired of the heavy weight of boats and coal-barges. What wonder? When I was a child, I used to fancy a look of weary, dumb appeal upon the face of the

---

1. "*Is . . . redress?*"] loosely based on lines from Tennyson's "In Memoriam."

negro-like river slavishly bearing its burden day after day. Something of the same idle notion comes to me to-day, when from the street-window I look on the slow stream of human life creeping past, night and morning, to the great mills. Masses of men, with dull, besotted faces bent to the ground, sharpened here and there by pain or cunning; skin and muscle and flesh begrimed with smoke and ashes; stooping all night over boiling caldrons of metal, laired by day in dens of drunkenness and infamy; breathing from infancy to death an air saturated with fog and grease and soot, vileness for soul and body. What do you make of a case like that, amateur psychologist? You call it an altogether serious thing to be alive: to these men it is a drunken jest, a joke, — horrible to angels perhaps, to them commonplace enough. My fancy about the river was an idle one: it is no type of such a life. What if it be stagnant and slimy here? It knows that beyond there waits for it odorous sunlight, — quaint old gardens, dusky with soft, green foliage of apple-trees, and flushing crimson with roses, — air, and fields, and mountains. The future of the Welsh puddler passing just now is not so pleasant. To be stowed away, after his grimy work is done, in a hole in the muddy graveyard, and after that, — *not* air, nor green fields, nor curious roses.

Can you see how foggy the day is? As I stand here, idly tapping the window-pane, and looking out through the rain at the dirty back-yard and the coal-boats below, fragments of an old story float up before me, — a story of this house into which I happened to come to-day. You may think it a tiresome story enough, as foggy as the day, sharpened by no sudden flashes of pain or pleasure. I know: only the outline of a dull life, that long since, with thousands of dull lives like its own, was vainly lived and lost: thousands of them, — massed, vile, slimy lives, like those of the torpid lizards in yonder stagnant water-butt. — Lost? There is a curious point for you to settle, my friend, who study psychology in a lazy, *dilettante* way. Stop a moment. I am going to be honest. This is what I want you to do. I want you to hide your disgust, take no heed to your clean clothes, and come right down with me, — here, into the thickest of the fog and mud and foul effluvia. I want you to hear this story. There is a secret down here, in this nightmare fog, that has lain dumb for centuries: I want to make it a real thing to you. You, Egoist, or Pantheist, or Arminian, busy in making straight paths for your feet on the hills, do not see it clearly, — this terrible question which men here have gone mad and died trying to answer. I dare not put this secret into words. I told you it was dumb. These men, going by with drunken faces, and brains full of unawakened power, do not ask it of Society or of God. Their lives ask it;

their deaths ask it. There is no reply. I will tell you plainly that I have a great hope; and I bring it to you to be tested. It is this: that this terrible dumb question is its own reply; that it is not the sentence of death we think it, but, from the very extremity of its darkness, the most solemn prophecy which the world has known of the Hope to come. I dare make my meaning no clearer, but will only tell my story. It will, perhaps, seem to you as foul and dark as this thick vapor about us, and as pregnant with death; but if your eyes are free as mine are to look deeper, no perfume-tinted dawn will be so fair with promise of the day that shall surely come.

My story is very simple, — only what I remember of the life of one of these men, — a furnace-tender in one of Kirby & John's rolling-mills, — Hugh Wolfe. You know the mills? They took the great order for the lower Virginia railroads there last winter; run usually with about a thousand men. I cannot tell why I choose the half-forgotten story of this Wolfe more than that of myriads of these furnace-hands. Perhaps because there is a secret, underlying sympathy between that story and this day with its impure fog and thwarted sunshine, — or perhaps simply for the reason that this house is the one where the Wolfes lived. There were the father and son, — both hands, as I said, in one of Kirby & John's mills for making railroad-iron, — and Deborah, their cousin, a picker in some of the cotton-mills. The house was rented then to half a dozen families. The Wolfes had two of the cellar-rooms. The old man, like many of the puddlers and feeders of the mills, was Welsh, — had spent half of his life in the Cornish tin-mines. You may pick the Welsh emigrants, Cornish miners, out of the throng passing the windows, any day. They are a trifle more filthy; their muscles are not so brawny; they stoop more. When they are drunk, they neither yell, nor shout, nor stagger, but skulk along like beaten hounds. A pure, unmixed blood, I fancy, shows itself in the slight angular bodies and sharply-cut facial lines. It is nearly thirty years since the Wolfes lived here. Their lives were like those of their class: incessant labor, sleeping in kennel-like rooms, eating rank pork and molasses, drinking—God and the distillers only know what; with an occasional night in jail, to atone for some drunken excess. Is that all of their lives? — of the portion given to them and these their duplicates swarming the streets to-day? — nothing beneath? — all? So many a political reformer will tell you, — and many a private reformer, too, who has gone among them with a heart tender with Christ's charity, and come out outraged, hardened.

One rainy night, about eleven o'clock, a crowd of half-clothed women stopped outside of the cellar-door. They were going home from the cotton-mill.

"Good-night, Deb," said one, a mulatto, steadying herself against the gas-post. She needed the post to steady her. So did more than one of them.

"Dah's a ball to Miss Potts' to-night. Ye'd best come."

"Inteet, Deb, if hur'll come, hur'll hef fun," said a shrill Welsh voice in the crowd.

Two or three dirty hands were thrust out to catch the gown of the woman, who was groping for the latch of the door.

"No."

"No? Where's Kit Small, then?"

"Begorra! on the spools. Alleys behint, though we helped her, we dud. An wid ye! Let Deb alone! It's ondacent frettin' a quite body. Be the powers, an' we'll have a night of it! there'll be lashin's o' drink, — the Vargent be blessed and praised for 't!"

They went on, the mulatto inclining for a moment to show fight, and drag the woman Wolfe off with them; but, being pacified, she staggered away.

Deborah groped her way into the cellar, and, after considerable stumbling, kindled a match, and lighted a tallow dip, that sent a yellow glimmer over the room. It was low, damp, — the earthen floor covered with a green, slimy moss, — a fetid air smothering the breath. Old Wolfe lay asleep on a heap of straw, wrapped in a torn horse-blanket. He was a pale, meek little man, with a white face and red rabbit-eyes. The woman Deborah was like him; only her face was even more ghastly, her lips bluer, her eyes more watery. She wore a faded cotton gown and a slouching bonnet. When she walked, one could see that she was deformed, almost a hunchback. She trod softly, so as not to waken him, and went through into the room beyond. There she found by the half-extinguished fire an iron saucepan filled with cold boiled potatoes, which she put upon a broken chair with a pint-cup of ale. Placing the old candlestick beside this dainty repast, she untied her bonnet, which hung limp and wet over her face, and prepared to eat her supper. It was the first food that had touched her lips since morning. There was enough of it, however: there is not always. She was hungry, — one could see that easily enough, — and not drunk, as most of her companions would have been found at this hour. She did not drink, this woman, — her face told that too, — nothing stronger than ale. Perhaps the weak, flaccid wretch had some stimulant in her pale life to keep her up, — some love or hope, it might be, or urgent need. When that stimulant was gone, she would take to whiskey. Man cannot live by work alone. While she was skinning the potatoes, and munching them, a noise behind her made her stop.

"Janey!" she called, lifting the candle and peering into the darkness. "Janey, are you there?".

A heap of ragged coats was heaved up, and the face of a young girl emerged, staring sleepily at the woman.

"Deborah," she said, at last, "I'm here the night."

"Yes, child. Hur's welcome," she said, quietly eating on.

The girl's face was haggard and sickly; her eyes were heavy with sleep and hunger: real Milesian eyes they were, dark, delicate blue, glooming out from black shadows with a pitiful fright.

"I was alone," she said, timidly.

"Where's the father?" asked Deborah, holding out a potato, which the girl greedily seized.

"He's beyant, — wid Haley, — in the stone house" (Did you ever hear the word *jail* from an Irish mouth?) "I came here. Hugh told me never to stay me-lone."

"Hugh?"

"Yes."

A vexed frown crossed her face. The girl saw it, and added quickly, —

"I have not seen Hugh the day, Deb. The old man says his watch lasts till the mornin'."

The woman sprang up, and hastily began to arrange some bread and flitch in a tin pail, and to pour her own measure of ale into a bottle. Tying on her bonnet, she blew out the candle.

"Lay ye down, Janey dear," she said, gently, covering her with the old rags. "Hur can eat the potatoes, if hur's hungry."

"Where are ye goin', Deb? The rain's sharp."

"To the mill, with Hugh's supper."

"Let him bide till th' morn. Sit ye down."

"No, no," — sharply pushing her off. "The boy'll starve."

She hurried from the cellar, while the child wearily coiled herself up for sleep. The rain was falling heavily, as the woman, pail in hand, emerged from the mouth of the alley, and turned down the narrow street, that stretched out, long and black, miles before her. Here and there a flicker of gas lighted an uncertain space of muddy footwalk and gutter; the long rows of houses, except an occasional lager-bier shop, were closed; now and then she met a band of mill-hands skulking to or from their work.

Not many even of the inhabitants of a manufacturing town know the vast machinery of system by which the bodies of workmen are governed, that goes on unceasingly from year to year. The hands of each mill are divided into watches that relieve each other as regularly as the sentinels of an army. By night and day the work goes on, the unsleeping engines groan and shriek, the fiery pools of metal boil and surge. Only for a day in the week, in half-courtesy to public censure, the fires are partially veiled; but as soon as the clock strikes midnight, the great furnaces break forth with renewed fury, the clamor begins with fresh, breathless vigor, the engines sob and shriek like "gods in pain."

As Deborah hurried down through the heavy rain, the noise of these thousand engines sounded through the sleep and shadow of the city like far-off thunder. The mill to which she was going lay on the river, a mile below the city-limits. It was far, and she was weak, aching from standing twelve hours at the spools. Yet it was her almost nightly walk to take this man his supper, though at every square she sat down to rest, and she knew she should receive small word of thanks.

Perhaps, if she had possessed an artist's eye, the picturesque oddity of the scene might have made her step stagger less, and the path seem shorter; but to her the mills were only "summat deilish to look at by night."

The road leading to the mills had been quarried from the solid rock, which rose abrupt and bare on one side of the cinder-covered road, while the river, sluggish and black, crept past on the other. The mills for rolling iron are simply immense tent-like roofs, covering acres of ground, open on every side. Beneath these roofs Deborah looked in on a city of fires, that burned hot and fiercely in the night. Fire in every horrible form: pits of flame waving in the wind; liquid metal-flames writhing in tortuous streams through the sand; wide caldrons filled with boiling fire, over which bent ghastly wretches stirring the strange brewing; and through all, crowds of half-clad men, looking like revengeful ghosts in the red light, hurried, throwing masses of glittering fire. It was like a street in Hell. Even Deborah muttered, as she crept through, "'T looks like t' Devil's place!" It did, — in more ways than one.

She found the man she was looking for, at last, heaping coal on a furnace. He had not time to eat his supper; so she went behind the furnace, and waited. Only a few men were with him, and they noticed her only by a "Hyur comes t' hunchback, Wolfe."

Deborah was stupid with sleep; her back pained her sharply; and her teeth chattered with cold, with the rain that soaked her clothes and dripped from her at every step. She stood, however, patiently holding the pail, and waiting.

"Hout, woman! ye look like a drowned cat. Come near to the fire," — said one of the men, approaching to scrape away the ashes.

She shook her head. Wolfe had forgotten her. He turned, hearing the man, and came closer.

"I did no' think; g' me my supper, woman."

She watched him eat with a painful eagerness. With a woman's quick instinct, she saw that he was not hungry, — was eating to please her. Her pale, watery eyes began to gather a strange light.

"Is 't good, Hugh? T' ale was a bit sour, I feared."

"No, good enough." He hesitated a moment. "Ye're tired, poor lass! Bide here till I go. Lay down there on that heap of ash, and go to sleep."

He threw her an old coat for a pillow, and turned to his work. The heap was the refuse of the burnt iron, and was not a hard bed; the half-smothered warmth, too, penetrated her limbs, dulling their pain and cold shiver.

Miserable enough she looked, lying there on the ashes like a limp, dirty rag, — yet not an unfitting figure to crown the scene of hopeless discomfort and veiled crime: more fitting, if one looked deeper into the heart of things, — at her thwarted woman's form, her colorless life, her waking stupor that smothered pain and hunger, — even more fit to be a type of her class. Deeper yet if one could look; was there nothing worth reading in this wet, faded thing, half covered with ashes? no story of a soul filled with groping, passionate love, heroic unselfishness, fierce jealousy? of years of weary trying to please the one human being whom she loved, to gain one look of real heart-kindness from him? If anything like this were hidden beneath the pale, bleared eyes, and dull, washed-out-looking face, no one had ever taken the trouble to read its faint signs: not the half-clothed furnace-tender, Wolfe, certainly. Yet he was kind to her: it was his nature to be kind, even to the very rats that swarmed in the cellar: kind to her in just the same way. She knew that. And it might be that very knowledge had given to her face its apathy and vacancy more than her low, torpid life. One sees that dead, vacant look steal sometimes over the rarest, finest of women's faces, — in the very midst, it may be, of their warmest summer's day; and then one can guess at the secret of intolerable solitude that lies hid beneath the delicate laces and brilliant smile. There was no warmth, no brilliancy, no summer for this woman; so the stupor and vacancy had time to gnaw into her face perpetually. She was young, too, though no one guessed it; so the gnawing was the fiercer.

She lay quiet in the dark corner, listening, through the monotonous din and uncertain glare of the works, to the dull plash of the rain in the far distance, — shrinking back whenever the man Wolfe happened to look towards her. She knew, in spite of all his kindness, that there was that in her face and form which made him loathe the sight of her. She felt by instinct, although she could not comprehend it, the finer nature of the man, which made him among his fellow-workmen something unique, set apart. She knew, that, down under all the vileness and coarseness of his life, there was a groping passion for whatever was beautiful and pure, — that his soul sickened with disgust at her deformity, even when his words were kindest. Through this dull consciousness, which never left her, came, like a sting, the recollection of the dark blue eyes and lithe figure of the little Irish girl she had left in the cellar. The recollection struck through even her stupid intellect with a vivid glow of beauty and of grace. Little Janey, timid, helpless, clinging to Hugh as her only friend: that was the sharp thought, the bitter thought, that drove into the glazed eyes a fierce light of pain. You laugh at it? Are pain and jealousy less savage realities down here in this place I am taking you to than in your own house or your own heart, — your heart, which they clutch at sometimes? The note is the same, I fancy, be the octave high or low.

If you could go into this mill where Deborah lay, and drag out from the hearts of these men the terrible tragedy of their lives, taking it as a symptom of the disease of their class, no ghost Horror would terrify you more. A reality of soul-starvation, of living death, that meets you every day under the besotted faces on the street — I can paint nothing of this, only give you the outside outlines of a night, a crisis in the life of one man: whatever muddy depth of soul-history lies beneath you can read according to the eyes God has given you.

Wolfe, while Deborah watched him as a spaniel its master, bent over the furnace with his iron pole, unconscious of her scrutiny, only stopping to receive orders. Physically, Nature had promised the man but little. He had already lost the strength and instinct vigor of a man, his muscles were thin, his nerves weak, his face (a meek, woman's face) haggard, yellow with consumption. In the mill he was known as one of the girl-men: "Molly Wolfe" was his *sobriquet*. He was never seen in the cockpit, did not own a terrier, drank but seldom; when he did, desperately. He fought sometimes, but was always thrashed, pommelled to a jelly. The man was game enough, when his blood was up: but he was no favorite in the mill; he had the taint of school-learning on him, — not to a dangerous extent, only a quarter or so in the free-school in fact, but enough to ruin him as a good hand in a fight.

For other reasons, too, he was not popular. Not one of themselves, they felt that, though outwardly as filthy and ash-covered; silent, with foreign thoughts and longings breaking out through his quietness in innumerable curious ways: this one, for instance. In the neighboring furnace-buildings lay great heaps of the refuse from the ore after the pig-metal is run. *Korl* we call it here: a light, porous substance, of a delicate, waxen, flesh-colored tinge. Out of the blocks of this korl, Wolfe, in his off-hours from the furnace, had a habit of chipping and moulding figures, — hideous, fantastic enough, but sometimes strangely beautiful: even the mill-men saw that, while they jeered at him. It was a curious fancy in the man, almost a passion. The few hours for rest he spent hewing and hacking with his blunt knife, never speaking, until his watch came again, — working at one figure for months, and, when it was finished, breaking it to pieces perhaps, in a fit of disappointment. A morbid, gloomy man, untaught, unled, left to feed his soul in grossness and crime, and hard, grinding labor.

I want you to come down and look at this Wolfe, standing there among the lowest of his kind, and see him just as he is, that you may judge him justly when you hear the story of this night. I want you to look back, as he does every day, at his birth in vice, his starved infancy; to remember the heavy years he has groped through as boy and man, — the slow, heavy years of constant, hot work. So long ago he began, that he thinks some-times he has worked there for ages. There is no hope that it will ever end. Think that God put into this man's soul a fierce thirst for beauty, — to know it, to create it; to *be* — something, he knows not what, — other than he is. There are moments when a passing cloud, the sun glinting on the purple thistles, a kindly smile, a child's face, will rouse him to a passion of pain, — when his nature starts up with a mad cry of rage against God, man, whoever it is that has forced this vile, slimy life upon him. With all this groping, this mad desire, a great blind intellect stumbling through wrong, a loving poet's heart, the man was by habit only a coarse, vulgar laborer, familiar with sights and words you would blush to name. Be just: when I tell you about this night, see him as he is. Be just, — not like man's law, which seizes on one isolated fact, but like God's judging angel, whose clear, sad eye saw all the countless cankering days of this man's life, all the countless nights, when, sick with starving, his soul fainted in him, before it judged him for this night, the saddest of all.

I called this night the crisis of his life. If it was, it stole on him unawares. These great turning-days of life cast no shadow before, slip by unconsciously. Only a trifle, a little turn of the rudder, and the ship goes to heaven or hell.

Wolfe, while Deborah watched him, dug into the furnace of melting iron with his pole, dully thinking only how many rails the lump would yield. It was late, — nearly Sunday morning; another hour, and the heavy work would be done, — only the furnaces to replenish and cover for the next day. The workmen were growing more noisy, shouting, as they had to do, to be heard over the deep clamor of the mills. Suddenly they grew less boisterous, — at the far end, entirely silent. Something unusual had happened. After a moment, the silence came nearer; the men stopped their jeers and drunken choruses. Deborah, stupidly lifting up her head, saw the cause of the quiet. A group of five or six men were slowly approaching, stopping to examine each furnace as they came. Visitors often came to see the mills after night: except by growing less noisy, the men took no notice of them. The furnace where Wolfe worked was near the bounds of the works; they halted there hot and tired: a walk over one of these great founderies is no trifling task. The woman, drawing out of sight, turned over to sleep. Wolfe, seeing them stop, suddenly roused from his indifferent stupor, and watched them keenly. He knew some of them: the overseer, Clarke, — a son of Kirby, one of the mill-owners, — and a Doctor May, one of the town-physicians. The other two were strangers. Wolfe came closer. He seized eagerly every chance that brought him into contact with this mysterious class that shone down on him perpetually with the glamour of another order of being. What made the difference between them? That was the mystery of his life. He had a vague notion that perhaps to-night he could find it out. One of the strangers sat down on a pile of bricks, and beckoned young Kirby to his side.

"This *is* hot, with a vengeance. A match, please?" — lighting his cigar. "But the walk is worth the trouble. If it were not that you must have heard it so often, Kirby, I would tell you that your works look like Dante's Inferno."

Kirby laughed.

"Yes. Yonder is Farinata himself in the burning tomb," — pointing to some figure in the shimmering shadows.

"Judging from some of the faces of your men," said the other, "they bid fair to try the reality of Dante's vision, some day."

Young Kirby looked curiously around, as if seeing the faces of his hands for the first time.

"They're bad enough, that's true. A desperate set, I fancy. Eh, Clarke?"

The overseer did not hear him. He was talking of net profits just then, — giving, in fact, a schedule of the annual business of the firm to a sharp peering little Yankee, who jotted down notes on a paper laid on the crown of his hat: a reporter for one of the city papers, getting up a series of reviews of the leading manufactories. The other gentlemen had accompanied them merely for amusement. They were silent until the notes were finished, drying their feet at the furnaces, and sheltering their faces from the intolerable heat. At last the overseer concluded with —

"I believe that is a pretty fair estimate, Captain."

"Here, some of you men!" said Kirby, "bring up those boards. We may as well sit down, gentlemen, until the rain is over. It cannot last much longer at this rate."

"Pig-metal," — mumbled the reporter, — "um! — coal facilities, — um! — hands employed, twelve hundred, — bitumen, — um! — all right, I believe, Mr. Clarke; — sinking-fund, — what did you say was your sinking-fund?"

"Twelve hundred hands?" said the stranger, the young man who had first spoken. "Do you control their votes, Kirby?"

"Control? No." The young man smiled complacently. "But my father brought seven hundred votes to the polls for his candidate last November. No force-work, you understand, — only a speech or two, a hint to form themselves into a society, and a bit of red and blue bunting to make them a flag. The Invincible Roughs, — I believe that is their name. I forget the motto: 'Our country's hope,' I think."

There was a laugh. The young man talking to Kirby sat with an amused light in his cool gray eye, surveying critically the half-clothed figures of the puddlers, and the slow swing of their brawny muscles. He was a stranger in the city, — spending a couple of months in the borders of a Slave State, to study the institutions of the South, — a brother-in-law of Kirby's, — Mitchell. He was an amateur gymnast, — hence his anatomical eye; a patron, in a *blasé* way, of the prize-ring; a man who sucked the essence out of a science or philosophy in an indifferent, gentlemanly way; who took Kant, Novalis, Humboldt, for what they were worth in his own scales; accepting all, despising nothing, in heaven, earth, or hell, but one-idea'd men; with a temper yielding and brilliant as summer water, until his Self was touched, when it was ice, though brilliant still. Such men are not rare in the States.

As he knocked the ashes from his cigar, Wolfe caught with a quick pleasure the contour of the white hand, the blood-glow of a red ring he wore. His voice, too, and that of Kirby's, touched him like music, — low, even, with chording cadences. About this man Mitchell hung the impalpable atmosphere belonging to the thoroughbred gentleman. Wolfe, scraping away the ashes beside him, was conscious of it, did obeisance to it with his artist sense, unconscious that he did so.

The rain did not cease. Clarke and the reporter left the mills; the others, comfortably seated near the furnace, lingered, smoking and talking in a desultory way. Greek would not have been more unintelligible to the furnace-tenders, whose presence they soon forgot entirely. Kirby drew out a newspaper from his pocket and read aloud some ·article, which they discussed eagerly. At every sentence, Wolfe listened more and more like a dumb, hopeless animal, with a duller, more stolid look creeping over his face, glancing now and then at Mitchell, marking acutely every smallest sign of refinement, then back to himself, seeing as in a mirror his filthy body, his more stained soul.

Never! He had no words for such a thought, but he knew now, in all the sharpness of the bitter certainty, that between them there was a great gulf never to be passed. Never!

The bell of the mills rang for midnight. Sunday morning had dawned. Whatever hidden message lay in the tolling bells floated past these men unknown. Yet it was there. Veiled in the solemn music ushering the risen Saviour was a key-note to solve the darkest secrets of a world gone wrong, — even this social riddle which the brain of the grimy puddler grappled with madly to-night.

The men began to withdraw the metal from the caldrons. The mills were deserted on Sundays, except by the hands who fed the fires, and those who had no lodgings and slept usually on the ash-heaps. The three strangers sat still during the next hour, watching the men cover the furnaces, laughing now and then at some jest of Kirby's.

"Do you know," said Mitchell, "I like this view of the works better than when the glare was fiercest? These heavy shadows and the amphitheatre of smothered fires are ghostly, unreal. One could fancy these red smouldering lights to be the half-shut eyes of wild beasts, and the spectral figures their victims in the den."

Kirby laughed. "You are fanciful. Come, let us get out of the den. The spectral figures, as you call them, are a little too real for me to fancy a close proximity in the darkness, — unarmed, too."

The others rose, buttoning their overcoats, and lighting cigars.

"Raining still," said Doctor May, "and hard. Where did we leave the coach, Mitchell?"

"At the other side of the works. — Kirby, what's that?"

Mitchell started back, half-frightened, as, suddenly turning a corner, the white figure of a woman faced him in the darkness, — a woman, white, of giant proportions, crouching on the ground, her arms flung out in some wild gesture of warning.

"Stop! Make that fire burn there!" cried Kirby, stopping short.

The flame burst out, flashing the gaunt figure into bold relief.

Mitchell drew a long breath.

"I thought it was alive," he said, going up curiously.

The others followed.

"Not marble, eh?" asked Kirby, touching it.

One of the lower overseers stopped.

"Korl, Sir."

"Who did it?"

"Can't say. Some of the hands; chipped it out in off-hours."

"Chipped to some purpose, I should say. What a flesh-tint the stuff has! Do you see, Mitchell?"

"I see."

He had stepped aside where the light fell boldest on the figure, looking at it in silence. There was not one line of beauty or grace in it: a nude woman's form, muscular, grown coarse with labor, the powerful limbs instinct with some one poignant longing. One idea: there it was in the tense, rigid muscles, the clutching hands, the wild, eager face, like that of a starving wolf's. Kirby and Doctor May walked around it, critical, curious. Mitchell stood aloof, silent. The figure touched him strangely.

"Not badly done," said Doctor May. "Where did the fellow learn that sweep of the muscles in the arm and hand? Look at them! They are groping, — do you see? — clutching: the peculiar action of a man dying of thirst."

"They have ample facilities for studying anatomy," sneered Kirby, glancing at the half-naked figures.

"Look," continued the Doctor, "at this bony wrist, and the strained sinews of the instep! A working-woman, — the very type of her class."

"God forbid!" muttered Mitchell.

"Why?" demanded May. "What does the fellow intend by the figure? I cannot catch the meaning."

"Ask him," said the other, dryly. "There he stands," — pointing to Wolfe, who stood with a group of men, leaning on his ash-rake.

The Doctor beckoned him with the affable smile which kind-hearted men put on, when talking to these people.

"Mr. Mitchell has picked you out as the man who did this, — I'm sure I don't know why. But what did you mean by it?"

"She be hungry."

Wolfe's eyes answered Mitchell, not the Doctor.

"Oh-h! But what a mistake you have made, my fine fellow! You have given no sign of starvation to the body. It is strong, — terribly strong. It has the mad, half-despairing gesture of drowning."

Wolfe stammered, glanced appealingly at Mitchell, who saw the soul of the thing, he knew. But the cool, probing eyes were turned on himself now, — mocking, cruel, relentless.

"Not hungry for meat," the furnace-tender said at last.

"What then? Whiskey?" jeered Kirby, with a coarse laugh.

Wolfe was silent a moment, thinking.

"I dunno," he said, with a bewildered look. "It mebbe. Summat to make her live, I think, — like you. Whiskey ull do it, in a way."

The young man laughed again. Mitchell flashed a look of disgust somewhere, — not at Wolfe.

"May," he broke out impatiently, "are you blind? Look at that woman's face! It asks questions of God, and says, 'I have a right to know.' Good God, how hungry it is!"

They looked a moment; then May turned to the mill-owner: —

"Have you many such hands as this? What are you going to do with them? Keep them at puddling iron?"

Kirby shrugged his shoulders. Mitchell's look had irritated him.

"*Ce n'est pas mon affaire.*[2] I have no fancy for nursing infant geniuses. I suppose there are some stray gleams of mind and soul among these wretches. The Lord will take care of his own; or else they can work out their own salvation. I have heard you call our American system a ladder which any man can scale. Do you doubt it? Or perhaps you want to banish all social ladders, and put us all on a flat table-land, — eh, May?"

The Doctor looked vexed, puzzled. Some terrible problem lay hid in this woman's face, and troubled these men. Kirby waited for an answer, and, receiving none, went on, warming with his subject.

"I tell you, there's something wrong that no talk of '*Liberté*' or '*Egalité*' will do away. If I had the making of men, these men who do the lowest

---

2. "*Ce . . . affaire.*"] "It's not my business."

part of the world's work should be machines, — nothing more, — hands.
It would be kindness. God help them! What are taste, reason, to crea-
tures who must live such lives as that?" He pointed to Deborah, sleeping
on the ash-heap. "So many nerves to sting them to pain. What if God
had put your brain, with all its agony of touch, into your fingers, and bid
you work and strike with that?"

"You think you could govern the world better?" laughed the Doctor.

"I do not think at all."

"That is true philosophy. Drift with the stream, because you cannot
dive deep enough to find bottom, eh?"

"Exactly," rejoined Kirby. "I do not think. I wash my hands of all social
problems, — slavery, caste, white or black. My duty to my operatives has
a narrow limit, — the pay-hour on Saturday night. Outside of that, if they
cut korl, or cut each other's throats, (the more popular amusement of
the two,) I am not responsible."

The Doctor sighed, — a good honest sigh, from the depths of his
stomach.

"God help us! Who is responsible?"

"Not I, I tell you," said Kirby, testily. "What has the man who pays
them money to do with their souls' concerns, more than the grocer or
butcher who takes it?"

"And yet," said Mitchell's cynical voice, "look at her! How hungry
she is!"

Kirby tapped his boot with his cane. No one spoke. Only the dumb
face of the rough image looking into their faces with the awful question,
"What shall we do to be saved?" Only Wolfe's face, with its heavy weight
of brain, its weak, uncertain mouth, its desperate eyes, out of which
looked the soul of his class, — only Wolfe's face turned towards Kirby's.
Mitchell laughed, — a cool, musical laugh.

"Money has spoken!" he said, seating himself lightly on a stone with
the air of an amused spectator at a play. "Are you answered?" — turning
to Wolfe his clear, magnetic face.

Bright and deep and cold as Arctic air, the soul of the man lay tranquil
beneath. He looked at the furnace-tender as he had looked at a rare mo-
saic in the morning; only the man was the more amusing study of the two.

"Are you answered? Why, May, look at him! '*De profundis clamavi*.'[3]
Or, to quote in English, 'Hungry and thirsty, his soul faints in him.' And

---

3. '*De . . . clamavi*.'] 'I called from the depths' (opening of Psalm 130).

so Money sends back its answer into the depths through you, Kirby! Very clear the answer, too! — I think I remember reading the same words somewhere: — washing your hands in Eau de Cologne, and saying, 'I am innocent of the blood of this man. See ye to it!' "

Kirby flushed angrily.

"You quote Scripture freely."

"Do I not quote correctly? I think I remember another line, which may amend my meaning: 'Inasmuch as ye did it unto one of the least of these, ye did it unto me.' Deist? Bless you, man, I was raised on the milk of the Word. Now, Doctor, the pocket of the world having uttered its voice, what has the heart to say? You are a philanthropist, in a small way, — *n'est ce pas?* Here, boy, this gentleman can show you how to cut korl better, — or your destiny. Go on, May!"

"I think a mocking devil possesses you to-night," rejoined the Doctor, seriously.

He went to Wolfe and put his hand kindly on his arm. Something of a vague idea possessed the Doctor's brain that much good was to be done here by a friendly word or two: a latent genius to be warmed into life by a waited-for sunbeam. Here it was: he had brought it. So he went on complacently: —

"Do you know, boy, you have it in you to be a great sculptor, a great man? — do you understand?" (talking down to the capacity of his hearer: it is a way people have with children, and men like Wolfe,) — "to live a better, stronger life than I, or Mr. Kirby here? A man may make himself anything he chooses. God has given you stronger powers than many men, — me, for instance."

May stopped, heated, glowing with his own magnanimity. And it was magnanimous. The puddler had drunk in every word, looking through the Doctor's flurry, and generous heat, and self-approval, into his will, with those slow, absorbing eyes of his.

"Make yourself what you will. It is your right."

"I know," quietly. "Will you help me?"

Mitchell laughed again. The Doctor turned now, in a passion, —

"You know, Mitchell, I have not the means. You know, if I had, it is in my heart to take this boy and educate him for — "

"The glory of God, and the glory of John May."

May did not speak for a moment; then, controlled, he said, —

"Why should one be raised, when myriads are left? — I have not the money, boy," to Wolfe, shortly.

"Money?" He said it over slowly, as one repeats the guessed answer to a riddle, doubtfully. "That is it? Money?"

"Yes, money, — that is it," said Mitchell, rising, and drawing his furred coat about him. "You've found the cure for all the world's diseases. — Come, May, find your good-humor, and come home. This damp wind chills my very bones. Come and preach your Saint-Simonian doctrines to-morrow to Kirby's hands. Let them have a clear idea of the rights of the soul, and I'll venture next week they'll strike for higher wages. That will be the end of it."

"Will you send the coach-driver to this side of the mills?" asked Kirby, turning to Wolfe.

He spoke kindly: it was his habit to do so. Deborah, seeing the puddler go, crept after him. The three men waited outside. Doctor May walked up and down, chafed. Suddenly he stopped.

"Go back, Mitchell! You say the pocket and the heart of the world speak without meaning to these people. What has its head to say? Taste, culture, refinement? Go!"

Mitchell was leaning against a brick wall. He turned his head indolently, and looked into the mills. There hung about the place a thick, unclean odor. The slightest motion of his hand marked that he perceived it, and his insufferable disgust. That was all. May said nothing, only quickened his angry tramp.

"Besides," added Mitchell, giving a corollary to his answer, "it would be of no use. I am not one of them."

"You do not mean" — said May, facing him.

"Yes, I mean just that. Reform is born of need, not pity. No vital movement of the people's has worked down, for good or evil; fermented, instead, carried up the heaving, cloggy mass. Think back through history, and you will know it. What will this lowest deep — thieves, Magdalens, negroes — do with the light filtered through ponderous Church creeds, Baconian theories, Goethe schemes? Some day, out of their bitter need will be thrown up their own light-bringer, — their Jean Paul, their Cromwell, their Messiah."

"Bah!" was the Doctor's inward criticism. However, in practice, he adopted the theory; for, when, night and morning, afterwards, he prayed that power might be given these degraded souls to rise, he glowed at heart, recognizing an accomplished duty.

Wolfe and the woman had stood in the shadow of the works as the coach drove off. The Doctor had held out his hand in a frank, generous way, telling him to "take care of himself, and to remember it was his right to rise." Mitchell had simply touched his hat, as to an equal, with a quiet look of thorough recognition. Kirby had thrown Deborah some money, which she found, and clutched eagerly enough. They were gone now, all of them. The man sat down on the cinder-road, looking up into the murky sky.

"'T be late, Hugh. Wunnot hur come?"

He shook his head doggedly, and the woman crouched out of his sight against the wall. Do you remember rare moments when a sudden light flashed over yourself, your world, God? when you stood on a mountain-peak, seeing your life as it might have been, as it is? one quick instant, when custom lost its force and every-day usage? when your friend, wife, brother, stood in a new light? your soul was bared, and the grave, — a foretaste of the nakedness of the Judgment-Day? So it came before him, his life, that night. The slow tides of pain he had borne gathered themselves up and surged against his soul. His squalid daily life, the brutal coarseness eating into his brain, as the ashes into his skin: before, these things had been a dull aching into his consciousness; to-night, they were reality. He griped the filthy red shirt that clung, stiff with soot, about him, and tore it savagely from his arm. The flesh beneath was muddy with grease and ashes, — and the heart beneath that! And the soul? God knows.

Then flashed before his vivid poetic sense the man who had left him, — the pure face, the delicate, sinewy limbs, in harmony with all he knew of beauty or truth. In his cloudy fancy he had pictured a Something like this. He had found it in this Mitchell, even when he idly scoffed at his pain: a Man all-knowing, all-seeing, crowned by Nature, reigning, — the keen glance of his eye falling like a sceptre on other men. And yet his instinct taught him that he too — He! He looked at himself with sudden loathing, sick, wrung his hands with a cry, and then was silent. With all the phantoms of his heated, ignorant fancy, Wolfe had not been vague in his ambitions. They were practical, slowly built up before him out of his knowledge of what he could do. Through years he had day by day made this hope a real thing to himself, — a clear, projected figure of himself, as he might become.

Able to speak, to know what was best, to raise these men and women working at his side up with him: sometimes he forgot this defined hope in the frantic anguish to escape, — only to escape, — out of the wet, the pain, the ashes, somewhere, anywhere, — only for one moment of free air on a hill-side, to lie down and let his sick soul throb itself out in the sunshine. But to-night he panted for life. The savage strength of his nature was roused; his cry was fierce to God for justice.

"Look at me!" he said to Deborah, with a low, bitter laugh, striking his puny chest savagely. "What am I worth, Deb? Is it my fault that I am no better? My fault? My fault?"

He stopped, stung with a sudden remorse, seeing her hunchback shape writhing with sobs. For Deborah was crying thankless tears, according to the fashion of women.

"God forgi' me, woman! Things go harder wi' you nor me. It's a worse share."

He got up and helped her to rise; and they went doggedly down the muddy street, side by side.

"It's all wrong," he muttered, slowly, — "all wrong! I dunnot understan'. But it'll end some day."

"Come home, Hugh!" she said, coaxingly; for he had stopped, looking around bewildered.

"Home, — and back to the mill!" He went on saying this over to himself, as if he would mutter down every pain in this dull despair.

She followed him through the fog, her blue lips chattering with cold. They reached the cellar at last. Old Wolfe had been drinking since she went out, and had crept nearer the door. The girl Janey slept heavily in the corner. He went up to her, touching softly the worn white arm with his fingers. Some bitterer thought stung him, as he stood there. He wiped the drops from his forehead, and went into the room beyond, livid, trembling. A hope, trifling, perhaps, but very dear, had died just then out of the poor puddler's life, as he looked at the sleeping, innocent girl, — some plan for the future, in which she had borne a part. He gave it up that moment, then and forever. Only a trifle, perhaps, to us: his face grew a shade paler, — that was all. But, somehow, the man's soul, as God and the angels looked down on it, never was the same afterwards.

Deborah followed him into the inner room. She carried a candle, which she placed on the floor, closing the door after her. She had seen the look on his face, as he turned away; her own grew deadly. Yet, as she came up to him, her eyes glowed. He was seated on an old chest, quiet, holding his face in his hands.

"Hugh!" she said, softly.

He did not speak.

"Hugh, did hur hear what the man said, — him with the clear voice? Did hur hear? Money, money, — that it wud do all?"

He pushed her away, — gently, but he was worn out; her rasping tone fretted him.

"Hugh!"

The candle flared a pale yellow light over the cobwebbed brick walls, and the woman standing there. He looked at her. She was young, in deadly earnest; her faded eyes, and wet, ragged figure caught from their frantic eagerness a power akin to beauty.

"Hugh, it is true! Money ull do it! Oh, Hugh, boy, listen till me! He said it true! It is money!"

"I know. Go back! I do not want you here."

"Hugh, it is t' last time. I'll never worrit hur again."

There were tears in her voice now, but she choked them back.

"Hear till me only to-night! If one of t' witch people wud come, them we heard of t' home, and gif hur all hur wants, what then? Say, Hugh!"

"What do you mean?"

"I mean money."

Her whisper shrilled through his brain.

"If one of t' witch dwarfs wud come from t' lane moors to-night, and gif hur money, to go out, — *out*, I say, — out, lad, where t' sun shines, and t' heath grows, and t' ladies walk in silken gownds, and God stays all t' time, — where t' man lives that talked to us to-night, — Hugh knows, — Hugh could walk there like a king!"

He thought the woman mad, tried to check her, but she went on, fierce in her eager haste.

"If *I* were t' witch dwarf, if I had t' money, wud hur thank me? Wud hur take me out o' this place wid hur and Janey? I wud not come into the gran' house hur wud build, to vex hur wid t' hunch, — only at night, when t' shadows were dark, stand far off to see hur."

"Poor Deb! poor Deb!" he said, soothingly.

"It is here," she said, suddenly jerking into his hand a small roll. "I took it! I did it! I shall be hanged! I shall be burnt in hell, if anybody knows I took it! Me, me! not hur! Out of his pocket, as he leaned against t' bricks. Hur knows?"

She thrust it into his hand, and then, her errand done, began to gather chips together to make a fire, choking down hysteric sobs.

"Has it come to this?"

That was all he said. The Welsh Wolfe blood was honest. The roll was a small green pocket-book containing one or two gold pieces, and a check for an incredible amount, as it seemed to the poor puddler. He laid it down, hiding his face again in his hands.

"Hugh, don't be angry wud me! It's only poor Deb,—hur knows?"

He took the long skinny fingers kindly in his.

"Angry? God help me, no! Let me sleep. I am tired."

He threw himself heavily down on the wooden bench, stunned with pain and weariness. She brought some old rags to cover him.

It was late on Sunday evening before he awoke. I tell God's truth, when I say he had then no thought of keeping this money. Deborah had hid it in his pocket. He found it there. She watched him eagerly, as he took it out.

"I must gif it to him," he said, reading her face.

"Hur knows," she said with a bitter sigh of disappointment. "But it is hur right to keep it."

His right! The word struck him. Doctor May had used the same. He washed himself, and went out to find this man Mitchell. His right! Why did this chance word cling to him so obstinately? Do you hear the fierce devils whisper in his ear, as he went slowly down the darkening street?

The evening came on, slow and calm. He seated himself at the end of an alley leading into one of the larger streets. His brain was clear tonight, keen, intent, mastering. It would not start back, cowardly, from any hellish temptation, but meet it face to face. Therefore the great temptation of his life came to him veiled by no sophistry, but bold, defiant, owning its own vile name, trusting to one bold blow for victory.

He did not deceive himself. Theft! That was it. At first the word sickened him; then he grappled with it. Sitting there on a broken cartwheel, the fading day, the noisy groups, the church-bells' tolling passed before him like a panorama, while the sharp struggle went on within. This money! He took it out, and looked at it. If he gave it back, what then? He was going to be cool about it.

People going by to church saw only a sickly mill-boy watching them quietly at the alley's mouth. They did not know that he was mad, or they would not have gone by so quietly: mad with hunger; stretching out his hands to the world, that had given so much to them, for leave to live the life God meant him to live. His soul within him was smothering to death; he wanted so much, thought so much, and *knew*—nothing. There was nothing of which he was certain, except the mill and things there. Of God and heaven he had heard so little, that they were to him what fairy-land is to a child: something real, but not here; very far off. His brain, greedy, dwarfed, full of thwarted energy and unused powers, questioned these men and women going by, coldly, bitterly, that night. Was it not his right to live as they,—a pure life, a good, true-hearted life, full of beauty and kind words? He only wanted to know how to use the strength within him. His heart warmed, as he thought of it. He suffered himself to think of it longer. If he took the money?

Then he saw himself as he might be, strong, helpful, kindly. The night crept on, as this one image slowly evolved itself from the crowd of other thoughts and stood triumphant. He looked at it. As he might be! What wonder, if it blinded him to delirium, — the madness that underlies all revolution, all progress, and all fall?

You laugh at the shallow temptation? You see the error underlying its argument so clearly, — that to him a true life was one of full development rather than self-restraint? that he was deaf to the higher tone in a cry of voluntary suffering for truth's sake than in the fullest flow of spontaneous harmony? I do not plead his cause. I only want to show you the mote in my brother's eye: then you can see clearly to take it out.

The money, — there it lay on his knee, a little blotted slip of paper, nothing in itself; used to raise him out of the pit; something straight from God's hand. A thief! Well, what was it to be a thief? He met the question at last face to face, wiping the clammy drops of sweat from his forehead. God made this money — the fresh air, too — for his children's use. He never made the difference between poor and rich. The Something who looked down on him that moment through the cool gray sky had a kindly face, he knew, — loved his children alike. Oh, he knew that!

There were times when the soft floods of color in the crimson and purple flames, or the clear depth of amber in the water below the bridge, had somehow given him a glimpse of another world than this, — of an infinite depth of beauty and of quiet somewhere, — somewhere, — a depth of quiet and rest and love. Looking up now, it became strangely real. The sun had sunk quite below the hills, but his last rays struck upward, touching the zenith. The fog had risen, and the town and river were steeped in its thick, gray damp; but overhead, the sun-touched smoke-clouds opened like a cleft ocean, — shifting, rolling seas of crimson mist, waves of billowy silver veined with blood-scarlet, inner depths unfathomable of glancing light. Wolfe's artist-eye grew drunk with color. The gates of that other world! Fading, flashing before him now! What, in that world of Beauty, Content, and Right, were the petty laws, the mine and thine, of mill-owners and mill-hands?

A consciousness of power stirred within him. He stood up. A man, — he thought, stretching out his hands, — free to work, to live, to love! Free! His right! He folded the scrap of paper in his hand. As his nervous fingers took it in, limp and blotted, so his soul took in the mean

temptation, lapped it in fancied rights, in dreams of improved exis-
tences, drifting and endless as the cloud-seas of color. Clutching it, as if
the tightness of his hold would strengthen his sense of possession, he
went aimlessly down the street. It was his watch at the mill. He need not
go, need never go again, thank God! — shaking off the thought with
unspeakable loathing.

Shall I go over the history of the hours of that night? how the man
wandered from one to another of his old haunts, with a half-
consciousness of bidding them farewell, — lanes and alleys and back-
yards where the mill-hands lodged, — noting, with a new eagerness, the
filth and drunkenness, the pig-pens, the ash-heaps covered with potato-
skins, the bloated, pimpled women at the doors, — with a new disgust,
a new sense of sudden triumph, and, under all, a new, vague dread,
unknown before, smothered down, kept under, but still there? It left
him but once during the night, when, for the second time in his life,
he entered a church. It was a sombre Gothic pile, where the stained
light lost itself in far-retreating arches; built to meet the requirements
and sympathies of a far other class than Wolfe's. Yet it touched, moved
him uncontrollably. The distances, the shadows, the still, marble figures, the mass of silent, kneeling worshippers, the mysterious music,
thrilled, lifted his soul with a wonderful pain. Wolfe forgot himself,
forgot the new life he was going to live, the mean terror gnawing
underneath. The voice of the speaker strengthened the charm; it was
clear, feeling, full, strong. An old man, who had lived much, suffered
much; whose brain was keenly alive, dominant; whose heart was
summer-warm with charity. He taught it to-night. He held up Human-
ity in its grand total; showed the great world-cancer to his people. Who
could show it better? He was a Christian reformer; he had studied the
age thoroughly; his outlook at man had been free, world-wide, over all
time. His faith stood sublime upon the Rock of Ages; his fiery zeal
guided vast schemes by which the Gospel was to be preached to all
nations. How did he preach it to-night? In burning, light-laden words
he painted Jesus, the incarnate Life, Love, the universal Man: words
that became reality in the lives of these people, — that lived again in
beautiful words and actions, trifling, but heroic. Sin, as he defined it,
was a real foe to them; their trials, temptations, were his. His words
passed far over the furnace-tender's grasp, toned to suit another class of
culture; they sounded in his ears a very pleasant song in an unknown
tongue. He meant to cure this world-cancer with a steady eye that had
never glared with hunger, and a hand that neither poverty nor

strychnine-whiskey had taught to shake. In this morbid, distorted heart of the Welsh puddler he had failed.

Eighteen centuries ago, the Master of this man tried reform in the streets of a city as crowded and vile as this, and did not fail. His disciple, showing Him to-night to cultured hearers, showing the clearness of the God-power acting through Him, shrank back from one coarse fact; that in birth and habit the man Christ was thrown up from the lowest of the people: his flesh, their flesh; their blood, his blood; tempted like them, to brutalize day by day; to lie, to steal: the actual slime and want of their hourly life, and the wine-press he trod alone.

Yet, is there no meaning in this perpetually covered truth? If the son of the carpenter had stood in the church that night, as he stood with the fishermen and harlots by the sea of Galilee, before His Father and their Father, despised and rejected of men, without a place to lay His head, wounded for their iniquities, bruised for their transgressions, would not that hungry mill-boy at least, in the back seat, have "known the man"? That Jesus did not stand there.

Wolfe rose at last, and turned from the church down the street. He looked up; the night had come on foggy, damp; the golden mists had vanished, and the sky lay dull and ash-colored. He wandered again aimlessly down the street, idly wondering what had become of the cloud-sea of crimson and scarlet. The trial-day of this man's life was over, and he had lost the victory. What followed was mere drifting circumstance, — a quicker walking over the path, — that was all. Do you want to hear the end of it? You wish me to make a tragic story out of it? Why, in the police-reports of the morning paper you can find a dozen such tragedies; hints of shipwrecks unlike any that ever befell on the high seas; hints that here a power was lost to heaven, — that there a soul went down where no tide can ebb or flow. Commonplace enough the hints are, — jocose sometimes, done up in rhyme.

Doctor May, a month after the night I have told you of, was reading to his wife at breakfast from this fourth column of the morning-paper: an unusual thing, — these police-reports not being, in general, choice reading for ladies; but it was only one item he read.

"Oh, my dear! You remember that man I told you of, that we saw at Kirby's mill? — that was arrested for robbing Mitchell? Here he is; just listen: — 'Circuit Court. Judge Day. Hugh Wolfe, operative in Kirby & John's Loudon Mills. Charge, grand larceny. Sentence, nineteen years hard labor in penitentiary.' — Scoundrel! Serves him right! After all our kindness that night! Picking Mitchell's pocket at the very time!"

His wife said something about the ingratitude of that kind of people, and then they began to talk of something else.

Nineteen years! How easy that was to read! What a simple word for Judge Day to utter! Nineteen years! Half a lifetime!

Hugh Wolfe sat on the window-ledge of his cell, looking out. His ankles were ironed. Not usual in such cases; but he had made two desperate efforts to escape. "Well," as Haley, the jailer, said, "small blame to him! Nineteen years' imprisonment was not a pleasant thing to look forward to." Haley was very good-natured about it, though Wolfe had fought him savagely.

"When he was first caught," the jailer said afterwards, in telling the story, "before the trial, the fellow was cut down at once, — laid there on that pallet like a dead man, with his hands over his eyes. Never saw a man so cut down in my life. Time of the trial, too, came the queerest dodge of any customer I ever had. Would choose no lawyer. Judge gave him one, of course. Gibson it was. He tried to prove the fellow crazy; but it would n't go. Thing was plain as daylight: check found on him. 'T was a hard sentence, — all the law allows; but it was for 'xample's sake. These mill-hands are gettin' onbearable. When the sentence was read, he just looked up, and said the money was his by rights, and that all the world had gone wrong. That night, after the trial, a gentleman came to see him here, name of Mitchell, — him as he stole from. Talked to him for an hour. Thought he came for curiosity, like. After he was gone, thought Wolfe was remarkable quiet, and went into his cell. Found him very low; bed all bloody. Doctor said he had been bleeding at the lungs. He was as weak as a cat; yet, if ye'll b'lieve me, he tried to get a-past me and get out. I just carried him like a baby, and threw him on the pallet. Three days after, he tried it again: that time reached the wall. Lord help you! he fought like a tiger, — giv' some terrible blows. Fightin' for life, you see; for he can't live long, shut up in the stone crib down yonder. Got a death-cough now. 'T took two of us to bring him down that day; so I just put the irons on his feet. There he sits, in there. Goin' to-morrow, with a batch more of 'em. That woman, hunchback, tried with him, — you remember? — she's only got three years. 'Complice. But *she's* a woman, you know. He's been quiet ever since I put on irons: giv' up, I suppose. Looks white, sick-lookin'. It acts different on 'em, bein' sentenced. Most of 'em gets reckless, devilish-like. Some prays awful, and sings them vile songs of the mills, all in a breath. That woman, now, she's desper't'. Been beggin' to see Hugh, as she calls him, for three days. I'm a-goin' to let her in. She don't go with him. Here she is in this next cell. I'm a-goin' now to let her in."

He let her in. Wolfe did not see her. She crept into a corner of the cell, and stood watching him. He was scratching the iron bars of the window with a piece of tin which he had picked up, with an idle, uncertain, vacant stare, just as a child or idiot would do.

"Tryin' to get out, old boy?" laughed Haley. "Them irons will need a crowbar beside your tin, before you can open 'em."

Wolfe laughed, too, in a senseless way.

"I think I'll get out," he said.

"I believe his brain's touched," said Haley, when he came out.

The puddler scraped away with the tin for half an hour. Still Deborah did not speak. At last she ventured nearer, and touched his arm.

"Blood?" she said, looking at some spots on his coat with a shudder.

He looked up at her. "Why, Deb!" he said, smiling, — such a bright, boyish smile, that it went to poor Deborah's heart directly, and she sobbed and cried out loud.

"Oh, Hugh, lad! Hugh! dunnot look at me, when it wur my fault! To think I brought hur to it! And I loved hur so! Oh lad, I dud!"

The confession, even in this wretch, came with the woman's blush through the sharp cry.

He did not seem to hear her, — scraping away diligently at the bars with the bit of tin.

Was he going mad? She peered closely into his face. Something she saw there made her draw suddenly back, — something which Haley had not seen, that lay beneath the pinched, vacant look it had caught since the trial, or the curious gray shadow that rested on it. That gray shadow, — yes, she knew what that meant. She had often seen it creeping over women's faces for months, who died at last of slow hunger or consumption. That meant death, distant, lingering: but this — Whatever it was the woman saw, or thought she saw, used as she was to crime and misery, seemed to make her sick with a new horror. Forgetting her fear of him, she caught his shoulders, and looked keenly, steadily, into his eyes.

"Hugh!" she cried, in a desperate whisper, — "oh, boy, not that! for God's sake, not *that!*"

The vacant laugh went off his face, and he answered her in a muttered word or two that drove her away. Yet the words were kindly enough. Sitting there on his pallet, she cried silently a hopeless sort of tears, but did not speak again. The man looked up furtively at her now and then. Whatever his own trouble was, her distress vexed him with a momentary sting.

It was market-day. The narrow window of the jail looked down directly on the carts and wagons drawn up in a long line, where they had unloaded. He could see, too, and hear distinctly the clink of money as it changed hands, the busy crowd of whites and blacks shoving, pushing one another, and the chaffering and swearing at the stalls. Somehow, the sound, more than anything else had done, wakened him up, — made the whole real to him. He was done with the world and the business of it. He let the tin fall, and looked out, pressing his face close to the rusty bars. How they crowded and pushed! And he, — he should never walk that pavement again! There came Neff Sanders, one of the feeders at the mill, with a basket on his arm. Sure enough, Neff was married the other week. He whistled, hoping he would look up; but he did not. He wondered if Neff remembered he was there, — if any of the boys thought of him up there, and thought that he never was to go down that old cinder-road again. Never again! He had not quite understood it before; but now he did. Not for days or years, but never! — that was it.

How clear the light fell on that stall in front of the market! and how like a picture it was, the dark-green heaps of corn, and the crimson beets, and golden melons! There was another with game: how the light flickered on that pheasant's breast, with the purplish blood dripping over the brown feathers! He could see the red shining of the drops, it was so near. In one minute he could be down there. It was just a step. So easy, as it seemed, so natural to go! Yet it could never be — not in all the thousands of years to come — that he should put his foot on that street again! He thought of himself with a sorrowful pity, as of some one else. There was a dog down in the market, walking after his master with such a stately, grave look! — only a dog, yet he could go backwards and forwards just as he pleased: he had good luck! Why, the very vilest cur, yelping there in the gutter, had not lived his life, had been free to act out whatever thought God had put into his brain; while he — No, he would not think of that! He tried to put the thought away, and to listen to a dispute between a countryman and a woman about some meat; but it would come back. He, what had he done to bear this?

Then came the sudden picture of what might have been, and now. He knew what it was to be in the penitentiary, — how it went with men there. He knew how in these long years he should slowly die, but not until soul and body had become corrupt and rotten, — how, when he came out, if he lived to come, even the lowest of the mill-hands would jeer him, — how his hands would be weak, and his brain senseless and stupid. He believed he was almost that now. He put his hand to his head, with a puzzled, weary look. It ached, his head, with thinking. He tried to quiet himself. It was only right, perhaps; he had done wrong. But was there right or wrong for such as he? What was right? And who had ever taught him? He thrust the whole matter away. A dark, cold quiet crept through his brain. It was all wrong; but let it be! It was nothing to him more than the others. Let it be!

The door grated, as Haley opened it.

"Come, my woman! Must lock up for t' night. Come, stir yerself!"

She went up and took Hugh's hand.

"Good-night, Deb," he said, carelessly.

She had not hoped he would say more; but the tired pain on her mouth just then was bitterer than death. She took his passive hand and kissed it.

"Hur'll never see Deb again!" she ventured, her lips growing colder and more bloodless.

What did she say that for? Did he not know it? Yet he would not be impatient with poor old Deb. She had trouble of her own, as well as he.

"No, never again," he said, trying to be cheerful.

She stood just a moment, looking at him. Do you laugh at her, standing there, with her hunchback, her rags, her bleared, withered face, and the great despised love tugging at her heart?

"Come you!" called Haley, impatiently.

She did not move.

"Hugh!" she whispered.

It was to be her last word. What was it?

"Hugh, boy, not THAT!"

He did not answer. She wrung her hands, trying to be silent, looking in his face in an agony of entreaty. He smiled again, kindly.

"It is best, Deb. I cannot bear to be hurted any more."

"Hur knows," she said, humbly.

"Tell my father good-by; and — and kiss little Janey."

She nodded, saying nothing, looked in his face again, and went out of the door. As she went, she staggered.

"Drinkin' to-day?" broke out Haley, pushing her before him. "Where the Devil did you get it? Here, in with ye!" and he shoved her into her cell, next to Wolfe's, and shut the door.

Along the wall of her cell there was a crack low down by the floor, through which she could see the light from Wolfe's. She had discovered it days before. She hurried in now, and, kneeling down by it, listened, hoping to hear some sound. Nothing but the rasping of the tin on the bars. He was at his old amusement again. Something in the noise jarred on her ear, for she shivered as she heard it. Hugh rasped away at the bars. A dull old bit of tin, not fit to cut korl with.

He looked out of the window again. People were leaving the market now. A tall mulatto girl, following her mistress, her basket on her head, crossed the street just below, and looked up. She was laughing; but, when she caught sight of the haggard face peering out through the bars, suddenly grew grave, and hurried by. A free, firm step, a clear-cut olive face, with a scarlet turban tied on one side, dark, shining eyes, and on the head the basket poised, filled with fruit and flowers, under which the scarlet turban and bright eyes looked out half-shadowed. The picture caught his eye. It was good to see a face like that. He would try to-morrow, and cut one like it. *To-morrow!* He threw down the tin, trembling, and covered his face with his hands. When he looked up again, the daylight was gone.

Deborah, crouching near by on the other side of the wall, heard no noise. He sat on the side of the low pallet, thinking. Whatever was the mystery which the woman had seen on his face, it came out now slowly, in the dark there, and became fixed, — a something never seen on his face before. The evening was darkening fast. The market had been over for an hour; the rumbling of the carts over the pavement grew more infrequent: he listened to each, as it passed, because he thought it was to be for the last time. For the same reason, it was, I suppose, that he strained his eyes to catch a glimpse of each passer-by, wondering who they were, what kind of homes they were going to, if they had children, — listening eagerly to every chance word in the street, as if — (God be merciful to the man! what strange fancy was this?) — as if he never should hear human voices again.

It was quite dark at last. The street was a lonely one. The last passenger, he thought, was gone. No, — there was a quick step: Joe Hill, lighting the lamps. Joe was a good old chap; never passed a fellow without some joke or other. He remembered once seeing the place where he lived with his wife. "Granny Hill" the boys called her. Bedridden she was; but so kind as Joe was to her! kept the room so clean! — and the old woman, when he was there, was laughing at "some of t' lad's foolishness." The step was far down the street; but he could see him place the ladder, run up, and light the gas. A longing seized him to be spoken to once more.

"Joe!" he called out of the grating. "Good-by, Joe!"

The old man stopped a moment, listening uncertainly; then hurried on. The prisoner thrust his hand out of the window, and called again, louder; but Joe was too far down the street. It was a little thing; but it hurt him, — this disappointment.

"Good-by, Joe!" he called, sorrowfully enough.

"Be quiet!" said one of the jailers, passing the door, striking on it with his club.

Oh, that was the last, was it?

There was an inexpressible bitterness on his face, as he lay down on the bed, taking the bit of tin, which he had rasped to a tolerable degree of sharpness, in his hand, — to play with, it may be. He bared his arms, looking intently at their corded veins and sinews. Deborah, listening in the next cell, heard a slight clicking sound, often repeated. She shut her lips tightly, that she might not scream; the cold drops of sweat broke over her, in her dumb agony.

"Hur knows best," she muttered at last, fiercely clutching the boards where she lay.

If she could have seen Wolfe, there was nothing about him to frighten her. He lay quite still, his arms outstretched, looking at the pearly stream of moonlight coming into the window. I think in that one hour that came then he lived back over all the years that had gone before. I think that all the low, vile life, all his wrongs, all his starved hopes, came then, and stung him with a farewell poison that made him sick unto death. He made neither moan nor cry, only turned his worn face now and then to the pure light, that seemed so far off, as one that said, "How long, O Lord? how long?"

The hour was over at last. The moon, passing over her nightly path, slowly came nearer, and threw the light across his bed on his feet. He watched it steadily, as it crept up, inch by inch, slowly. It seemed to him to carry with it a great silence. He had been so hot and tired there always in the mills! The years had been so fierce and cruel! There was coming now quiet and coolness and sleep. His tense limbs relaxed, and settled in a calm languor. The blood ran fainter and slow from his heart. He did not think now with a savage anger of what might be and was not; he was conscious only of deep stillness creeping over him. At first he saw a sea of faces: the mill-men, — women he had known, drunken and bloated, — Janey's timid and pitiful, — poor old Deb's: then they floated together like a mist, and faded away, leaving only the clear, pearly moonlight.

Whether, as the pure light crept up the stretched-out figure, it brought with it calm and peace, who shall say? His dumb soul was alone with God in judgment. A Voice may have spoken for it from far-off

Calvary, "Father, forgive them, for they know not what they do!" Who
dare say? Fainter and fainter the heart rose and fell, slower and slower
the moon floated from behind a cloud, until, when at last its full tide of
white splendor swept over the cell, it seemed to wrap and fold into a
deeper stillness the dead figure that never should move again. Silence
deeper than the Night! Nothing that moved, save the black, nauseous
stream of blood dripping slowly from the pallet to the floor!

There was outcry and crowd enough in the cell the next day. The
coroner and his jury, the local editors, Kirby himself, and boys with their
hands thrust knowingly into their pockets and heads on one side,
jammed into the corners. Coming and going all day. Only one woman.
She came late, and outstayed them all. A Quaker, or Friend, as they call
themselves. I think this woman was known by that name in heaven. A
homely body, coarsely dressed in gray and white. Deborah (for Haley
had let her in) took notice of her. She watched them all — sitting on the
end of the pallet, holding his head in her arms — with the ferocity of a
watch-dog, if any of them touched the body. There was no meekness, no
sorrow, in her face; the stuff out of which murderers are made, instead.
All the time Haley and the woman were laying straight the limbs and
cleaning the cell, Deborah sat still, keenly watching the Quaker's face.
Of all the crowd there that day, this woman alone had not spoken to
her, — only once or twice had put some cordial to her lips. After they all
were gone, the woman, in the same still, gentle way, brought a vase of
wood-leaves and berries, and placed it by the pallet, then opened the
narrow window. The fresh air blew in, and swept the woody fragrance
over the dead face. Deborah looked up with a quick wonder.

"Did hur know my boy wud like it? Did hur know Hugh?"

"I know Hugh now."

The white fingers passed in a slow, pitiful way over the dead, worn
face. There was a heavy shadow in the quiet eyes.

"Did hur know where they'll bury Hugh?" said Deborah in a shrill
tone, catching her arm.

This had been the question hanging on her lips all day.

"In t' town-yard? Under t' mud and ash? T' lad 'll smother, woman!
He wur born on t' lane moor, where t' air is frick and strong. Take hur
out, for God's sake, take hur out where t' air blows!"

The Quaker hesitated, but only for a moment. She put her strong arm
around Deborah and led her to the window.

"Thee sees the hills, friend, over the river? Thee sees how the light lies
warm there, and the winds of God blow all the day? I live there, — where

the blue smoke is, by the trees. Look at me." She turned Deborah's face to her own, clear and earnest. "Thee will believe me? I will take Hugh and bury him there to-morrow."

Deborah did not doubt her. As the evening wore on, she leaned against the iron bars, looking at the hills that rose far off, through the thick sodden clouds, like a bright, unattainable calm. As she looked, a shadow of their solemn repose fell on her face: its fierce discontent faded into a pitiful, humble quiet. Slow, solemn tears gathered in her eyes: the poor weak eyes turned so hopelessly to the place where Hugh was to rest, the grave heights looking higher and brighter and more solemn than ever before. The Quaker watched her keenly. She came to her at last, and touched her arm.

"When thee comes back," she said, in a low, sorrowful tone, like one who speaks from a strong heart deeply moved with remorse or pity, "thee shall begin thy life again, — there on the hills. I came too late; but not for thee, — by God's help, it may be."

Not too late. Three years after, the Quaker began her work. I end my story here. At evening-time it was light. There is no need to tire you with the long years of sunshine, and fresh air, and slow, patient Christ-love, needed to make healthy and hopeful this impure body and soul. There is a homely pine house, on one of these hills, whose windows overlook broad, wooded slopes and clover-crimsoned meadows, — niched into the very place where the light is warmest, the air freest. It is the Friends' meeting-house. Once a week they sit there, in their grave, earnest way, waiting for the Spirit of Love to speak, opening their simple hearts to receive His words. There is a woman, old, deformed, who takes a humble place among them: waiting like them: in her gray dress, her worn face, pure and meek, turned now and then to the sky. A woman much loved by these silent, restful people; more silent than they, more humble, more loving. Waiting: with her eyes turned to hills higher and purer than these on which she lives, — dim and far off now, but to be reached some day. There may be in her heart some latent hope to meet there the love denied her here, — that she shall find him whom she lost, and that then she will not be all-unworthy. Who blames her? Something is lost in the passage of every soul from one eternity to the other, — something pure and beautiful, which might have been and was not: a hope, a talent, a love, over which the soul mourns, like Esau deprived of his birthright. What blame to the meek Quaker, if she took her lost hope to make the hills of heaven more fair?

Nothing remains to tell that the poor Welsh puddler once lived, but this figure of the mill-woman cut in korl. I have it here in a corner of my library. I keep it hid behind a curtain, — it is such a rough, ungainly thing. Yet there are about it touches, grand sweeps of outline, that show a master's hand. Sometimes, — to-night, for instance, — the curtain is accidentally drawn back, and I see a bare arm stretched out imploringly in the darkness, and an eager, wolfish face watching mine: a wan, woful face, through which the spirit of the dead korl-cutter looks out, with its thwarted life, its mighty hunger, its unfinished work. Its pale, vague lips seem to tremble with a terrible question. "Is this the End?" — they say, — "nothing beyond? — no more?" Why, you tell me you have seen that look in the eyes of dumb brutes, — horses dying under the lash. I know.

The deep of the night is passing while I write. The gas-light wakens from the shadows here and there the objects which lie scattered through the room: only faintly, though; for they belong to the open sunlight. As I glance at them, they each recall some task or pleasure of the coming day. A half-moulded child's head; Aphrodite; a bough of forest-leaves; music; work; homely fragments, in which lie the secrets of all eternal truth and beauty. Prophetic all! Only this dumb, woful face seems to belong to and end with the night. I turn to look at it. Has the power of its desperate need commanded the darkness away? While the room is yet steeped in heavy shadow, a cool, gray light suddenly touches its head like a blessing hand, and its groping arm points through the broken cloud to the far East, where, in the flickering, nebulous crimson, God has set the promise of the Dawn.

Louisa May Alcott

(1832–1888)

FOR MANY YEARS, Louisa May Alcott was regarded primarily as a children's author. The longstanding popularity of such novels as *Little Women* (1869), *Little Men* (1871) and *Jo's Boys* (1886) attests to her talents in that genre, but these works have overshadowed Alcott's other writing. Recent scholarship by such critics as Madeleine B. Stern and Elaine Showalter has prompted a reassessment of Alcott's "alternative" fiction, including the sensational thrillers she published anonymously.

Alcott wrote her first book, a collection of children's stories entitled *Flower Fables* (published in 1855), when she was only 16. A prolific and determined author, Alcott was often forced to put aside her writing to fulfill household responsibilities. While her father, Bronson Alcott, was a respected and popular member of the Transcendental group that included Ralph Waldo Emerson and Henry David Thoreau, he was not well suited to the role of family provider. Alcott, her mother and four sisters all worked to stave off financial ruin. Rather than abandon her writerly aspirations, however, Alcott transformed her experiences into the autobiographical fictions that earned her literary success. The widely read *Hospital Sketches* (1863), based on letters Alcott wrote during her service as a military nurse in Washington during the Civil War, was one such work.

"Transcendental Wild Oats" is also autobiographical, based on her family's experience at Bronson Alcott's commune Fruitlands, one of many utopian communities that sprang up in New England at the height of the Transcendental Movement. Alcott's portrayal of the failed experiment has its tragic and comic sides. The depiction of Mrs. Lamb — a thinly veiled portrait of Alcott's mother — reveals Alcott's ambivalence toward the assumption that a woman should follow "wheresoever her husband led." Underlying the sketch's humor, one detects a bitterness over her father's determination to follow his philosophical callings at the expense of his family's well-being.

Transcendental Wild Oats

ON THE FIRST day of June, 184–, a large wagon, drawn by a small horse and containing a motley load, went lumbering over certain New England hills, with the pleasing accompaniments of wind, rain, and hail. A serene man with a serene child upon his knee was driving, or rather being driven, for the small horse had it all his own way. A brown boy with a William Penn style of countenance sat beside him, firmly embracing a bust of Socrates. Behind them was an energetic-looking woman, with a benevolent brow, satirical mouth, and eyes brimful of hope and courage. A baby reposed upon her lap, a mirror leaned against her knee, and a basket of provisions danced about at her feet, as she struggled with a large, unruly umbrella. Two blue-eyed little girls, with hands full of childish treasures, sat under one old shawl, chatting happily together.

In front of this lively party stalked a tall, sharp-featured man, in a long blue cloak; and a fourth small girl trudged along beside him through the mud as if she rather enjoyed it.

The wind whistled over the bleak hills; the rain fell in a despondent drizzle, and twilight began to fall. But the calm man gazed as tranquilly into the fog as if he beheld a radiant bow of promise spanning the gray sky. The cheery woman tried to cover every one but herself with the big umbrella. The brown boy pillowed his head on the bald pate of Socrates and slumbered peacefully. The little girls sang lullabies to their dolls in soft, maternal murmurs. The sharp-nosed pedestrian marched steadily on, with the blue cloak streaming out behind him like a banner; and the lively infant splashed through the puddles with a duck-like satisfaction pleasant to behold.

Thus these modern pilgrims journeyed hopefully out of the old world, to found a new one in the wilderness.

The editors of *The Transcendental Tripod* had received from Messrs. Lion and Lamb (two of the aforesaid pilgrims) a communication from which the following statement is an extract: —

"We have made arrangements with the proprietor of an estate of about one hundred acres which liberates this tract from human ownership. Here we shall prosecute our effort to initiate a Family in harmony with the primitive instincts of man.

"Ordinary secular farming is not our object. Fruit, grain, pulse, herbs, flax, and other vegetable products, receiving assiduous attention, will afford ample manual occupation, and chaste supplies for the bodily needs. It is intended to adorn the pastures with orchards, and to supersede the labor of cattle by the spade and the pruning-knife.

"Consecrated to human freedom, the land awaits the sober culture of devoted men. Beginning with small pecuniary means, this enterprise must be rooted in a reliance on the succors of an ever-bounteous Providence, whose vital affinities being secured by this union with uncorrupted field and unworldly persons, the cares and injuries of a life of gain are avoided.

"The inner nature of each member of the Family is at no time neglected. Our plan contemplates all such disciplines, cultures, and habits as evidently conduce to the purifying of the inmates.

"Pledged to the spirit alone, the founders anticipate no hasty or numerous addition to their numbers. The kingdom of peace is entered only through the gates of self-denial; and felicity is the test and the reward of loyalty to the unswerving law of Love."

This prospective Eden at present consisted of an old red farm-house, a dilapidated barn, many acres of meadowland, and a grove. Ten ancient apple-trees were all the "chaste supply" which the place afforded as yet; but, in the firm belief that plenteous orchards were soon to be evoked from their inner consciousness, these sanguine founders had christened their domain Fruitlands.

Here Timon Lion intended to found a colony of Latter Day Saints, who, under his patriarchal sway, should regenerate the world and glorify his name forever. Here Abel Lamb, with the devoutest faith in the high ideal which was to him a living truth, desired to plant a Paradise, where Beauty, Virtue, Justice, and Love might live happily together, without the possibility of a serpent entering in. And here his wife, unconverted but faithful to the end, hoped, after many wanderings over the face of the earth, to find rest for herself and a home for her children.

"There is our new abode," announced the enthusiast, smiling with a satisfaction quite undamped by the drops dripping from his hat-brim, as they turned at length into a cart-path that wound along a steep hillside into a barren-looking valley.

"A little difficult of access," observed his practical wife, as she endeavored to keep her various household goods from going overboard with every lurch of the laden ark.

"Like all good things. But those who earnestly desire and patiently seek will soon find us," placidly responded the philosopher from the mud, through which he was now endeavoring to pilot the much-enduring horse.

"Truth lies at the bottom of a well, Sister Hope," said Brother Timon, pausing to detach his small comrade from a gate, whereon she was perched for a clearer gaze into futurity.

"That's the reason we so seldom get at it, I suppose," replied Mrs. Hope, making a vain clutch at the mirror, which a sudden jolt sent flying out of her hands.

"We want no false reflections here," said Timon, with a grim smile, as he crunched the fragments under foot in his onward march.

Sister Hope held her peace, and looked wistfully through the mist at her promised home. The old red house with a hospitable glimmer at its windows cheered her eyes; and, considering the weather, was a fitter refuge than the sylvan bowers some of the more ardent souls might have preferred.

The new-comers were welcomed by one of the elect precious,—a regenerate farmer, whose idea of reform consisted mainly in wearing white cotton raiment and shoes of untanned leather. This costume, with a snowy beard, gave him a venerable, and at the same time a somewhat bridal appearance.

The goods and chattels of the Society not having arrived, the weary family reposed before the fire on blocks of wood, while Brother Moses White regaled them with roasted potatoes, brown bread and water, in two plates, a tin pan, and one mug—his table service being limited. But, having cast the forms and vanities of a depraved world behind them, the elders welcomed hardship with the enthusiasm of new pioneers, and the children heartily enjoyed this foretaste of what they believed was to be a sort of perpetual picnic.

During the progress of this frugal meal, two more brothers appeared. One a dark, melancholy man, clad in homespun, whose peculiar mission was to turn his name hind part before and use as few words as possible. The other was a bland, bearded Englishman, who expected to be saved by eating uncooked food and going without clothes. He had not yet adopted the primitive costume, however; but contented himself with meditatively chewing dry beans out of a basket.

"Every meal should be a sacrament, and the vessels used should be beautiful and symbolical," observed Brother Lamb mildly, righting the tin pan slipping about on his knees. "I priced a silver service when in town, but it was too costly; so I got some graceful cups and vases of Britannia ware."

"Hardest things in the world to keep bright. Will whiting be allowed in the community?" inquired Sister Hope, with a housewife's interest in labor-saving institutions.

"Such trivial questions will be discussed at a more fitting time," answered Brother Timon, sharply, as he burnt his fingers with a very hot potato. "Neither sugar, molasses, milk, butter, cheese nor flesh are to be used among us, for nothing is to be admitted which has caused wrong or death to man or beast."

"Our garments are to be linen till we learn to raise our own cotton or some substitute for woolen fabrics," added Brother Abel, blissfully basking in an imaginary future as warm and brilliant as the generous fire before him.

"Haou abaout shoes?" asked Brother Moses, surveying his own with interest.

"We must yield that point till we can manufacture an innocent substitute for leather. Bark, wood, or some durable fabric will be invented in time. Meanwhile, those who desire to carry out our idea to the fullest extent can go barefooted," said Lion, who liked extreme measures.

"I never will, nor let my girls," murmured rebellious Sister Hope, under her breath.

"Haou do you cattle'ate to treat the ten-acre lot? Ef things ain't 'tended to right smart, we shan't hev no crops," observed the practical patriarch in cotton.

"We shall spade it," replied Abel, in such perfect good faith that Moses said no more, though he indulged in a shake of the head as he glanced at hands that had held nothing heavier than a pen for years. He was a paternal old soul and regarded the younger men as promising boys on a new sort of lark.

"What shall we do for lamps, if we cannot use any animal substance? I do hope light of some sort is to be thrown upon the enterprise," said Mrs.

Lamb, with anxiety, for in those days kerosene and camphene were not, and gas unknown in the wilderness.

"We shall go without till we have discovered some vegetable oil or wax to serve us," replied Brother Timon, in a decided tone, which caused Sister Hope to resolve that her private lamp should be always trimmed, if not burning.

"Each member is to perform the work for which experience, strength, and taste best fit him," continued Director Lion. "Thus drudgery and disorder will be avoided and harmony prevail. We shall rise at dawn, begin the day by bathing, followed by music, and then a chaste repast of fruit and bread. Each one finds congenial employment till the meridian meal; when some deep-searching conversation gives rest to the body and development to the mind. Healthful labor again engages us till the last meal, when we assemble in social communion, prolonged till sunset, when we retire to sweet repose, ready for the next day's activity."

"What part of the work do you incline to yourself?" asked Sister Hope, with a humorous glimmer in her keen eyes.

"I shall wait till it is made clear to me. Being in preference to doing is the great aim, and this comes to us rather by a resigned willingness than a wilful activity, which is a check to all divine growth," responded Brother Timon.

"I thought so." And Mrs. Lamb sighed audibly, for during the year he had spent in her family Brother Timon had so faithfully carried out his idea of "being, not doing," that she had found his "divine growth" both an expensive and unsatisfactory process.

Here her husband struck into the conversation, his face shining with the light and joy of the splendid dreams and high ideals hovering before him.

"In these steps of reform, we do not rely so much on scientific reasoning or physiological skill as on the spirit's dictates. The greater part of man's duty consists in leaving alone much that he now does. Shall I stimulate with tea, coffee, or wine? No. Shall I consume flesh? Not if I value health. Shall I subjugate cattle? Shall I claim property in any created thing? Shall I trade? Shall I adopt a form of religion? Shall I interest myself in politics? To how many of these questions — could we ask them deeply enough and could they be heard as having relation to our eternal welfare — would the response be 'Abstain'?"

A mild snore seemed to echo the last word of Abel's rhapsody, for Brother Moses had succumbed to mundane slumber and sat nodding like a massive ghost. Forest Absalom, the silent man, and John Pease, the

English member, now departed to the barn; and Mrs. Lamb led her flock to a temporary fold, leaving the founders of the "Consociate Family" to build castles in the air till the fire went out and the symposium ended in smoke.

The furniture arrived next day, and was soon bestowed; for the principal property of the community consisted in books. To this rare library was devoted the best room in the house, and the few busts and pictures that still survived many flittings were added to beautify the sanctuary, for here the family was to meet for amusement, instruction, and worship.

Any housewife can imagine the emotions of Sister Hope, when she took possession of a large, dilapidated kitchen, containing an old stove and the peculiar stores out of which food was to evolve for her little family of eleven. Cakes of maple sugar, dried peas and beans, barley and hominy, meal of all sorts, potatoes, and dried fruit. No milk, butter, cheese, tea, or meat appeared. Even salt was considered a useless luxury and spice entirely forbidden by these lovers of Spartan simplicity. A ten years' experience of vegetarian vagaries had been good training for this new freak, and her sense of the ludicrous supported her through many trying scenes.

Unleavened bread, porridge, and water for breakfast; bread, vegetables, and water for dinner; bread, fruit, and water for supper was the bill of fare ordained by the elders. No teapot profaned that sacred stove, no gory steak cried aloud for vengeance from her chaste gridiron; and only a brave woman's taste, time, and temper were sacrificed on that domestic altar.

The vexed question of light was settled by buying a quantity of bayberry wax for candles; and, on discovering that no one knew how to make them, pine knots were introduced, to be used when absolutely necessary. Being summer the evenings were not long, and the weary fraternity found it no great hardship to retire with the birds. The inner light was sufficient for most of them. But Mrs. Lamb rebelled. Evening was the only time she had to herself, and while the tired feet rested the skilful hands mended torn frocks and little stockings, or anxious heart forgot its burden in a book.

So "mother's lamp" burned steadily, while the philosophers built a new heaven and earth by moonlight; and through all the metaphysical mists and philanthropic pyrotechnics of that period Sister Hope played her own little game of "throwing light," and none but the moths were the worse for it.

Such farming probably was never seen before since Adam delved.

The band of brothers began by spading garden and field; but a few days of it lessened their ardor amazingly. Blistered hands and aching backs suggested the expediency of permitting the use of cattle till the workers were better fitted for noble toil by a summer of the new life.

Brother Moses brought a yoke of oxen from his farm, — at least, the philosophers thought so till it was discovered that one of the animals was a cow; and Moses confessed that he "must be let down easy, for he couldn't live on garden sarse entirely."

Great was Dictator Lion's indignation at this lapse from virtue. But time pressed, the work must be done; so the meek cow was permitted to wear the yoke and the recreant brother continued to enjoy forbidden draughts in the barn, which dark proceeding caused the children to regard him as one set apart for destruction.

The sowing was equally peculiar, for, owing to some mistake, the three brethren, who devoted themselves to this graceful task, found when about half through the job that each had been sowing a different sort of grain in the same field; a mistake which caused much perplexity, as it could not be remedied; but, after a long consultation and a good deal of laughter, it was decided to say nothing and see what would come of it.

The garden was planted with a generous supply of useful roots and herbs; but, as manure was not allowed to profane the virgin soil, few of these vegetable treasures ever came up. Purslane reigned supreme, and the disappointed planters ate it philosophically, deciding that Nature knew what was best for them, and would generously supply their needs, if they could only learn to digest her "sallets" and wild roots.

The orchard was laid out, a little grafting done, new trees and vines set, regardless of the unfit season and entire ignorance of the husband-men, who honestly believed that in the autumn they would reap a bounteous harvest.

Slowly things got into order, and rapidly rumors of the new experi-ment went abroad, causing many strange spirits to flock thither, for in those days communities were the fashion and transcendentalism raged wildly. Some came to look on and laugh, some to be supported in poetic idleness, a few to believe sincerely and work heartily. Each member was allowed to mount his favorite hobby and ride it to his heart's content. Very queer were some of the riders, and very rampant some of the hobbies.

One youth, believing that language was of little consequence if the spirit was only right, startled new-comers by blandly greeting them with

"Good-morning, damn you," and other remarks of an equally mixed order. A second irrepressible being held that all the emotions of the soul should be freely expressed, and illustrated his theory by antics that would have sent him to a lunatic asylum, if, as an unregenerate wag said, he had not already been in one. When his spirit soared, he climbed trees and shouted; when doubt assailed him, he lay upon the floor and groaned lamentably. At joyful periods he raced, leaped, and sang; when sad, he wept aloud; and when a great thought burst upon him in the watches of the night, he crowed like a jocund cockerel, to the great delight of the children and the great annoyance of their elders. One musical brother fiddled whenever so moved, sang sentimentally to the four little girls, and put a music-box on the wall when he hoed corn.

Brother Pease ground away at his uncooked food, or browsed over the farm on sorrel, mint, green fruit, and new vegetables. Occasionally he took his walks abroad, airily attired in an unbleached cotton *poncho*, which was the nearest approach to the primeval costume he was allowed to indulge in. At midsummer he retired to the wilderness, to try his plan where the woodchucks were without prejudices and huckleberry-bushes were hospitably full. A sun-stroke unfortunately spoiled his plan, and he returned to semi-civilization a sadder and wiser man.

Forest Absalom preserved his Pythagorean silence, cultivated his fine dark locks, and worked like a beaver, setting an excellent example of brotherly love, justice, and fidelity by his upright life. He it was who helped overworked Sister Hope with her heavy washes, kneaded the endless succession of batches of bread, watched over the children, and did the many tasks left undone by the brethren, who were so busy discussing and defining great duties that they forgot to perform the small ones.

Moses White placidly plodded about, "chorin' raound," as he called it, looking like an old-time patriarch, with his silver hair and flowing beard, and saving the community from many a mishap by his thrift and Yankee shrewdness.

Brother Lion domineered over the whole concern; for, having put the most money into the speculation, he was resolved to make it pay, — as if anything founded on an ideal basis could be expected to do so by any but enthusiasts.

Abel Lamb simply revelled in the Newness, firmly believing that his dream was to be beautifully realized and in time not only little Fruit-lands, but the whole earth, be turned into a Happy Valley. He worked with every muscle of his body, for *he* was in deadly earnest. He taught with his whole head and heart; planned and sacrificed, preached and prophesied, with a soul full of the purest aspirations, most unselfish purposes, and desires for a life devoted to God and man, too high and tender to bear the rough usage of this world.

It was a little remarkable that only one woman ever joined this community. Mrs. Lamb merely followed wheresoever her husband led, — "as ballast for his balloon," as she said, in her bright way.

Miss Jane Gage was a stout lady of mature years, sentimental, amiable, and lazy. She wrote verses copiously, and had vague yearnings and graspings after the unknown, which led her to believe herself fitted for a higher sphere than any she had yet adorned.

Having been a teacher, she was set to instructing the children in the common branches. Each adult member took a turn at the infants; and, as each taught in his own way, the result was a chronic state of chaos in the minds of these much-afflicted innocents.

Sleep, food, and poetic musings were the desires of dear Jane's life, and she shirked all duties as clogs upon her spirit's wings. Any thought of lending a hand with the domestic drudgery never occurred to her; and when to the question, "Are there any beasts of burden on the place?" Mrs. Lamb answered, with a face that told its own tale, "Only one woman!" the buxom Jane took no shame to herself, but laughed at the joke, and let the stout-hearted sister tug on alone.

Unfortunately, the poor lady hankered after the flesh-pots, and endeavored to stay herself with private sips of milk, crackers, and cheese, and on one dire occasion she partook of fish at a neighbor's table.

One of the children reported this sad lapse from virtue, and poor Jane was publicly reprimanded by Timon.

"I only took a little bit of the tail!" sobbed the penitent poetess.

"Yes, but the whole fish had to be tortured and slain that you might tempt your carnal appetite with that one taste of the tail. Know ye not, consumers of flesh meat, that ye are nourishing the wolf and the tiger in your bosoms?"

At this awful question and the peal of laughter which arose from some of the younger brethren, tickled by the ludicrous contrast between the stout sinner, the stern judge, and the naughty satisfaction of the young detective, poor Jane fled from the room to pack her trunk and return to a world where fishes' tails were not forbidden fruit.

Transcendental wild oats were sown broadcast that year, and the fame thereof has not yet ceased in the land; for, futile as this crop seemed to outsiders, it bore an invisible harvest, worth much to those who planted in earnest. As none of the members of this particular community have ever recounted their experiences before, a few of them may not be amiss, since the interest in these attempts has never died out and Fruitlands was the most ideal of all these castles in Spain.

A new dress was invented, since cotton, silk, and wool were forbidden as the product of slave-labor, worm-slaughter, and sheep-robbery. Tunics and trowsers of brown linen were the only wear. The women's skirts were longer, and their straw hat-brims wider than the men's, and this was the only difference. Some persecution lent a charm to the costume, and the long-haired, linen-clad reformers quite enjoyed the mild martyrdom they endured when they left home.

Money was abjured, as the root of all evil. The produce of the land was to supply most of their wants, or be exchanged for the few things they could not grow. This idea had its inconveniences; but self-denial was the fashion, and it was surprising how many things one can do without. When they desired to travel, they walked, if possible, begged the loan of a vehicle or boldly entered car or coach, and, stating their principles to the officials, took the consequences. Usually their dress, their earnest frankness, and gentle resolution won them a passage; but now and then they met with hard usage and had the satisfaction of suffering for their principles.

On one of these penniless pilgrimages they took passage on a boat, and, when fare was demanded, artlessly offered to talk, instead of pay. As the boat was well under way and they actually had not a cent, there was no help for it. So Brothers Lion and Lamb held forth to the assembled passengers in their most eloquent style. There must have been something effective in this conversation, for the listeners were moved to take up a contribution for these inspired lunatics, who preached peace on earth and good-will to man so earnestly, with empty pockets. A goodly sum was collected; but when the captain presented it the reformers proved that they were consistent even in their madness, for not a penny would they accept, saying, with a look at the group about them, whose indifference or contempt had changed to interest and respect, "You see how well we get on without money"; and so went serenely on their way, with their linen blouses flapping airily in the cold October wind.

They preached vegetarianism everywhere and resisted all temptations of the flesh, contentedly eating apples and bread at well-spread tables, and much afflicting hospitable hostesses by denouncing their food and taking away their appetites, discussing the "horrors of shambles," the "incorporation of the brute in man," and "on elegant abstinence the sign of a pure soul." But, when the perplexed or offended ladies asked what they should eat, they got in reply a bill of fare consisting of "bowls of sunrise for breakfast," "solar seeds of the sphere," "dishes from Plutarch's chaste table," and other viands equally hard to find in any modern market.

Reform conventions of all sorts were haunted by these brethren, who said many wise things and did many foolish ones. Unfortunately, these wanderings interfered with their harvest at home; but the rule was to do what the spirit moved, so they left their crops to Providence and went a-reaping in wider and, let us hope, more fruitful fields than their own.

Luckily, the earthly providence who watched over Abel Lamb was at hand to glean the scanty crop yielded by the "uncorrupted land," which, "consecrated to human freedom," had received "the sober culture of devout men."

About the time the grain was ready to house, some call of the Oversoul wafted all the men away. An easterly storm was coming up and the yellow stacks were sure to be ruined. Then Sister Hope gathered her forces. Three little girls, one boy (Timon's son), and herself, harnessed to clothes-baskets and Russia-linen sheets, were the only teams she could command; but with these poor appliances the indomitable woman got in the grain and saved food for her young, with the instinct and energy of a mother-bird with a brood of hungry nestlings to feed.

This attempt at regeneration had its tragic as well as comic side, though the world only saw the former.

With the first frosts, the butterflies, who had sunned themselves in the new light through the summer, took flight, leaving the few bees to see what honey they had stored for winter use. Precious little appeared beyond the satisfaction of a few months of holy living.

At first it seemed as if a chance to try holy dying also was to be offered them. Timon, much disgusted with the failure of the scheme, decided to retire to the Shakers, who seemed to be the only successful community going.

"What is to become of us?" asked Mrs. Hope, for Abel was heart-broken at the bursting of his lovely bubble.

"You can stay here, if you like, till a tenant is found. No more wood must be cut, however, and no more corn ground. All I have must be sold to pay the debts of the concern, as the responsibility rests with me," was the cheering reply.

"Who is to pay us for what we have lost? I gave all I had, — furniture, time, strength, six months of my children's lives, — and all are wasted.

Abel gave himself body and soul, and is almost wrecked by hard work and disappointment. Are we to have no return for this, but leave to starve and freeze in an old house, with winter at hand, no money, and hardly a friend left, for this wild scheme has alienated nearly all we had. You talk much about justice. Let us have a little, since there is nothing else left."

But the woman's appeal met with no reply but the old one: "It was an experiment. We all risked something, and must bear our losses as we can."

With this cold comfort, Timon departed with his son, and was absorbed into the Shaker brotherhood, where he soon found that the order of things was reversed, and it was all work and no play.

Then the tragedy began for the forsaken little family. Desolation and despair fell upon Abel. As his wife said, his new beliefs had alienated many friends. Some thought him mad, some unprincipled. Even the most kindly thought him a visionary, whom it was useless to help till he took more practical views of life. All stood aloof, saying: "Let him work out his own ideas, and see what they are worth."

He had tried, but it was a failure. The world was not ready for Utopia yet, and those who attempted to found it only got laughed at for their pains. In other days, men could sell all and give to the poor, lead lives devoted to holiness and high thought, and, after the persecution was over, find themselves honored as saints or martyrs. But in modern times these things are out of fashion. To live for one's principles, at all costs, is a dangerous speculation; and the failure of an ideal, no matter how humane and noble, is harder for the world to forgive and forget than bank robbery or the grand swindles of corrupt politicians.

Deep waters now for Abel, and for a time there seemed no passage through. Strength and spirits were exhausted by hard work and too much thought. Courage failed when, looking about for help, he saw no sympathizing face, no hand outstretched to help him, no voice to say cheerily, "We all make mistakes, and it takes many experiences to shape a life. Try again, and let us help you."

Every door was closed, every eye averted, every heart cold, and no way open whereby he might earn bread for his children. His principles would not permit him to do many things that others did; and in the few fields where conscience would allow him to work, who would employ a man who had flown in the face of society, as he had done?

Then this dreamer, whose dream was the life of his life, resolved to carry out his idea to the bitter end. There seemed no place for him here, — no work, no friend. To go begging conditions was as ignoble as to go begging money. Better perish of want than sell one's soul for the sustenance of the body. Silently he lay down upon his bed, turned his face to the wall, and waited with pathetic patience for death to cut the knot which he could not untie. Days and nights went by, and neither food nor water passed his lips. Soul and body were dumbly struggling together, and no word of complaint betrayed what either suffered.

His wife, when tears and prayers were unavailing, sat down to wait the end with a mysterious awe and submission; for in this entire resignation of all things there was an eloquent significance to her who knew him as no other human being did.

"Leave all to God," was his belief; and in this crisis the loving soul clung to this faith, sure that the Allwise Father would not desert this child who tried to live so near to Him. Gathering her children about her, she waited the issue of the tragedy that was being enacted in that solitary room, while the first snow fell outside, untrodden by the footprints of a single friend.

But the strong angels who sustain and teach perplexed and troubled souls came and went, leaving no trace without, but working miracles within. For, when all other sentiments had faded into dimness, all other hopes died utterly; when the bitterness of death was nearly over, when body was past any pang of hunger or thirst, and soul stood ready to depart, the love that outlives all else refused to die. Head had bowed to defeat, hand had grown weary with too heavy tasks, but heart could not grow cold to those who lived in its tender depths, even when death touched it.

"My faithful wife, my little girls, — they have not forsaken me, they are mine by ties that none can break. What right have I to leave them alone? What right to escape from the burden and the sorrow I have helped to bring? This duty remains to me, and I must do it manfully. For their sakes, the world will forgive me in time; for their sakes, God will sustain me now."

Too feeble to rise, Abel groped for the food that always lay within his reach, and in the darkness and solitude of that memorable night ate and drank what was to him the bread and wine of a new communion, a new dedication of heart and life to the duties that were left him when the dreams fled.

In the early dawn, when that sad wife crept fearfully to see what change had come to the patient face on the pillow, she found it smiling at her, saw a wasted hand outstretched to her, and heard a feeble voice cry bravely, "Hope!"

What passed in that little room is not to be recorded except in the hearts of those who suffered and endured much for love's sake. Enough for us to know that soon the wan shadow of a man came forth, leaning on the arm that never failed him, to be welcomed and cherished by the children, who never forgot the experiences of that time.

"Hope" was the watchword now; and, while the last logs blazed on the hearth, the last bread and apples covered the table, the new commander, with renewed courage, said to her husband, —

"Leave all to God — and me. He has done his part, now I will do mine."

"But we have no money, dear."

"Yes, we have, I sold all we could spare, and have enough to take us away from this snow-bank."

"Where can we go?"

"I have engaged four rooms at our good neighbor, Lovejoy's. There we can live cheaply till spring. Then for new plans and a home of our own, please God."

"But, Hope, your little store won't last long, and we have no friends."

"I can sew and you can chop wood. Lovejoy offers you the same pay as he gives his other men; my old friend, Mrs. Truman, will send me all the work I want; and my blessed brother stands by us to the end. Cheer up, dear heart, for while there is work and love in the world we shall not suffer."

"And while I have my good angel Hope, I shall not despair, even if I wait another thirty years before I step beyond the circle of the sacred little world in which I still have a place to fill."

So one bleak December day, with their few possessions piled on an oxsled, the rosy children perched atop, the parents trudging arm in arm behind, the exiles left their Eden and faced the world again.

"Ah me! my happy dream. How much I leave behind that can never be mine again," said Abel, looking back at the lost Paradise, lying white and chill in its shroud of snow.

"Yes, dear; but how much we bring away," answered brave-hearted Hope, glancing from husband to children.

"Poor Fruitlands! The name was as great a failure as the rest!" continued Abel, with a sigh, as a frostbitten apple fell from a leafless bough at his feet.

But the sigh changed to a smile as his wife added, in a half-tender, half-satirical tone, —

"Don't you think Apple Slump would be a better name for it, dear?"

Sarah Orne Jewett

(1849–1909)

As a child Sarah Orne Jewett accompanied her father, a prosperous physician, on his rural rounds, and thus developed her appreciation of the people and customs of the remote villages of southern Maine. Though Jewett was viewed in her lifetime as a regional writer, Willa Cather's two-volume collection *The Best Short Stories of Sarah Orne Jewett* (1925) placed her work in a broader context. As critic Marjorie Pryse notes, Jewett's attention to physical setting marks her as one of America's earliest realists.

Jewett began publishing fiction at 19, when she submitted her short story "Mr. Bruce" to William Dean Howells at the *Atlantic Monthly*. Howells' appreciation of his "discovery" increased over the years, and in 1877 she published *Deephaven*, a compilation of stories and sketches that had appeared in the magazine. *The Country of the Pointed Firs* (1896), one of Jewett's four novels, is considered her masterpiece.

While critics of her day praised Jewett for her ability to evoke a particular time and place, they were also quick to note the limitations of regional fiction, primarily its lack of universal appeal. But, as "A White Heron" (1886) demonstrates, Jewett's fiction transcends the bounds of physical setting. In the tradition of the *Bildungsroman*, the story traces the coming of age of Sylvia, a young girl living on a remote farm with her grandmother. Torn between a desire to keep the secret of the white heron and the "dream of love" inspired by the young hunter who wants to learn what she knows, Sylvia gains an awareness both sexual and spiritual. Jewett's sensitive treatment of female adolescence and sexuality is unique in nineteenth-century fiction.

A White Heron

I

THE WOODS WERE already filled with shadows one June evening, just before eight o'clock, though a bright sunset still glimmered faintly among the trunks of the trees. A little girl was driving home her cow, a plodding, dilatory, provoking creature in her behavior, but a valued companion for all that. They were going away from whatever light there was, and striking deep into the woods, but their feet were familiar with the path, and it was no matter whether their eyes could see it or not.

There was hardly a night the summer through when the old cow could be found waiting at the pasture bars; on the contrary, it was her greatest pleasure to hide herself away among the huckleberry bushes, and though she wore a loud bell she had made the discovery that if one stood perfectly still it would not ring. So Sylvia had to hunt for her until she found her, and call Co'! Co'! with never an answering Moo, until her childish patience was quite spent. If the creature had not given good milk and plenty of it, the case would have seemed very different to her owners. Besides, Sylvia had all the time there was, and very little use to make of it. Sometimes in pleasant weather it was a consolation to look upon the cow's pranks as an intelligent attempt to play hide and seek, and as the child had no playmates she lent herself to this amusement with a good deal of zest. Though this chase had been so long that the wary animal herself had given an unusual signal of her whereabouts, Sylvia had only laughed when she came upon Mistress Moolly at the swampside, and urged her affectionately homeward with a twig of birch leaves. The old cow was not inclined to wander farther, she even turned in the right direction for once as they left the pasture, and stepped along the road at a good pace. She was quite ready to be milked now, and seldom stopped to browse. Sylvia wondered what her grandmother

51

would say because they were so late. It was a great while since she had left home at half-past five o'clock, but everybody knew the difficulty of making this errand a short one. Mrs. Tilley had chased the hornéd torment too many summer evenings herself to blame any one else for lingering, and was only thankful as she waited that she had Sylvia, nowadays, to give such valuable assistance. The good woman suspected that Sylvia loitered occasionally on her own account; there never was such a child for straying about out-of-doors since the world was made! Everybody said that it was a good change for a little maid who had tried to grow for eight years in a crowded manufacturing town, but, as for Sylvia herself, it seemed as if she never had been alive at all before she came to live at the farm. She thought often with wistful compassion of a wretched geranium that belonged to a town neighbor.

" 'Afraid of folks,' " old Mrs. Tilley said to herself, with a smile, after she had made the unlikely choice of Sylvia from her daughter's houseful of children, and was returning to the farm. " 'Afraid of folks,' they said! I guess she won't be troubled no great with 'em up to the old place!" When they reached the door of the lonely house and stopped to unlock it, and the cat came to purr loudly, and rub against them, a deserted pussy, indeed, but fat with young robins, Sylvia whispered that this was a beautiful place to live in, and she never should wish to go home.

The companions followed the shady woodroad, the cow taking slow steps and the child very fast ones. The cow stopped long at the brook to drink, as if the pasture were not half a swamp, and Sylvia stood still and waited, letting her bare feet cool themselves in the shoal water, while the great twilight moths struck softly against her. She waded on through the brook as the cow moved away, and listened to the thrushes with a heart that beat fast with pleasure. There was a stirring in the great boughs overhead. They were full of little birds and beasts that seemed to be wide awake, and going about their world, or else saying good-night to each other in sleepy twitters. Sylvia herself felt sleepy as she walked along. However, it was not much farther to the house, and the air was soft and sweet. She was not often in the woods so late as this, and it made her feel as if she were a part of the gray shadows and the moving leaves. She was just thinking how long it seemed since she first came to the farm a year ago, and wondering if everything went on in the noisy town just the same as when she was there; the thought of the great red-faced boy who used to chase and frighten her made her hurry along the path to escape from the shadow of the trees.

Suddenly this little woods-girl is horror-stricken to hear a clear whistle not very far away. Not a bird's-whistle, which would have a sort of friendliness, but a boy's whistle, determined, and somewhat aggressive. Sylvia left the cow to whatever sad fate might await her, and stepped discreetly aside into the bushes, but she was just too late. The enemy had discovered her, and called out in a very cheerful and persuasive tone, "Halloa, little girl, how far is it to the road?" and trembling Sylvia answered almost inaudibly, "A good ways."

She did not dare to look boldly at the tall young man, who carried a gun over his shoulder, but she came out of her bush and again followed the cow, while he walked alongside.

"I have been hunting for some birds," the stranger said kindly, "and I have lost my way, and need a friend very much. Don't be afraid," he added gallantly. "Speak up and tell me what your name is, and whether you think I can spend the night at your house, and go out gunning early in the morning."

Sylvia was more alarmed than before. Would not her grandmother consider her much to blame? But who could have foreseen such an accident as this? It did not seem to be her fault, and she hung her head as if the stem of it were broken, but managed to answer "Sylvy," with much effort when her companion again asked her name.

Mrs. Tilley was standing in the doorway when the trio came into view. The cow gave a loud moo by way of explanation.

"Yes, you'd better speak up for yourself, you old trial! Where'd she tucked herself away this time, Sylvy?" But Sylvia kept an awed silence; she knew by instinct that her grandmother did not comprehend the gravity of the situation. She must be mistaking the stranger for one of the farmer-lads of the region.

The young man stood his gun beside the door, and dropped a lumpy game-bag beside it; then he bade Mrs. Tilley good-evening, and repeated his wayfarer's story, and asked if he could have a night's lodging.

"Put me anywhere you like," he said. "I must be off early in the morning, before day; but I am very hungry, indeed. You can give me some milk at any rate, that's plain."

"Dear sakes, yes," responded the hostess, whose long slumbering hospitality seemed to be easily awakened. "You might fare better if you went out to the main road a mile or so, but you're welcome to what we've got. I'll milk right off, and you make yourself at home. You can sleep on husks or feathers," she proffered graciously. "I raised them all myself. There's good pasturing for geese just below here towards the ma'sh. Now step round and set a plate for the gentleman, Sylvy!" And Sylvia promptly stepped. She was glad to have something to do, and she was hungry herself.

It was a surprise to find so clean and comfortable a little dwelling in this New England wilderness. The young man had known the horrors of its most primitive housekeeping, and the dreary squalor of that level of society which does not rebel at the companionship of hens. This was the best thrift of an old-fashioned farmstead, though on such a small scale that it seemed like a hermitage. He listened eagerly to the old woman's quaint talk, he watched Sylvia's pale face and shining gray eyes with ever growing enthusiasm, and insisted that this was the best supper he had eaten for a month, and afterward the new-made friends sat down in the door-way together while the moon came up.

Soon it would be berry-time, and Sylvia was a great help at picking. The cow was a good milker, though a plaguy thing to keep track of, the hostess gossiped frankly, adding presently that she had buried four children, so Sylvia's mother, and a son (who might be dead) in California were all the children she had left. "Dan, my boy, was a great hand to go gunning," she explained sadly. "I never wanted for pa'tridges or gray squer'ls while he was to home. He's been a great wand'rer, I expect, and he's no hand to write letters. There, I don't blame him, I'd ha' seen the world myself if it had been so I could."

"Sylvy takes after him," the grandmother continued affectionately, after a minute's pause. "There ain't a foot o' ground she don't know her way over, and the wild creatur's counts her one o' themselves. Squer'ls she'll tame to come an' feed right out o' her hands, and all sorts o' birds. Last winter she got the jaybirds to bangeing[1] here, and I believe she'd 'a' scanted herself of her own meals to have plenty to throw out amongst 'em, if I had n't kep' watch. Anything but crows, I tell her, I'm willin' to help support — though Dan he had a tamed one o' them that did seem to have reason same as folks. It was round here a good spell after he went away. Dan an' his father they did n't hitch, — but he never held up his head ag'in after Dan had dared him an' gone off."

The guest did not notice this hint of family sorrows in his eager interest in something else.

"So Sylvy knows all about birds, does she?" he exclaimed, as he looked round at the little girl who sat, very demure but increasingly

---

1. *bangeing*] regional term meaning lounging around, loafing.

sleepy, in the moonlight. "I am making a collection of birds myself. I have been at it ever since I was a boy." (Mrs. Tilley smiled.) "There are two or three very rare ones I have been hunting for these five years. I mean to get them on my own ground if they can be found."

"Do you cage 'em up?" asked Mrs. Tilley doubtfully, in response to this enthusiastic announcement.

"Oh no, they're stuffed and preserved, dozens and dozens of them," said the ornithologist, "and I have shot or snared every one myself. I caught a glimpse of a white heron a few miles from here on Saturday, and I have followed it in this direction. They have never been found in this district at all. The little white heron, it is," and he turned again to look at Sylvia with the hope of discovering that the rare bird was one of her acquaintances.

But Sylvia was watching a hop-toad in the narrow footpath.

"You would know the heron if you saw it," the stranger continued eagerly. "A queer tall white bird with soft feathers and long thin legs. And it would have a nest perhaps in the top of a high tree, made of sticks, something like a hawk's nest."

Sylvia's heart gave a wild beat; she knew that strange white bird, and had once stolen softly near where it stood in some bright green swamp grass, away over at the other side of the woods. There was an open place where the sunshine always seemed strangely yellow and hot, where tall, nodding rushes grew, and her grandmother had warned her that she might sink in the soft black mud underneath and never be heard of more. Not far beyond were the salt marshes just this side the sea itself, which Sylvia wondered and dreamed much about, but never had seen, whose great voice could sometimes be heard above the noise of the woods on stormy nights.

"I can't think of anything I should like so much as to find that heron's nest," the handsome stranger was saying. "I would give ten dollars to anybody who could show it to me," he added desperately, "and I mean to spend my whole vacation hunting for it if need be. Perhaps it was only migrating, or had been chased out of its own region by some bird of prey."

Mrs. Tilley gave amazed attention to all this, but Sylvia still watched the toad, not divining, as she might have done at some calmer time, that the creature wished to get to its hole under the door-step, and was much hindered by the unusual spectators at that hour of the evening. No amount of thought, that night, could decide how many wished-for treasures the ten dollars, so lightly spoken of, would buy.

The next day the young sportsman hovered about the woods, and Sylvia kept him company, having lost her first fear of the friendly lad, who proved to be most kind and sympathetic. He told her many things about the birds and what they knew and where they lived and what they did with themselves. And he gave her a jack-knife, which she thought as great a treasure as if she were a desert-islander. All day long he did not once make her troubled or afraid except when he brought down some unsuspecting singing creature from its bough. Sylvia would have liked him vastly better without his gun; she could not understand why he killed the very birds he seemed to like so much. But as the day waned, Sylvia still watched the young man with loving admiration. She had never seen anybody so charming and delightful; the woman's heart, asleep in the child, was vaguely thrilled by a dream of love. Some premonition of that great power stirred and swayed these young crea-tures who traversed the solemn woodlands with soft-footed silent care. They stopped to listen to a bird's song; they pressed forward again eagerly, parting the branches — speaking to each other rarely and in whispers; the young man going first and Sylvia following, fascinated, a few steps behind, with her gray eyes dark with excitement.

She grieved because the longed-for white heron was elusive, but she did not lead the guest, she only followed, and there was no such thing as speaking first. The sound of her own unquestioned voice would have terrified her — it was hard enough to answer yes or no when there was need of that. At last evening began to fall, and they drove the cow home together, and Sylvia smiled with pleasure when they came to the place where she heard the whistle and was afraid only the night before.

II

Half a mile from home, at the farther edge of the woods, where the land was highest, a great pine-tree stood, the last of its generation. Whether it was left for a boundary mark, or for what reason, no one could say; the wood-choppers who had felled its mates were dead and gone long ago, and a whole forest of sturdy trees, pines and oaks and maples, had grown again. But the stately head of this old pine towered above them all and made a landmark for sea and shore miles and miles away. Sylvia knew it well. She had always believed that whoever climbed to the top of it could see the ocean; and the little girl had often laid her hand on the great rough trunk and looked up wistfully at those dark boughs that the wind always stirred, no matter how hot and still the air might be below. Now she thought of the tree with a new excitement, for why, if one climbed it at break of day could not one see all the world, and easily discover from whence the white heron flew, and mark the place, and find the hidden nest?

What a spirit of adventure, what wild ambition! What fancied triumph and delight and glory for the later morning when she could make known the secret! It was almost too real and too great for the childish heart to bear.

All night the door of the little house stood open and the whippoorwills came and sang upon the very step. The young sportsman and his old hostess were sound asleep, but Sylvia's great design kept her broad awake and watching. She forgot to think of sleep. The short summer night seemed as long as the winter darkness, and at last when the whippoorwills ceased, and she was afraid the morning would after all come too soon, she stole out of the house and followed the pasture path through the woods, hastening toward the open ground beyond, listening with a sense of comfort and companionship to the drowsy twitter of a half-awakened bird, whose perch she had jarred in passing. Alas, if the great wave of human interest which flooded for the first time this dull little life should sweep away the satisfactions of an existence heart to heart with nature and the dumb life of the forest!

There was the huge tree asleep yet in the paling moonlight, and small and silly Sylvia began with utmost bravery to mount to the top of it, with tingling, eager blood coursing the channels of her whole frame, with her bare feet and fingers, that pinched and held like bird's claws to the monstrous ladder reaching up, up, almost to the sky itself. First she must mount the white oak tree that grew alongside, where she was almost lost among the dark branches and the green leaves heavy and wet with dew; a bird fluttered off its nest, and a red squirrel ran to and fro and scolded pettishly at the harmless housebreaker. Sylvia felt her way easily. She had often climbed there, and knew that higher still one of the oak's upper branches chafed against the pine trunk, just where its lower boughs were set close together. There, when she made the dangerous pass from one tree to the other, the great enterprise would really begin.

She crept out along the swaying oak limb at last, and took the daring step across into the old pine-tree. The way was harder than she thought;

she must reach far and hold fast, the sharp dry twigs caught and held her and scratched her like angry talons, the pitch made her thin little fingers clumsy and stiff as she went round and round the tree's great stem, higher and higher upward. The sparrows and robins in the woods below were beginning to wake and twitter to the dawn, yet it seemed much lighter there aloft in the pine-tree, and the child knew she must hurry if her project were to be of any use.

The tree seemed to lengthen itself out as she went up, and to reach farther and farther upward. It was like a great main-mast to the voyaging earth; it must truly have been amazed that morning through all its ponderous frame as it felt this determined spark of human spirit wending its way from higher branch to branch. Who knows how steadily the least twigs held themselves to advantage this light, weak creature on her way! The old pine must have loved his new dependent. More than all the hawks, and bats, and moths, and even the sweet voiced thrushes, was the brave, beating heart of the solitary gray-eyed child. And the tree stood still and frowned away the winds that June morning while the dawn grew bright in the east.

Sylvia's face was like a pale star, if one had seen it from the ground, when the last thorny bough was past, and she stood trembling and tired but wholly triumphant, high in the treetop. Yes, there was the sea with the dawning sun making a golden dazzle over it, and toward that glorious east flew two hawks with slow-moving pinions. How low they looked in the air from that height when one had only seen them before far up, and dark against the blue sky. Their gray feathers were as soft as moths; they seemed only a little way from the tree, and Sylvia felt as if she too could go flying away among the clouds. Westward, the woodlands and farms reached miles and miles into the distance; here and there were church steeples, and white villages, truly it was a vast and awesome world!

The birds sang louder and louder. At last the sun came up bewilderingly bright. Sylvia could see the white sails of ships out at sea, and the clouds that were purple and rose-colored and yellow at first began to fade away. Where was the white heron's nest in the sea of green branches, and was this wonderful sight and pageant of the world the only reward for having climbed to such a giddy height? Now look down again, Sylvia, where the green marsh is set among the shining birches and dark hemlocks; there where you saw the white heron once you will see him again; look, look! a white spot of him like a single floating feather comes up from the dead hemlock and grows larger, and rises, and comes close at last, and goes by the landmark pine with steady sweep of wing and outstretched slender neck and crested head. And wait! wait! do not move a foot or a finger, little girl, do not send an arrow of light and consciousness from your two eager eyes, for the heron has perched on a pine bough not far beyond yours, and cries back to his mate on the nest and plumes his feathers for the new day!

The child gives a long sigh a minute later when a company of shouting cat-birds comes also to the tree, and vexed by their fluttering and lawlessness the solemn heron goes away. She knows his secret now, the wild, light, slender bird that floats and wavers, and goes back like an arrow presently to his home in the green world beneath. Then Sylvia, well satisfied, makes her perilous way down again, not daring to look far below the branch she stands on, ready to cry sometimes because her fingers ache and her lamed feet slip. Wondering over and over again what the stranger would say to her, and what he would think when she told him how to find his way straight to the heron's nest.

"Sylvy, Sylvy!" called the busy old grandmother again and again, but nobody answered, and the small husk bed was empty and Sylvia had disappeared.

The guest waked from a dream, and remembering his day's pleasure hurried to dress himself that it might sooner begin. He was sure from the way the shy little girl looked once or twice yesterday that she had at least seen the white heron, and now she must really be made to tell. Here she comes now, paler than ever, and her worn old frock is torn and tattered, and smeared with pine pitch. The grandmother and the sportsman stand in the door together and question her, and the splendid moment has come to speak of the dead hemlock-tree by the green marsh.

But Sylvia does not speak after all, though the old grandmother fretfully rebukes her, and the young man's kind, appealing eyes are looking straight in her own. He can make them rich with money; he has promised it, and they are poor now. He is so well worth making happy, and he waits to hear the story she can tell.

No, she must keep silence! What is it that suddenly forbids her and makes her dumb? Has she been nine years growing and now, when the great world for the first time puts out a hand to her, must she thrust it aside for a bird's sake? The murmur of the pine's green branches is in her ears, she remembers how the white heron came flying through the golden air and how they watched the sea and the morning together, and Sylvia cannot speak; she cannot tell the heron's secret and give its life away.

Dear loyalty, that suffered a sharp pang as the guest went away disappointed later in the day, that could have served and followed him and loved him as a dog loves! Many a night Sylvia heard the echo of his whistle haunting the pasture path as she came home with the loitering cow. She forgot even her sorrow at the sharp report of his gun and the sight of thrushes and sparrows dropping silent to the ground, their songs hushed and their pretty feathers stained and wet with blood. Were the birds better friends than their hunter might have been, — who can tell? Whatever treasures were lost to her, woodlands and summer-time, remember! Bring your gifts and graces and tell your secrets to this lonely country child!

Mary E. Wilkins Freeman

(1852–1930)

MARY ELEANOR WILKINS FREEMAN began her literary career writing stories and verse for children. The first story she published for adults, "A Shadow Family," appeared in a Boston newspaper, followed by "Two Old Lovers," published in the March 31, 1883 issue of *Harper's Bazaar*. Though Freeman also wrote several novels, her best work appears in two volumes of stories, *A Humble Romance and Other Stories* (1887) and *A New England Nun and Other Stories* (1891).

Her mother's death in 1880, followed by that of her father three years later, left Freeman financially dependent on her writing. Fortunately, her fiction — particularly the short stories — was well received, and Freeman enjoyed a successful literary career; in 1926 she was awarded the (William Dean) Howells Medal for Fiction. That same year, she and Edith Wharton became the first women elected to membership in the National Institute of Arts and Letters.

Freeman's protagonists, usually older women who view life resolutely rather than through a veil of sentimentality, departed from more typical heroines of the period. By portraying women who endure their lot in life but retain their dignity, Freeman's fiction pointed up new possibilities for female characters. Louisa Ellis, heroine of "A New England Nun," is representative of Freeman's heroines. After fourteen years spent waiting for her fiancé to return, Louisa has adapted to her isolated existence and has come to find a certain comfort and contentment in it. When she is finally confronted with her prospective bridegroom, she determines to face her impending nuptials with the same stoic determination that his absence elicited. As in many of Freeman's works, a masculine presence is perceived by the heroine as a disruptive force, and Louisa's "noble" gesture at the story's conclusion constitutes a guarantee of the way of life she has grown to cherish.

A New England Nun

IT WAS LATE in the afternoon, and the light was waning. There was a difference in the look of the tree shadows out in the yard. Somewhere in the distance cows were lowing and a little bell was tinkling; now and then a farm-wagon tilted by, and the dust flew; some blue-shirted laborers with shovels over their shoulders plodded past; little swarms of flies were dancing up and down before the people's faces in the soft air. There seemed to be a gentle stir arising over everything for the mere sake of subsidence — a very premonition of rest and hush and night.

This soft diurnal commotion was over Louisa Ellis also. She had been peacefully sewing at her sitting-room window all the afternoon. Now she quilted her needle carefully into her work, which she folded precisely, and laid in a basket with her thimble and thread and scissors. Louisa Ellis could not remember that ever in her life she had mislaid one of these little feminine appurtenances, which had become, from long use and constant association, a very part of her personality.

Louisa tied a green apron round her waist, and got out a flat straw hat with a green ribbon. Then she went into the garden with a little blue crockery bowl, to pick some currants for her tea. After the currants were picked she sat on the back door-step and stemmed them, collecting the stems carefully in her apron, and afterwards throwing them into the hen-coop. She looked sharply at the grass beside the step to see if any had fallen there.

Louisa was slow and still in her movements; it took her a long time to prepare her tea; but when ready it was set forth with as much grace as if she had been a veritable guest to her own self. The little square table stood exactly in the centre of the kitchen, and was covered with a starched linen cloth whose border pattern of flowers glistened. Louisa had a damask napkin on her tea-tray, where were arranged a cut-glass tumbler full of teaspoons, a silver cream-pitcher, a china sugar-bowl, and one pink china cup and saucer. Louisa used china every day — something which none of her neighbors did. They whispered about it among themselves. Their daily tables were laid with common crockery, their sets of best china stayed in the parlor closet, and Louisa Ellis was no richer nor better bred than they. Still she would use the china. She had for her supper a glass dish full of sugared currants, a plate of little cakes, and one of light white biscuits. Also a leaf or two of lettuce, which she cut up daintily. Louisa was very fond of lettuce, which she raised to perfection in her little garden. She ate quite heartily, though in a delicate, pecking way; it seemed almost surprising that any considerable bulk of the food should vanish.

After tea she filled a plate with nicely baked thin corn-cakes, and carried them out into the back-yard.

"Cæsar!" she called. "Cæsar! Cæsar!"

There was a little rush, and the clank of a chain, and a large yellow-and-white dog appeared at the door of his tiny hut, which was half hidden among the tall grasses and flowers. Louisa patted him and gave him the corn-cakes. Then she returned to the house and washed the tea-things, polishing the china carefully. The twilight had deepened; the chorus of the frogs floated in at the open window wonderfully loud and shrill, and once in a while a long sharp drone from a tree-toad pierced it. Louisa took off her green gingham apron, disclosing a shorter one of pink-and-white print. She lighted her lamp, and sat down again with her sewing.

In about half an hour Joe Dagget came. She heard his heavy step on the walk, and rose and took off her pink-and-white apron. Under that was still another — white linen with a little cambric edging on the bottom; that was Louisa's company apron. She never wore it without her calico sewing apron over it unless she had a guest. She had barely folded the pink-and-white one with methodical haste and laid it in a table-drawer when the door opened and Joe Dagget entered.

He seemed to fill up the whole room. A little yellow canary that had been asleep in his green cage at the south window woke up and fluttered wildly, beating his little yellow wings against the wires. He always did so when Joe Dagget came into the room.

"Good-evening," said Louisa. She extended her hand with a kind of solemn cordiality.

"Good-evening, Louisa," returned the man, in a loud voice.

She placed a chair for him, and they sat facing each other, with the table between them. He sat bolt-upright, toeing out his heavy feet squarely, glancing with a good-humored uneasiness around the room. She sat gently erect, folding her slender hands in her white-linen lap.

"Been a pleasant day," remarked Dagget.

"Real pleasant," Louisa assented, softly. "Have you been haying?" she asked, after a little while.

"Yes, I've been haying all day, down in the ten-acre lot. Pretty hot work."

"It must be."

"Yes, it's pretty hot work in the sun."

"Is your mother well to-day?"

"Yes, mother's pretty well."

"I suppose Lily Dyer's with her now?"

Dagget colored. "Yes, she's with her," he answered, slowly.

He was not very young, but there was a boyish look about his large face. Louisa was not quite as old as he, her face was fairer and smoother, but she gave people the impression of being older.

"I suppose she's a good deal of help to your mother," she said, further.

"I guess she is; I don't know how mother'd get along without her," said Dagget, with a sort of embarrassed warmth.

"She looks like a real capable girl. She's pretty-looking too," remarked Louisa.

"Yes, she is pretty fair looking."

Presently Dagget began fingering the books on the table. There was a square red autograph album, and a Young Lady's Gift-Book which had belonged to Louisa's mother. He took them up one after the other and opened them; then laid them down again, the album on the Gift-Book.

Louisa kept eying them with mild uneasiness. Finally she rose and changed the position of the books, putting the album underneath. That was the way they had been arranged in the first place.

Dagget gave an awkward little laugh. "Now what difference did it make which book was on top?" said he.

Louisa looked at him with a deprecating smile. "I always keep them that way," murmured she.

"You do beat everything," said Dagget, trying to laugh again. His large face was flushed.

He remained about an hour longer, then rose to take leave. Going out, he stumbled over a rug, and trying to recover himself, hit Louisa's work-basket on the table, and knocked it on the floor.

He looked at Louisa, then at the rolling spools; he ducked himself awkwardly toward them, but she stopped him. "Never mind," said she; "I'll pick them up after you're gone."

She spoke with a mild stiffness. Either she was a little disturbed, or his nervousness affected her, and made her seem constrained in her effort to reassure him.

When Joe Dagget was outside he drew in the sweet evening air with a sigh, and felt much as an innocent and perfectly well-intentioned bear might after his exit from a china shop.

Louisa, on her part, felt much as the kind-hearted, long-suffering owner of the china shop might have done after the exit of the bear.

She tied on the pink, then the green apron, picked up all the scattered treasures and replaced them in her work-basket, and straightened the rug. Then she set the lamp on the floor, and began sharply examining the carpet. She even rubbed her fingers over it, and looked at them.

"He's tracked in a good deal of dust," she murmured. "I thought he must have."

Louisa got a dust-pan and brush, and swept Joe Dagget's track carefully.

If he could have known it, it would have increased his perplexity and uneasiness, although it would not have disturbed his loyalty in the least. He came twice a week to see Louisa Ellis, and every time, sitting there in her delicately sweet room, he felt as if surrounded by a hedge of lace. He was afraid to stir lest he should put a clumsy foot or hand through the fairy web, and he had always the consciousness that Louisa was watching fearfully lest he should.

Still the lace and Louisa commanded perforce his perfect respect and patience and loyalty. They were to be married in a month, after a singular courtship which had lasted for a matter of fifteen years. For fourteen out of the fifteen years the two had not once seen each other, and they had seldom exchanged letters. Joe had been all those years in Australia, where he had gone to make his fortune, and where he had stayed until he made it. He would have stayed fifty years if it had taken so long, and come home feeble and tottering, or never come home at all, to marry Louisa.

But the fortune had been made in the fourteen years, and he had come home now to marry the woman who had been patiently and unquestioningly waiting for him all that time.

Shortly after they were engaged he had announced to Louisa his determination to strike out into new fields, and secure a competency before they should be married. She had listened and assented with the

sweet serenity which never failed her, not even when her lover set forth
on that long and uncertain journey. Joe, buoyed up as he was by his
sturdy determination, broke down a little at the last, but Louisa kissed
him with a mild blush, and said good-by.

"It won't be for long," poor Joe had said, huskily; but it was for
fourteen years.

In that length of time much had happened. Louisa's mother and
brother had died, and she was all alone in the world. But greatest
happening of all — a subtle happening which both were too simple to
understand — Louisa's feet had turned into a path, smooth maybe under
a calm, serene sky, but so straight and unswerving that it could only meet
a check at her grave, and so narrow that there was no room for any one at
her side.

Louisa's first emotion when Joe Dagget came home (he had not
apprised her of his coming) was consternation, although she would not
admit it to herself, and he never dreamed of it. Fifteen years ago she had
been in love with him — at least she considered herself to be. Just at that
time, gently acquiescing with and falling into the natural drift of girl-
hood, she had seen marriage ahead as a reasonable feature and a
probable desirability of life. She had listened with calm docility to her
mother's views upon the subject. Her mother was remarkable for
her cool sense and sweet, even temperament. She talked wisely to her
daughter when Joe Dagget presented himself, and Louisa accepted him
with no hesitation. He was the first lover she had ever had.

She had been faithful to him all these years. She had never dreamed
of the possibility of marrying any one else. Her life, especially for the last
seven years, had been full of a pleasant peace, she had never felt
discontented nor impatient over her lover's absence; still she had always
looked forward to his return and their marriage as the inevitable conclusion of things. However, she had fallen into a way of placing it so far in
the future that it was almost equal to placing it over the boundaries of
another life.

When Joe came she had been expecting him, and expecting to be
married for fourteen years, but she was as much surprised and taken
aback as if she had never thought of it.

Joe's consternation came later. He eyed Louisa with an instant confir-
mation of his old admiration. She had changed but little. She still kept
her pretty manner and soft grace, and was, he considered, every whit as
attractive as ever. As for himself, his stent was done; he had turned his
face away from fortune-seeking, and the old winds of romance whistled

as loud and sweet as ever through his ears. All the song which he had been wont to hear in them was Louisa; he had for a long time a loyal belief that he heard it still, but finally it seemed to him that although the winds sang always that one song, it had another name. But for Louisa the wind had never more than murmured; now it had gone down, and everything was still. She listened for a little while with half-wistful attention; then she turned quietly away and went to work on her wedding clothes.

Joe had made some extensive and quite magnificent alterations in his house. It was the old homestead; the newly-married couple would live there, for Joe could not desert his mother, who refused to leave her old home. So Louisa must leave hers. Every morning, rising and going about among her neat maidenly possessions, she felt as one looking her last upon the faces of dear friends. It was true that in a measure she could take them with her, but, robbed of their old environments, they would appear in such new guises that they would almost cease to be themselves. Then there were some peculiar features of her happy solitary life which she would probably be obliged to relinquish altogether. Sterner tasks than these graceful but half-needless ones would probably devolve upon her. There would be a large house to care for; there would be company to entertain; there would be Joe's rigours and feeble old mother to wait upon; and it would be contrary to all thrifty village traditions for her to keep more than one servant. Louisa had a little still, and she used to occupy herself pleasantly in summer weather with distilling the sweet and aromatic essences from roses and peppermint and spearmint. By-and-by her still must be laid away. Her store of essences was already considerable, and there would be no time for her to distil for the mere pleasure of it. Then Joe's mother would think it foolishness; she had already hinted her opinion in the matter. Louisa dearly loved to sew a linen seam, not always for use, but for the simple, mild pleasure which she took in it. She would have been loath to confess how more than once she had ripped a seam for the mere delight of sewing it together again. Sitting at her window during long sweet afternoons, drawing her needle gently through the dainty fabric, she was peace itself. But there was small chance of such foolish comfort in the future. Joe's mother, domineering, shrewd old matron that she was even in her old age, and very likely even Joe himself, with his honest masculine rudeness, would laugh and frown down all these pretty but senseless old maiden ways.

Louisa had almost the enthusiasm of an artist over the mere order and cleanliness of her solitary home. She had throbs of genuine triumph at the sight of the window-panes which she had polished until they shone like jewels. She gloated gently over her orderly bureau-drawers, with their exquisitely folded contents redolent with lavender and sweet clover and very purity. Could she be sure of the endurance of even this? She had visions, so startling that she half repudiated them as indelicate, of coarse masculine belongings strewn about in endless litter; of dust and disorder arising necessarily from a coarse masculine presence in the midst of all this delicate harmony.

Among her forebodings of disturbance, not the least was with regard to Cæsar. Cæsar was a veritable hermit of a dog. For the greater part of his life he had dwelt in his secluded hut, shut out from the society of his kind and all innocent canine joys. Never had Cæsar since his early youth watched at a woodchuck's hole; never had he known the delights of a stray bone at a neighbor's kitchen door. And it was all on account of a sin committed when hardly out of his puppyhood. No one knew the possible depth of remorse of which this mild-visaged, altogether innocent-looking old dog might be capable; but whether or not he had encountered remorse, he had encountered a full measure of righteous retribution. Old Cæsar seldom lifted up his voice in a growl or a bark; he was fat and sleepy; there were yellow rings which looked like spectacles around his dim old eyes; but there was a neighbor who bore on his hand the imprint of several of Cæsar's sharp white youthful teeth, and for that he had lived at the end of a chain, all alone in a little hut, for fourteen years. The neighbor, who was choleric and smarting with the pain of his wound, had demanded either Cæsar's death or complete ostracism. So Louisa's brother, to whom the dog had belonged, had built him his little kennel and tied him up. It was now fourteen years since, in a flood of youthful spirits, he had inflicted that memorable bite and with the exception of short excursions, always at the end of the chain, under the strict guardianship of his master or Louisa, the old dog had remained a close prisoner. It is doubtful if, with his limited ambition, he took much pride in the fact, but it is certain that he was possessed of considerable cheap fame. He was regarded by all the children in the village and by many adults as a very monster of ferocity. St. George's dragon could hardly have surpassed in evil repute Louisa Ellis's old yellow dog. Mothers charged their children with solemn emphasis not to go too near him, and the children listened and believed greedily, with a fascinated appetite for terror, and ran by Louisa's house stealthily, with many sidelong and backward glances at the terrible dog. If perchance he sounded a hoarse bark, there was a panic. Wayfarers chancing into Louisa's yard eyed him with respect, and inquired if the chain were stout. Cæsar at large might have seemed a very ordinary dog, and excited no comment whatever; chained, his reputation overshadowed him, so that he lost his own proper outlines and looked darkly vague and enormous. Joe Dagget, however, with his good-humored sense and shrewdness, saw him as he was. He strode valiantly up to him and patted him on the head, in spite of Louisa's soft clamor of warning, and even attempted to set him loose. Louisa grew so alarmed that he desisted, but kept announcing his opinion in the matter quite forcibly at intervals. "There ain't a better-natured dog in town," he would say, "and it's downright cruel to keep him tied up there. Some day I'm going to take him out."

Louisa had very little hope that he would not, one of these days, when their interests and possessions should be more completely fused in one. She pictured to herself Cæsar on the rampage through the quiet and unguarded village. She saw innocent children bleeding in his path. She was herself very fond of the old dog, because he had belonged to her dead brother, and he was always very gentle with her; still she had great faith in his ferocity. She always warned people not to go too near him. She fed him on ascetic fare of corn-mush and cakes, and never fired his dangerous temper with heating and sanguinary diet of flesh and bones. Louisa looked at the old dog munching his simple fare, and thought of her approaching marriage and trembled. Still no anticipation of disorder and confusion in lieu of sweet peace and harmony, no forebodings of Cæsar on the rampage, no wild fluttering of her little yellow canary, were sufficient to turn her a hair's-breadth. Joe Dagget had been fond of her and working for her all these years. It was not for her, whatever came to pass, to prove untrue and break his heart. She put the exquisite little stitches into her wedding-garments, and the time went on until it was only a week before her wedding-day. It was a Tuesday evening, and the wedding was to be a week from Wednesday.

There was a full moon that night. About nine o'clock Louisa strolled down the road a little way. There were harvest-fields on either hand, bordered by low stone walls. Luxuriant clumps of bushes grew beside the wall, and trees — wild cherry and old apple-trees — at intervals. Presently Louisa sat down on the wall and looked about her with mildly sorrowful reflectiveness. Tall shrubs of blueberry and meadow-sweet, all woven together and tangled with blackberry vines and horsebriers, shut her in on either side. She had a little clear space between. Opposite her, on the other side of the road, was a spreading tree; the moon shone between its boughs, and the leaves twinkled like silver. The road was bespread with a beautiful shifting dapple of silver and shadow; the air was full of a mysterious sweetness. "I wonder if it's wild grapes?" murmured Louisa. She sat there some time. She was just thinking of rising, when she heard footsteps and low voices, and remained quiet. It was a lonely place, and she felt a little timid. She thought she would keep still in the shadow and let the persons, whoever they might be, pass her.

But just before they reached her the voices ceased, and the footsteps. She understood that their owners had also found seats upon the stone wall. She was wondering if she could not steal away unobserved, when the voice broke the stillness. It was Joe Dagget's. She sat still and listened.

The voice was announced by a loud sigh, which was as familiar as itself. "Well," said Dagget, "you've made up your mind, then, I suppose?"

"Yes," returned another voice; "I'm going day after to-morrow."

"That's Lily Dyer," thought Louisa to herself. The voice embodied itself in her mind. She saw a girl tall and full-figured, with a firm, fair face, looking fairer and firmer in the moonlight, her strong yellow hair braided in a close knot. A girl full of a calm rustic strength and bloom, with a masterful way which might have beseemed a princess. Lily Dyer was a favorite with the village folk; she had just the qualities to arouse the admiration. She was good and handsome and smart. Louisa had often heard her praises sounded.

"Well," said Joe Dagget, "I ain't got a word to say."

"I don't know what you could say," returned Lily Dyer.

"Not a word to say," repeated Joe, drawing out the words heavily. Then there was silence. "I ain't sorry," he began at last, "that that happened yesterday—that we kind of let on how we felt to each other. I guess it's just as well we knew. Of course I can't do anything any different. I'm going right on an' get married next week. I ain't going back on a woman that's waited for me fourteen years, an' break her heart."

"If you should jilt her to-morrow, I wouldn't have you," spoke up the girl, with sudden vehemence.

"Well, I ain't going to give you the chance," said he; "but I don't believe you would, either."

"You'd see I wouldn't. Honor's honor, an' right's right. An' I'd never think anything of any man that went against 'em for me or any other girl; you'd find that out, Joe Dagget."

"Well, you'll find out fast enough that I ain't going against 'em for you or any other girl," returned he. Their voices sounded almost as if they were angry with each other. Louisa was listening eagerly.

"I'm sorry you feel as if you must go away," said Joe, "but I don't know but it's best."

"Of course it's best. I hope you and I have got common-sense."

"Well, I suppose you're right." Suddenly Joe's voice got an undertone of tenderness. "Say, Lily," said he, "I'll get along well enough myself, but I can't bear to think—You don't suppose you're going to fret much over it?"

"I guess you'll find out I sha'n't fret much over a married man."

"Well, I hope you won't—I hope you won't, Lily. God knows I do. And—I hope—one of these days—you'll—come across somebody else—"

"I don't see any reason why I shouldn't." Suddenly her tone changed. She spoke in a sweet, clear voice, so loud that she could have been heard across the street. "No, Joe Dagget," said she, "I'll never marry any other man as long as I live. I've got good sense, an' I ain't going to break my heart nor make a fool of myself; but I'm never going to be married, you can be sure of that. I ain't that sort of a girl to feel this way twice."

Louisa heard an exclamation and a soft commotion behind the bushes; then Lily spoke again—the voice sounded as if she had risen. "This must be put a stop to," said she. "We've stayed here long enough. I'm going home."

Louisa sat there in a daze, listening to their retreating steps. After a while she got up and slunk softly home herself. The next day she did her housework methodically; that was as much a matter of course as breathing; but she did not sew on her wedding-clothes. She sat at her window and meditated. In the evening Joe came. Louisa Ellis had never known that she had any diplomacy in her, but when she came to look for it that night she found it, although meek of its kind, among her little feminine weapons. Even now she could hardly believe that she had heard aright, and that she would not do Joe a terrible injury should she break her troth-plight. She wanted to sound him without betraying too soon her own inclinations in the matter. She did it successfully, and they finally came to an understanding; but it was a difficult thing, for he was as afraid of betraying himself as she.

She never mentioned Lily Dyer. She simply said that while she had no cause of complaint against him, she had lived so long in one way that she shrank from making a change.

"Well, I never shrank, Louisa," said Dagget. "I'm going to be honest enough to say that I think maybe it's better this way; but if you'd wanted to keep on, I'd have stuck to you till my dying day. I hope you know that."

"Yes, I do," said she.

That night she and Joe parted more tenderly than they had done for a long time. Standing in the door, holding each other's hands, a last great wave of regretful memory swept over them.

"Well, this ain't the way we've thought it was all going to end, is it, Louisa?" said Joe.

She shook her head. There was a little quiver on her placid face.

"You let me know if there's ever anything I can do for you," said he. "I ain't ever going to forget you, Louisa." Then he kissed her, and went down the path.

Louisa, all alone by herself that night, wept a little, she hardly knew why; but the next morning, on waking, she felt like a queen who, after fearing lest her domain be wrested away from her, sees it firmly insured in her possession.

Now the tall weeds and grasses might cluster around Cæsar's little hermit hut, the snow might fall on its roof year in and year out, but he never would go on a rampage through the unguarded village. Now the little canary might turn itself into a peaceful yellow ball night after night, and have no need to wake and flutter with wild terror against its bars. Louisa could sew linen seams, and distil roses, and dust and polish and fold away in lavender, as long as she listed. That afternoon she sat with her needle-work at the window, and felt fairly steeped in peace. Lily Dyer, tall and erect and blooming, went past; but she felt no qualm. If Louisa Ellis had sold her birthright she did not know it, the taste of the pottage was so delicious, and had been her sole satisfaction for so long. Serenity and placid narrowness had become to her as the birthright itself. She gazed ahead through a long reach of future days strung together like pearls in a rosary, every one like the others, and all smooth and flawless and innocent, and her heart went up in thankfulness. Outside was the fervid summer afternoon; the air was filled with the sounds of the busy harvest of men and birds and bees; there were halloos, metallic clatterings, sweet calls, and long hummings. Louisa sat, prayerfully numbering her days, like an uncloistered nun.

Charlotte Perkins Gilman

(1860–1935)

CHARLOTTE PERKINS GILMAN was the second child of Frederic Beecher Perkins—nephew of Harriet Beecher Stowe—and Mary A. Fitch. Shortly after her birth, Perkins abandoned his family, and Gilman's mother was left to support her two children.

As a young woman, Gilman earned her living as a governess, art teacher and greeting-card designer. She married another artist, Charles Stetson, in 1884 and shortly after gave birth to their daughter Katharine. Suffering from what was most likely postpartum depression, Gilman followed her husband's suggestion and consulted with the famous physician S. Weir Mitchell, author of *Lectures on the Diseases of the Nervous System, Especially in Women* (1881). After undergoing Mitchell's renowned Rest Cure, which prescribed complete bed rest, Gilman was advised to live "as domestic a life" as possible, to keep her child with her at all times and to avoid any intellectual stimulation whatsoever. "The Yellow Wall-Paper"—published in 1892, the same year that Gilman was granted a divorce from her first husband—is Gilman's semi-autobiographical account of the disastrous effects of Mitchell's "cure." Related in the first person, the story traces a woman's descent into madness under the care of her well-intentioned husband.

Gilman's text is an example of what critic Michelle Massé calls marital gothic. Whereas marriage provided the resolution of conventional gothic, in "The Yellow Wall-Paper" it is a source of—rather than sanctuary from—horror. And though the narrator's husband loves her, he remains oblivious, thereby contributing, to the real cause of his wife's illness.

Gilman was one of the foremost feminists at the turn of the century. In addition to "The Yellow Wall-Paper," her most famous work of fiction, she published a large body of polemical work, including *Women and Economics* (1898), a fundamental text of the early women's movement in America, *Herland* (1915) and *His Religion and Hers* (1923).

The Yellow Wall-Paper

IT IS VERY seldom that mere ordinary people like John and myself secure ancestral halls for the summer.

A colonial mansion, a hereditary estate, I would say a haunted house, and reach the height of romantic felicity — but that would be asking too much of fate!

Still I will proudly declare that there is something queer about it.

Else, why should it be let so cheaply? And why have stood so long untenanted?

John laughs at me, of course, but one expects that in marriage.

John is practical in the extreme. He has no patience with faith, an intense horror of superstition, and he scoffs openly at any talk of things not to be felt and seen and put down in figures.

John is a physician, and *perhaps* — (I would not say it to a living soul, of course, but this is dead paper and a great relief to my mind —) *perhaps* that is one reason I do not get well faster.

You see he does not believe I am sick!

And what can one do?

If a physician of high standing, and one's own husband, assures friends and relatives that there is really nothing the matter with one but temporary nervous depression — a slight hysterical tendency — what is one to do?

My brother is also a physician, and also of high standing, and he says the same thing.

So I take phosphates or phosphites — whichever it is, and tonics, and journeys, and air, and exercise, and am absolutely forbidden to "work" until I am well again.

Personally, I disagree with their ideas.

Personally, I believe that congenial work, with excitement and change, would do me good.

But what is one to do?

I did write for a while in spite of them; but it *does* exhaust me a good deal—having to be so sly about it, or else meet with heavy opposition.

I sometimes fancy that in my condition if I had less opposition and more society and stimulus—but John says the very worst thing I can do is to think about my condition, and I confess it always makes me feel bad.

So I will let it alone and talk about the house.

The most beautiful place! It is quite alone, standing well back from the road, quite three miles from the village. It makes me think of English places that you read about, for there are hedges and walls and gates that lock, and lots of separate little houses for the gardeners and people.

There is a *delicious* garden! I never saw such a garden—large and shady, full of box-bordered paths, and lined with long grape-covered arbors with seats under them.

There were greenhouses, too, but they are all broken now.

There was some legal trouble, I believe, something about the heirs and coheirs; anyhow, the place has been empty for years.

That spoils my ghostliness, I am afraid, but I don't care—there is something strange about the house—I can feel it.

I even said so to John one moonlight evening, but he said what I felt was a *draught*, and shut the window.

I get unreasonably angry with John sometimes. I'm sure I never used to be so sensitive. I think it is due to this nervous condition.

But John says if I feel so, I shall neglect proper self-control; so I take pains to control myself—before him, at least, and that makes me very tired.

I don't like our room a bit. I wanted one downstairs that opened on the piazza and had roses all over the window, and such pretty old-fashioned chintz hangings! but John would not hear of it.

He said there was only one window and not room for two beds, and no near room for him if he took another.

He is very careful and loving, and hardly lets me stir without special direction.

I have a schedule prescription for each hour in the day; he takes all care from me, and so I feel basely ungrateful not to value it more.

He said we came here solely on my account, that I was to have perfect rest and all the air I could get. "Your exercise depends on your strength, my dear," said he, "and your food somewhat on your appetite; but air you can absorb all the time." So we took the nursery at the top of the house.

It is a big, airy room, the whole floor nearly, with windows that look all ways, and air and sunshine galore. It was nursery first and then playroom and gymnasium, I should judge; for the windows are barred for little children, and there are rings and things in the walls.

The paint and paper look as if a boys' school had used it. It is stripped off — the paper — in great patches all around the head of my bed, about as far as I can reach, and in a great place on the other side of the room low down. I never saw a worse paper in my life.

One of those sprawling flamboyant patterns committing every artistic sin.

It is dull enough to confuse the eye in following, pronounced enough to constantly irritate and provoke study, and when you follow the lame uncertain curves for a little distance they suddenly commit suicide — plunge off at outrageous angles, destroy themselves in unheard of contradictions.

The color is repellant, almost revolting; a smouldering unclean yellow, strangely faded by the slow-turning sunlight.

It is a dull yet lurid orange in some places, a sickly sulphur tint in others.

No wonder the children hated it! I should hate it myself if I had to live in this room long.

There comes John, and I must put this away, — he hates to have me write a word.

* * *

We have been here two weeks, and I haven't felt like writing before, since that first day.

I am sitting by the window now, up in this atrocious nursery, and there is nothing to hinder my writing as much as I please, save lack of strength.

John is away all day, and even some nights when his cases are serious.

I am glad my case is not serious!

But these nervous troubles are dreadfully depressing.

John does not know how much I really suffer. He knows there is no *reason* to suffer, and that satisfies him.

Of course it is only nervousness. It does weigh on me so not to do my duty in any way!

I meant to be such a help to John, such a real rest and comfort, and here I am a comparative burden already!

Nobody would believe what an effort it is to do what little I am able, —
to dress and entertain, and order things.

It is fortunate Mary is so good with the baby. Such a dear baby!

And yet I *cannot* be with him, it makes me so nervous.

I suppose John never was nervous in his life. He laughs at me so about
this wall-paper!

At first he meant to repaper the room, but afterwards he said that I was
letting it get the better of me, and that nothing was worse for a nervous
patient than to give way to such fancies.

He said that after the wall-paper was changed it would be the heavy
bedstead, and then the barred windows, and then that gate at the head of
the stairs, and so on.

"You know the place is doing you good," he said, "and really, dear, I
don't care to renovate the house just for a three months' rental."

"Then do let us go downstairs," I said, "there are such pretty rooms
there."

Then he took me in his arms and called me a blessed little goose, and
said he would go down cellar, if I wished, and have it whitewashed into
the bargain.

But he is right enough about the beds and windows and things.

It is an airy and comfortable room as any one need wish, and, of
course, I would not be so silly as to make him uncomfortable just for a
whim.

I'm really getting quite fond of the big room, all but that horrid paper.

Out of one window I can see the garden, those mysterious deep-
shaded arbors, the riotous old-fashioned flowers, and bushes and gnarly
trees.

Out of another I get a lovely view of the bay and a little private wharf
belonging to the estate. There is a beautiful shaded lane that runs down
there from the house. I always fancy I see people walking in these
numerous paths and arbors, but John has cautioned me not to give way
to fancy in the least. He says that with my imaginative power and habit of
story-making, a nervous weakness like mine is sure to lead to all manner
of excited fancies, and that I ought to use my will and good sense to
check the tendency. So I try.

I think sometimes that if I were only well enough to write a little it
would relieve the press of ideas and rest me.

But I find I get pretty tired when I try.

It is so discouraging not to have any advice and companionship about
my work. When I get really well, John says we will ask Cousin Henry and

Julia down for a long visit; but he says he would as soon put fireworks in my pillow-case as to let me have those stimulating people about now.

I wish I could get well faster.

But I must not think about that. This paper looks to me as if it *knew* what a vicious influence it had!

There is a recurrent spot where the pattern lolls like a broken neck and two bulbous eyes stare at you upside down.

I get positively angry with the impertinence of it and the everlasting-ness. Up and down and sideways they crawl, and those absurd, un-blinking eyes are everywhere. There is one place where two breadths didn't match, and the eyes go all up and down the line, one a little higher than the other.

I never saw so much expression in an inanimate thing before, and we all know how much expression they have! I used to lie awake as a child and get more entertainment and terror out of blank walls and plain furniture than most children could find in a toy-store.

I remember what a kindly wink the knobs of our big, old bureau used to have, and there was one chair that always seemed like a strong friend.

I used to feel that if any of the other things looked too fierce I could always hop into that chair and be safe.

The furniture in this room is no worse than inharmonious, however, for we had to bring it all from downstairs. I suppose when this was used as a playroom they had to take the nursery things out, and no wonder! I never saw such ravages as the children have made here.

The wall-paper, as I said before, is torn off in spots, and it sticketh closer than a brother — they must have had perseverance as well as hatred.

Then the floor is scratched and gouged and splintered, the plaster itself is dug out here and there, and this great heavy bed which is all we found in the room, looks as if it had been through the wars.

But I don't mind it a bit — only the paper.

There comes John's sister. Such a dear girl as she is, and so careful of me! I must not let her find me writing.

She is a perfect and enthusiastic housekeeper, and hopes for no better profession. I verily believe she thinks it is the writing which made me sick!

But I can write when she is out, and see her a long way off from these windows.

There is one that commands the road, a lovely shaded winding road, and one that just looks off over the country. A lovely country, too, full of great elms and velvet meadows.

This wall-paper has a kind of subpattern in a different shade, a particularly irritating one, for you can only see it in certain lights, and not clearly then.

But in the places where it isn't faded and where the sun is just so — I can see a strange, provoking, formless sort of figure, that seems to skulk about behind that silly and conspicuous front design.

There's sister on the stairs!

* * *

Well, the Fourth of July is over! The people are all gone and I am tired out. John thought it might do me good to see a little company, so we just had mother and Nellie and the children down for a week.

Of course I didn't do a thing. Jennie sees to everything now.

But it tired me all the same.

John says if I don't pick up faster he shall send me to Weir Mitchell in the fall.

But I don't want to go there at all. I had a friend who was in his hands once, and she says he is just like John and my brother, only more so!

Besides, it is such an undertaking to go so far.

I don't feel as if it was worth while to turn my hand over for anything, and I'm getting dreadfully fretful and querulous.

I cry at nothing, and cry most of the time.

Of course I don't when John is here, or anybody else, but when I am alone.

And I am alone a good deal just now. John is kept in town very often by serious cases, and Jennie is good and lets me alone when I want her to.

So I walk a little in the garden or down that lovely lane, sit on the porch under the roses, and lie down up here a good deal.

I'm getting really fond of the room in spite of the wall-paper. Perhaps *because* of the wall-paper.

It dwells in my mind so!

I lie here on this great immovable bed — it is nailed down, I believe — and follow that pattern about by the hour. It is as good as gymnastics, I assure you. I start, we'll say, at the bottom, down in the corner over there where it has not been touched, and I determine for the thousandth time that I *will* follow that pointless pattern to some sort of a conclusion.

I know a little of the principle of design, and I know this thing was not arranged on any laws of radiation, or alternation, or repetition, or symmetry, or anything else that I ever heard of.

It is repeated, of course, by the breadths, but not otherwise.

Looked at in one way each breadth stands alone, the bloated curves and flourishes—a kind of "debased Romanesque" with *delirium tremens*—go waddling up and down in isolated columns of fatuity.

But, on the other hand, they connect diagonally, and the sprawling outlines run off in great slanting waves of optic horror, like a lot of wallowing seaweeds in full chase.

The whole thing goes horizontally, too, at least it seems so, and I exhaust myself in trying to distinguish the order of its going in that direction.

They have used a horizontal breadth for a frieze, and that adds wonderfully to the confusion.

There is one end of the room where it is almost intact, and there, when the crosslights fade and the low sun shines directly upon it, I can almost fancy radiation after all,—the interminable grotesque seems to form around a common centre and rush off in headlong plunges of equal distraction.

It makes me tired to follow it. I will take a nap I guess.

*   *   *

I don't know why I should write this.

I don't want to.

I don't feel able.

And I know John would think it absurd. But I *must* say what I feel and think in some way—it is such a relief!

But the effort is getting to be greater than the relief.

Half the time now I am awfully lazy, and lie down ever so much.

John says I mustn't lose my strength, and has me take cod liver oil and lots of tonics and things, to say nothing of ale and wine and rare meat.

Dear John! He loves me very dearly, and hates to have me sick. I tried to have a real earnest reasonable talk with him the other day, and tell him how I wish he would let me go and make a visit to Cousin Henry and Julia.

But he said I wasn't able to go, nor able to stand it after I got there; and I did not make out a very good case for myself, for I was crying before I had finished.

It is getting to be a great effort for me to think straight. Just this nervous weakness I suppose.

And dear John gathered me up in his arms, and just carried me upstairs and laid me on the bed, and sat by me and read to me till it tired my head.

He said I was his darling and his comfort and all he had, and that I must take care of myself for his sake, and keep well.

He says no one but myself can help me out of it, that I must use my will and self-control and not let any silly fancies run away with me.

There's one comfort, the baby is well and happy, and does not have to occupy this nursery with the horrid wall-paper.

If we had not used it, that blessed child would have! What a fortunate escape! Why, I wouldn't have a child of mine, an impressionable little thing, live in such a room for worlds.

I never thought of it before, but it is lucky that John kept me here after all, I can stand it so much easier than a baby, you see.

Of course I never mention it to them any more — I am too wise, — but I keep watch of it all the same.

There are things in that paper that nobody knows but me, or ever will.

Behind that outside pattern the dim shapes get clearer every day.

It is always the same shape, only very numerous.

And it is like a woman stooping down and creeping about behind that pattern. I don't like it a bit. I wonder — I begin to think — I wish John would take me away from here!

* * *

It is so hard to talk with John about my case, because he is so wise, and because he loves me so.

But I tried it last night.

It was moonlight. The moon shines in all around just as the sun does.

I hate to see it sometimes, it creeps so slowly, and always comes in by one window or another.

John was asleep and I hated to waken him, so I kept still and watched the moonlight on that undulating wall-paper till I felt creepy.

The faint figure behind seemed to shake the pattern, just as if she wanted to get out.

I got up softly and went to feel and see if the paper *did* move, and when I came back John was awake.

"What is it, little girl?" he said. "Don't go walking about like that — you'll get cold."

I thought it was a good time to talk, so I told him that I really was not gaining here, and that I wished he would take me away.

"Why, darling!" said he, "our lease will be up in three weeks, and I can't see how to leave before.

"The repairs are not done at home, and I cannot possibly leave town just now. Of course if you were in any danger, I could and would, but you really are better, dear, whether you can see it or not. I am a doctor, dear, and I know. You are gaining flesh and color, your appetite is better, I feel really much easier about you."

"I don't weigh a bit more," said I, "nor as much; and my appetite may be better in the evening when you are here, but it is worse in the morning when you are away!"

"Bless her little heart!" said he with a big hug, "she shall be as sick as she pleases! But now let's improve the shining hours by going to sleep, and talk about it in the morning!"

"And you won't go away?" I asked gloomily.

"Why, how can I, dear? It is only three weeks more and then we will take a nice little trip of a few days while Jennie is getting the house ready. Really dear you are better!"

"Better in body perhaps — " I began, and stopped short, for he sat up straight and looked at me with such a stern, reproachful look that I could not say another word.

"My darling," said he, "I beg of you, for my sake and for our child's sake, as well as for your own, that you will never for one instant let that idea enter your mind! There is nothing so dangerous, so fascinating, to a temperament like yours. It is a false and foolish fancy. Can you not trust me as a physician when I tell you so?"

So of course I said no more on that score, and we went to sleep before long. He thought I was asleep first, but I wasn't, and lay there for hours trying to decide whether that front pattern and the back pattern really did move together or separately.

*   *   *

On a pattern like this, by daylight, there is a lack of sequence, a defiance of law, that is a constant irritant to a normal mind.

The color is hideous enough, and unreliable enough, and infuriating enough, but the pattern is torturing.

You think you have mastered it, but just as you get well underway in following, it turns a back-somersault and there you are. It slaps you in the face, knocks you down, and tramples upon you. It is like a bad dream.

The outside pattern is a florid arabesque, reminding one of a fungus. If you can imagine a toadstool in joints, an interminable string of toadstools, budding and sprouting in endless convolutions — why, that is something like it.

That is, sometimes!

There is one marked peculiarity about this paper, a thing nobody seems to notice but myself, and that is that it changes as the light changes.

When the sun shoots in through the east window — I always watch for that first long, straight ray — it changes so quickly that I never can quite believe it.

That is why I watch it always.

By moonlight — the moon shines in all night when there is a moon — I wouldn't know it was the same paper.

At night in any kind of light, in twilight, candlelight, lamplight, and worst of all by moonlight, it becomes bars! The outside pattern I mean, and the woman behind it is as plain as can be.

I didn't realize for a long time what the thing was that showed behind, that dim sub-pattern, but now I am quite sure it is a woman.

By daylight she is subdued, quiet. I fancy it is the pattern that keeps her so still. It is so puzzling. It keeps me quiet by the hour.

I lie down ever so much now. John says it is good for me, and to sleep all I can.

Indeed he started the habit by making me lie down for an hour after each meal.

It is a very bad habit I am convinced, for you see I don't sleep.

And that cultivates deceit, for I don't tell them I'm awake — O no!

The fact is I am getting a little afraid of John.

He seems very queer sometimes, and even Jennie has an inexplicable look.

It strikes me occasionally, just as a scientific hypothesis, — that perhaps it is the paper!

I have watched John when he did not know I was looking, and come into the room suddenly on the most innocent excuses, and I've caught him several times *looking at the paper!* And Jennie too. I caught Jennie with her hand on it once.

She didn't know I was in the room, and when I asked her in a quiet, a very quiet voice, with the most restrained manner possible, what she was doing with the paper — she turned around as if she had been caught stealing, and looked quite angry — asked me why I should frighten her so!

Then she said that the paper stained everything it touched, that she had found yellow smooches on all my clothes and John's, and she wished we would be more careful!

Did not that sound innocent? But I know she was studying that pattern, and I am determined that nobody shall find it out but myself!

* * *

Life is very much more exciting now than it used to be. You see I have something more to expect, to look forward to, to watch. I really do eat better, and am more quiet than I was.

John is so pleased to see me improve! He laughed a little the other day, and said I seemed to be flourishing in spite of my wall-paper.

I turned it off with a laugh. I had no intention of telling him it was *because* of the wall-paper — he would make fun of me. He might even want to take me away.

I don't want to leave now until I have found it out. There is a week more, and I think that will be enough.

* * *

I'm feeling ever so much better! I don't sleep much at night, for it is so interesting to watch developments; but I sleep a good deal in the daytime.

In the daytime it is tiresome and perplexing.

There are always new shoots on the fungus, and new shades of yellow all over it. I cannot keep count of them, though I have tried conscientiously.

It is the strangest yellow, that wall-paper! It makes me think of all the yellow things I ever saw — not beautiful ones like buttercups, but old foul, bad yellow things.

But there is something else about that paper — the smell! I noticed it the moment we came into the room, but with so much air and sun it was not bad. Now we have had a week of fog and rain, and whether the windows are open or not, the smell is here.

It creeps all over the house.

I find it hovering in the dining-room, skulking in the parlor, hiding in the hall, lying in wait for me on the stairs.

It gets into my hair.

Even when I go to ride, if I turn my head suddenly and surprise it — there is that smell!

Such a peculiar odor, too! I have spent hours in trying to analyze it, to find what it smelled like.

It is not bad — at first, and very gentle, but quite the subtlest, most enduring odor I ever met.

In this damp weather it is awful, I wake up in the night and find it hanging over me.

It used to disturb me at first. I thought seriously of burning the house — to reach the smell.

But now I am used to it. The only thing I can think of that it is like is the *color* of the paper! A yellow smell.

There is a very funny mark on this wall, low down, near the mopboard. A streak that runs round the room. It goes behind every piece of furniture, except the bed, a long, straight, even *smooch*, as if it had been rubbed over and over.

I wonder how it was done and who did it, and what they did it for. Round and round and round — round and round and round — it makes me dizzy!

*   *   *

I really have discovered something at last.

Through watching so much at night, when it changes so, I have finally found out.

The front pattern *does* move — and no wonder! The woman behind shakes it!

Sometimes I think there are a great many women behind, and sometimes only one, and she crawls around fast, and her crawling shakes it all over.

Then in the very bright spots she keeps still, and in the very shady spots she just takes hold of the bars and shakes them hard.

And she is all the time trying to climb through. But nobody could climb through that pattern — it strangles so; I think that is why it has so many heads.

They get through, and then the pattern strangles them off and turns them upside down, and makes their eyes white!

If those heads were covered or taken off it would not be half so bad.

*   *   *

I think that woman gets out in the daytime!

And I'll tell you why — privately — I've seen her!

I can see her out of every one of my windows!

It is the same woman, I know, for she is always creeping, and most women do not creep by daylight.

I see her in that long shaded lane, creeping up and down. I see her in those dark grape arbors, creeping all around the garden.

I see her on that long road under the trees, creeping along, and when a carriage comes she hides under the blackberry vines.

I don't blame her a bit. It must be very humiliating to be caught creeping by daylight!

I always lock the door when I creep by daylight. I can't do it at night, for I know John would suspect something at once.

And John is so queer now, that I don't want to irritate him. I wish he would take another room! Besides, I don't want anybody to get that woman out at night but myself.

I often wonder if I could see her out of all the windows at once.

But, turn as fast as I can, I can only see out of one at one time.

And though I always see her, she *may* be able to creep faster than I can turn!

I have watched her sometimes away off in the open country, creeping as fast as a cloud shadow in a high wind.

*   *   *

If only that top pattern could be gotten off from the under one! I mean to try it, little by little.

I have found out another funny thing, but I shan't tell it this time! It does not do to trust people too much.

There are only two more days to get this paper off, and I believe John is beginning to notice. I don't like the look in his eyes.

And I heard him ask Jennie a lot of professional questions about me. She had a very good report to give.

She said I slept a good deal in the daytime.

John knows I don't sleep very well at night, for all I'm so quiet!

He asked me all sorts of questions, too, and pretended to be very loving and kind.

As if I couldn't see through him!

Still, I don't wonder he acts so, sleeping under this paper for three months.

It only interests me, but I feel sure John and Jennie are secretly affected by it.

*   *   *

Hurrah! This is the last day, but it is enough. John is to stay in town over night, and won't be out until this evening.

Jennie wanted to sleep with me — the sly thing! but I told her I should undoubtedly rest better for a night all alone.

That was clever, for really I wasn't alone a bit! As soon as it was moonlight and that poor thing began to crawl and shake the pattern, I got up and ran to help her.

I pulled and she shook, I shook and she pulled, and before morning we had peeled off yards of that paper.

A strip about as high as my head and half around the room.

And then when the sun came and that awful pattern began to laugh at me, I declared I would finish it to-day!

We go away to-morrow, and they are moving all my furniture down again to leave things as they were before.

Jennie looked at the wall in amazement, but I told her merrily that I did it out of pure spite at the vicious thing.

She laughed and said she wouldn't mind doing it herself, but I must not get tired.

How she betrayed herself that time!

But I am here, and no person touches this paper but me, — not *alive!*

She tried to get me out of the room — it was too patent! But I said it was so quiet and empty and clean now that I believed I would lie down again and sleep all I could; and not to wake me even for dinner — I would call when I woke.

So now she is gone, and the servants are gone, and the things are gone, and there is nothing left but that great bedstead nailed down, with the canvas mattress we found on it.

We shall sleep downstairs to-night, and take the boat home to-morrow.

I quite enjoy the room, now it is bare again.

How those children did tear about here!

This bedstead is fairly gnawed!

But I must get to work.

I have locked the door and thrown the key down into the front path.

I don't want to go out, and I don't want to have anybody come in, till John comes.

I want to astonish him.

I've got a rope up here that even Jennie did not find. If that woman does get out, and tries to get away, I can tie her!

But I forgot I could not reach far without anything to stand on!

This bed will *not* move!

I tried to lift and push it until I was lame, and then I got so angry I bit off a little piece at one corner — but it hurt my teeth.

Then I peeled off all the paper I could reach standing on the floor. It sticks horribly and the pattern just enjoys it! All those strangled heads and bulbous eyes and waddling fungus growths just shriek with derision!

I am getting angry enough to do something desperate. To jump out of the window would be admirable exercise, but the bars are too strong even to try.

Besides I wouldn't do it. Of course not. I know well enough that a step like that is improper and might be misconstrued.

I don't like to *look* out of the windows even — there are so many of those creeping women, and they creep so fast.

I wonder if they all come out of that wall-paper as I did?

But I am securely fastened now by my well-hidden rope — you don't get *me* out in the road there!

I suppose I shall have to get back behind the pattern when it comes night, and that is hard!

It is so pleasant to be out in this great room and creep around as I please!

I don't want to go outside. I won't, even if Jennie asks me to.

For outside you have to creep on the ground, and everything is green instead of yellow.

But here I can creep smoothly on the floor, and my shoulder just fits in that long smooch around the wall, so I cannot lose my way.

Why there's John at the door!

It is no use, young man, you can't open it!

How he does call and pound!

Now he's crying for an axe.

It would be a shame to break down that beautiful door!

"John dear!" said I in the gentlest voice, "the key is down by the front steps, under a plantain leaf!"

That silenced him for a few moments.

Then he said — very quietly indeed, "Open the door, my darling!"

"I can't," said I. "The key is down by the front door under a plantain leaf!"

And then I said it again, several times, very gently and slowly, and said it so often that he had to go and see, and he got it of course, and came in. He stopped short by the door.

"What is the matter?" he cried. "For God's sake, what are you doing!"

I kept on creeping just the same, but I looked at him over my shoulder.

"I've got out at last," said I, "in spite of you and Jane. And I've pulled off most of the paper, so you can't put me back!"

Now why should that man have fainted? But he did, and right across my path by the wall, so that I had to creep over him every time!

Kate Chopin

(1851–1904)

KATE CHOPIN did not begin writing for publication until 1889, when she was 38 years old. The mother of six children, Chopin had been widowed six years earlier, when her husband died of swamp fever. The family was then living on a small plantation in Cloutierville, Louisiana, but after her husband's death Chopin returned to St. Louis where she had grown up.

Chopin's own mother had been widowed at a young age, before Chopin was five years old. Raised in a household of strong women — her French-speaking great-grandmother, grandmother and mother — Chopin was well acquainted with the independent spirit that character-izes her fictional heroines. As with Jewett and Freeman, Chopin's depth of psychological realism was often overlooked by those who regarded her as a regional colorist. Best known for her depictions of the Cajuns and Creoles of Louisiana, Chopin shocked critics with her novel *The Awakening* (1899), in which she frankly portrays one woman's passions and sexual awakening. Edna Pontellier's story scandalized reviewers who considered the novel immoral "poison."

Chopin wrote "The Storm" in 1898, while waiting for *The Awakening* to come out. Like the novel, the story deals openly with female sexuality. Calixta, a happily married woman, is nevertheless attracted to another man. Daring for its time, Chopin's story ends happily for all the charac-ters, and no disastrous consequences attend Calixta's passionate en-counter with Alcée.

The harsh criticism that *The Awakening* received had such a negative influence on Chopin that she never published again. "The Storm" remained unpublished until it was included in *The Complete Works of Kate Chopin* (1969; ed. Per Seyersted).

The Storm

I

THE LEAVES WERE so still that even Bibi thought it was going to rain. Bobinôt, who was accustomed to converse on terms of perfect equality with his little son, called the child's attention to certain sombre clouds that were rolling with sinister intention from the west, accompanied by a sullen, threatening roar. They were at Friedheimer's store and decided to remain there till the storm had passed. They sat within the door on two empty kegs. Bibi was four years old and looked very wise.

"Mama'll be 'fraid, yes," he suggested with blinking eyes.

"She'll shut the house. Maybe she got Sylvie helpin' her this evenin'," Bobinôt responded reassuringly.

"No; she ent got Sylvie. Sylvie was helpin' her yistiday," piped Bibi.

Bobinôt arose and going across to the counter purchased a can of shrimps, of which Calixta was very fond. Then he returned to his perch on the keg and sat stolidly holding the can of shrimps while the storm burst. It shook the wooden store and seemed to be ripping great furrows in the distant field. Bibi laid his little hand on his father's knee and was not afraid.

II

Calixta, at home, felt no uneasiness for their safety. She sat at a side window sewing furiously on a sewing machine. She was greatly occupied and did not notice the approaching storm. But she felt very warm and often stopped to mop her face on which the perspiration gathered in beads. She unfastened her white sacque at the throat. It began to grow dark, and suddenly realizing the situation she got up hurriedly and went about closing windows and doors.

Out on the small front gallery she had hung Bobinôt's Sunday clothes to air and she hastened out to gather them before the rain fell. As she stepped outside, Alcée Laballière rode in at the gate. She had not seen him very often since her marriage, and never alone. She stood there with Bobinôt's coat in her hands, and the big rain drops began to fall. Alcée rode his horse under the shelter of a side projection where the chickens had huddled and there were plows and a harrow piled up in the corner.

"May I come and wait on your gallery till the storm is over, Calixta?" he asked.

"Come 'long in, M'sieur Alcée."

His voice and her own startled her as if from a trance, and she seized Bobinôt's vest. Alcée, mounting to the porch, grabbed the trousers and snatched Bibi's braided jacket that was about to be carried away by a sudden gust of wind. He expressed an intention to remain outside, but it was soon apparent that he might as well have been out in the open: the water beat in upon the boards in driving sheets, and he went inside, closing the door after him. It was even necessary to put something beneath the door to keep the water out.

"My! what a rain! It's good two years sence it rain' like that," exclaimed Calixta as she rolled up a piece of bagging and Alcée helped her to thrust it beneath the crack.

She was a little fuller of figure than five years before when she married; but she had lost nothing of her vivacity. Her blue eyes still retained their melting quality; and her yellow hair, dishevelled by the wind and rain, kinked more stubbornly than ever about her ears and temples.

The rain beat upon the low, shingled roof with a force and clatter that threatened to break an entrance and deluge them there. They were in the dining room — the sitting room — the general utility room. Adjoining was her bed room, with Bibi's couch along side her own. The door stood open, and the room with its white, monumental bed, its closed shutters, looked dim and mysterious.

Alcée flung himself into a rocker and Calixta nervously began to gather up from the floor the lengths of a cotton sheet which she had been sewing.

"If this keeps up, *Dieu sait*[1] if the levees goin' to stan' it!" she exclaimed.

"What have you got to do with the levees?"

---

1. *Dieu sait*] God knows.

"I got enough to do! An' there's Bobinôt with Bibi out in that storm — if he only didn' left Friedheimer's!"

"Let us hope, Calixta, that Bobinôt's got sense enough to come in out of a cyclone."

She went and stood at the window with a greatly disturbed look on her face. She wiped the frame that was clouded with moisture. It was stiflingly hot. Alcée got up and joined her at the window, looking over her shoulder. The rain was coming down in sheets obscuring the view of far-off cabins and enveloping the distant wood in a gray mist. The playing of the lightning was incessant. A bolt struck a tall chinaberry tree at the edge of the field. It filled all visible space with a blinding glare and the crash seemed to invade the very boards they stood upon.

Calixta put her hands to her eyes, and with a cry, staggered backward. Alcée's arm encircled her, and for an instant he drew her close and spasmodically to him.

"*Bonté!*"[2] she cried, releasing herself from his encircling arm and retreating from the window, "the house'll go next! If I only knew w'ere Bibi was!" She would not compose herself; she would not be seated. Alcée clasped her shoulders and looked into her face. The contact of her warm, palpitating body when he had unthinkingly drawn her into his arms, had aroused all the old-time infatuation and desire for her flesh.

"Calixta," he said, "don't be frightened. Nothing can happen. The house is too low to be struck, with so many tall trees standing about. There! aren't you going to be quiet? say, aren't you?" He pushed her hair back from her face that was warm and steaming. Her lips were as red and moist as pomegranate seed. Her white neck and a glimpse of her full, firm bosom disturbed him powerfully. As she glanced up at him the fear in her liquid blue eyes had given place to a drowsy gleam that unconsciously betrayed a sensuous desire. He looked down into her eyes and there was nothing for him to do but to gather her lips in a kiss. It reminded him of Assumption.

"Do you remember — in Assumption, Calixta?" he asked in a low voice broken by passion. Oh! she remembered; for in Assumption he had kissed her and kissed and kissed her; until his senses would well nigh fail, and to save her he would resort to a desperate flight. If she was not an immaculate dove in those days, she was still inviolate; a passionate creature whose very defenselessness had made her defense, against which his honor forbade him to prevail. Now — well, now — her lips

2. "*Bonté!*"] "Goodness!"

seemed in a manner free to be tasted, as well as her round, white throat and her whiter breasts.

They did not heed the crashing torrents, and the roar of the elements made her laugh as she lay in his arms. She was a revelation in that dim, mysterious chamber; as white as the couch she lay upon. Her firm, elastic flesh that was knowing for the first time its birthright, was like a creamy lily that the sun invites to contribute its breath and perfume to the undying life of the world.

The generous abundance of her passion, without guile or trickery, was like a white flame which penetrated and found response in depths of his own sensuous nature that had never yet been reached.

When he touched her breasts they gave themselves up in quivering ecstasy, inviting his lips. Her mouth was a fountain of delight. And when he possessed her, they seemed to swoon together at the very borderland of life's mystery.

He stayed cushioned upon her, breathless, dazed, enervated, with his heart beating like a hammer upon her. With one hand she clasped his head, her lips lightly touching his forehead. The other hand stroked with a soothing rhythm his muscular shoulders.

The growl of the thunder was distant and passing away. The rain beat softly upon the shingles, inviting them to drowsiness and sleep. But they dared not yield.

The rain was over; and the sun was turning the glistening green world into a palace of gems. Calixta, on the gallery, watched Alcée ride away. He turned and smiled at her with a beaming face; and she lifted her pretty chin in the air and laughed aloud.

III

Bobinôt and Bibi, trudging home, stopped without at the cistern to make themselves presentable.

"My! Bibi, w'at will yo' mama say! You ought to be ashame'. You oughtn' put on those good pants. Look at 'em! An' that mud on yo' collar! How you got that mud on yo' collar, Bibi? I never saw such a boy!" Bibi was the picture of pathetic resignation. Bobinôt was the embodiment of serious solicitude as he strove to remove from his own person and his son's the signs of their tramp over heavy roads and through wet fields. He scraped the mud off Bibi's bare legs and feet with a stick and carefully removed all traces from his heavy brogans. Then, prepared for the worst — the meeting with an over-scrupulous house-wife, they entered cautiously at the back door.

Calixta was preparing supper. She had set the table and was dripping coffee at the hearth. She sprang up as they came in.

"Oh, Bobinôt! You back! My! but I was uneasy. W'ere you been during the rain? An' Bibi? he ain't wet? he ain't hurt?" She had clasped Bibi and was kissing him effusively. Bobinôt's explanations and apologies which he had been composing all along the way, died on his lips as Calixta felt him to see if he were dry, and seemed to express nothing but satisfaction at their safe return.

"I brought you some shrimps, Calixta," offered Bobinôt, hauling the can from his ample side pocket and laying it on the table.

"Shrimps! Oh, Bobinôt! you too good fo' anything!" and she gave him a smacking kiss on the cheek that resounded. "*J'vous réponds,*[3] we'll have a feas' to-night! umph-umph!"

Bobinôt and Bibi began to relax and enjoy themselves, and when the three seated themselves at table they laughed much and so loud that anyone might have heard them as far away as Laballière's.

IV

Alcée Laballière wrote to his wife, Clarisse, that night. It was a loving letter, full of tender solicitude. He told her not to hurry back, but if she and the babies liked it at Biloxi, to stay a month longer. He was getting on nicely; and though he missed them, he was willing to bear the separation a while longer — realizing that their health and pleasure were the first things to be considered.

V

As for Clarisse, she was charmed upon receiving her husband's letter. She and the babies were doing well. The society was agreeable; many of her old friends and acquaintances were at the bay. And the first free breath since her marriage seemed to restore the pleasant liberty of her maiden days. Devoted as she was to her husband, their intimate conjugal life was something which she was more than willing to forego for a while.

So the storm passed and every one was happy.

3. "*J'vous réponds*"] "You bet!"

Edith Wharton

(1862–1937)

FOR MANY YEARS, Edith Wharton lived a life suited to her position as a wealthy socialite. Born into a prominent New York family, Wharton was educated privately, debuted at 17 and married wealthy Bostonian Edward (Teddy) Wharton when she was 23. For a time, the couple lived like others in their social set, but Wharton became disenchanted with what she perceived as the intellectual torpor of high society. Nevertheless her position helped her develop the keen sense of satire that is so central to her writing.

In 1891 Wharton published her first short story, "Mrs. Manstey's View," in *Scribner's* magazine and her first collection of stories, *The Greater Inclination,* appeared in 1899. Other collections followed, along with novels now deemed classics, such as *The House of Mirth* (1905), *Ethan Frome* (1911) and *The Age of Innocence* (1920).

Despite the success of her novels, Wharton felt most confident writing short fiction. Ironically, most of her stories are set in the same confining social circles from which she had escaped. But Wharton achieves her own brand of realism through her protagonists' struggles within and against conventional morality and the demands of an unsympathetic society.

"The Angel at the Grave" features a heroine who struggles against "duty." Paulina Anson, granddaughter of the great philosopher Orestes Anson, has spent her life preserving his reputation — only to learn the once-celebrated man has been forgotten by the rest of the world. Like Mrs. Amyot in "The Pelican" and Mary Anerton in "The Muse's Tragedy," Paulina Anson must come to terms with the consequences of her sacrifices.

The Angel at the Grave

I

THE HOUSE STOOD a few yards back from the elm-shaded village street, in that semi-publicity sometimes cited as a democratic protest against old-world standards of domestic exclusiveness. This candid exposure to the public eye is more probably a result of the gregariousness which, in the New England bosom, oddly coexists with a shrinking from direct social contact; most of the inmates of such houses preferring that furtive intercourse which is the result of observations through shuttered windows and a categorical acquaintance with the neighboring clothes-lines. The House, however, faced its public with a difference. For sixty years it had written itself with a capital letter, had self-consciously squared itself in the eye of an admiring nation. The most searching inroads of village intimacy hardly counted in a household that opened on the universe; and a lady whose door-bell was at any moment liable to be rung by visitors from London or Vienna was not likely to flutter up-stairs when she observed a neighbor "stepping over."

The solitary inmate of the Anson House owed this induration of the social texture to the most conspicuous accident in her annals: the fact that she was the only granddaughter of the great Orestes Anson. She had been born, as it were, into a museum, and cradled in a glass case with a label; the first foundations of her consciousness being built on the rock of her grandfather's celebrity. To a little girl who acquires her earliest knowledge of literature through a *Reader* embellished with fragments of her ancestor's prose, that personage necessarily fills an heroic space in the foreground of life. To communicate with one's past through the impressive medium of print, to have, as it were, a footing in every library in the country, and an acknowledged kinship with that world-diffused clan, the descendants of the great, was to be pledged to a standard of manners that amazingly simplified the lesser relations of life. The village street on which Paulina Anson's youth looked out led to all the capitals of Europe; and over the roads of intercommunication unseen caravans bore back to the elm-shaded House the tribute of an admiring world.

Fate seemed to have taken a direct share in fitting Paulina for her part as the custodian of this historic dwelling. It had long been secretly regarded as a "visitation" by the great man's family that he had left no son and that his daughters were not "intellectual." The ladies themselves were the first to lament their deficiency, to own that nature had denied them the gift of making the most of their opportunities. A profound veneration for their parent and an unswerving faith in his doctrines had not amended their congenital incapacity to understand what he had written. Laura, who had her moments of mute rebellion against destiny, had sometimes thought how much easier it would have been if their progenitor had been a poet; for she could recite, with feeling, portions of *The Culprit Fay* and of the poems of Mrs. Hemans; and Phœbe, who was more conspicuous for memory than imagination, kept an album filled with "selections." But the great man was a philosopher; and to both daughters respiration was difficult on the cloudy heights of metaphysic. The situation would have been intolerable but for the fact that, while Phœbe and Laura were still at school, their father's fame had passed from the open ground of conjecture to the chill privacy of certitude. Dr. Anson had in fact achieved one of those anticipated immortalities not uncommon at a time when people were apt to base their literary judgments on their emotions, and when to affect plain food and despise England went a long way toward establishing a man's intellectual pre-eminence. Thus, when the daughters were called on to strike a filial attitude about their parent's pedestal, there was little to do but to pose gracefully and point upward; and there are spines to which the immobility of worship is not a strain. A legend had by this time crystallized about the great Orestes, and it was of more immediate interest to the public to hear what brand of tea he drank, and whether he took off his boots in the hall, than to rouse the drowsy echo of his dialectic. A great man never draws so near his public as when it has become unnecessary to read his books and is still interesting to know what he eats for breakfast.

As recorders of their parent's domestic habits, as pious scavengers of his waste-paper basket, the Misses Anson were unexcelled. They always had an interesting anecdote to impart to the literary pilgrim, and the tact with which, in later years, they intervened between the public and the growing inaccessibility of its idol, sent away many an enthusiast satisfied to have touched the veil before the sanctuary. Still it was felt, especially by old Mrs. Anson, who survived her husband for some years, that Phœbe and Laura were not worthy of their privileges. There had been a third daughter so unworthy of hers that she had married a distant cousin, who had taken her to live in a new Western community where the *Works of Orestes Anson* had not yet become a part of the civic consciousness; but of this daughter little was said, and she was tacitly understood to be excluded from the family heritage of fame. In time, however, it appeared that the traditional penny with which she had been cut off had been invested to unexpected advantage; and the interest on it, when she died, returned to the Anson House in the shape of a granddaughter who was at once felt to be what Mrs. Anson called a "compensation." It was Mrs. Anson's firm belief that the remotest operations of nature were governed by the centripetal force of her husband's greatness and that Paulina's exceptional intelligence could be explained only on the ground that she was designed to act as the guardian of the family temple.

The House, by the time Paulina came to live in it, had already acquired the publicity of a place of worship; not the perfumed chapel of a romantic idolatry but the cold clean empty meeting-house of ethical enthusiasms. The ladies lived on its outskirts, as it were, in cells that left the central fane undisturbed. The very position of the furniture had come to have a ritual significance: the sparse ornaments were the offerings of kindred intellects, the steel engravings by Raphael Morghen marked the Via Sacra of a European tour, and the black-walnut desk with its bronze ink-stand modelled on the Pantheon was the altar of this bleak temple of thought.

To a child compact of enthusiasms, and accustomed to pasture them on the scanty herbage of a new social soil, the atmosphere of the old house was full of floating nourishment. In the compressed perspective of Paulina's outlook it stood for a monument of ruined civilizations, and its white portico opened on legendary distances. Its very aspect was impressive to eyes that had first surveyed life from the jig-saw "residence" of a raw-edged Western town. The high-ceilinged rooms, with their panelled walls, their polished mahogany, their portraits of triple-stocked ancestors and of ringleted "females" in crayon, furnished the child with the historic scenery against which a young imagination constructs its vision of the past. To other eyes the cold spotless thinly-furnished interior might have suggested the shuttered mind of a maiden-lady who associates fresh air and sunlight with dust and discoloration;

but it is the eye which supplies the coloring-matter, and Paulina's brimmed with the richest hues.

Nevertheless, the House did not immediately dominate her. She had her confused out-reachings toward other centres of sensation, her vague intuition of a heliocentric system; but the attraction of habit, the steady pressure of example, gradually fixed her roving allegiance and she bent her neck to the yoke. Vanity had a share in her subjugation; for it had early been discovered that she was the only person in the family who could read her grandfather's works. The fact that she had perused them with delight at an age when (even presupposing a metaphysical bias) it was impossible for her to understand them, seemed to her aunts and grandmother sure evidence of predestination. Paulina was to be the interpreter of the oracle, and the philosophic fumes so vertiginous to meaner minds would throw her into the needed condition of clairvoyance. Nothing could have been more genuine than the emotion on which this theory was based. Paulina, in fact, delighted in her grandfather's writings. His sonorous periods, his mystic vocabulary, his bold flights into the rarefied air of the abstract, were thrilling to a fancy unhampered by the need of definitions. This purely verbal pleasure was supplemented later by the excitement of gathering up crumbs of meaning from the rhetorical board. What could have been more stimulating than to construct the theory of a girlish world out of the fragments of this Titanic cosmogony? Before Paulina's opinions had reached the stage when ossification sets in their form was fatally predetermined.

The fact that Dr. Anson had died and that his apotheosis had taken place before his young priestess's induction to the temple, made her ministrations easier and more inspiring. There were no little personal traits — such as the great man's manner of helping himself to salt, or the guttural cluck that started the wheels of speech — to distract the eye of young veneration from the central fact of his divinity. A man whom one knows only through a crayon portrait and a dozen yellowing tomes on free-will and intuition is at least secure from the belittling effects of intimacy.

Paulina thus grew up in a world readjusted to the fact of her grandfather's greatness; and as each organism draws from its surroundings the kind of nourishment most needful to its growth, so from this somewhat colorless conception she absorbed warmth, brightness and variety. Paulina was the type of woman who transmutes thought into sensation and nurses a theory in her bosom like a child.

In due course Mrs. Anson "passed away" — no one died in the Anson vocabulary — and Paulina became more than ever the foremost figure of the commemorative group. Laura and Phœbe, content to leave their father's glory in more competent hands, placidly lapsed into needlework and fiction, and their niece stepped into immediate prominence as the chief "authority" on the great man. Historians who were "getting up" the period wrote to consult her and to borrow documents; ladies with inexplicable yearnings begged for an interpretation of phrases which had "influenced" them, but which they had not quite understood; critics applied to her to verify some doubtful citation or to decide some disputed point in chronology; and the great tide of thought and investigation kept up a continuous murmur on the quiet shores of her life.

An explorer of another kind disembarked there one day in the shape of a young man to whom Paulina was primarily a kissable girl, with an after-thought in the shape of a grandfather. From the outset it had been impossible to fix Hewlett Winsloe's attention on Dr. Anson. The young man behaved with the innocent profanity of infants sporting on a tomb. His excuse was that he came from New York, a Cimmerian outskirt which survived in Paulina's geography only because Dr. Anson had gone there once or twice to lecture. The curious thing was that she should have thought it worth while to find excuses for young Winsloe. The fact that she did so had not escaped the attention of the village; but people, after a gasp of awe, said it was the most natural thing in the world that a girl like Paulina Anson should think of marrying. It would certainly seem a little odd to see a man in the House, but young Winsloe would of course understand that the Doctor's books were not to be disturbed, and that he must go down to the orchard to smoke — . The village had barely framed this *modus vivendi* when it was convulsed by the announcement that young Winsloe declined to live in the House on any terms. Hang going down to the orchard to smoke! He meant to take his wife to New York. The village drew its breath and watched.

Did Persephone, snatched from the warm fields of Enna, peer half-consentingly down the abyss that opened at her feet? Paulina, it must be owned, hung a moment over the black gulf of temptation. She would have found it easy to cope with a deliberate disregard of her grandfather's rights; but young Winsloe's unconsciousness of that shadowy claim was as much a natural function as the falling of leaves on a grave. His love was an embodiment of the perpetual renewal which to some tender spirits seems a crueller process than decay.

On women of Paulina's mould this piety toward implicit demands, toward the ghosts of dead duties walking unappeased among usurping passions, has a stronger hold than any tangible bond. People said that she gave up young Winsloe because her aunts disapproved of her leaving them; but such disapproval as reached her was an emanation from the walls of the House, from the bare desk, the faded portraits, the dozen yellowing tomes that no hand but hers ever lifted from the shelf.

II

After that the House possessed her. As if conscious of its victory, it imposed a conqueror's claims. It had once been suggested that she should write a life of her grandfather, and the task from which she had shrunk as from a too-oppressive privilege now shaped itself into a justification of her course. In a burst of filial pantheism she tried to lose herself in the vast ancestral consciousness. Her one refuge from scepticism was a blind faith in the magnitude and the endurance of the idea to which she had sacrificed her life, and with a passionate instinct of self-preservation she labored to fortify her position.

The preparations for the *Life* led her through by-ways that the most scrupulous of the previous biographers had left unexplored. She accumulated her material with a blind animal patience unconscious of fortuitous risks. The years stretched before her like some vast blank page spread out to receive the record of her toil; and she had a mystic conviction that she would not die till her work was accomplished.

The aunts, sustained by no such high purpose, withdrew in turn to their respective divisions of the Anson "plot," and Paulina remained alone with her task. She was forty when the book was completed. She had travelled little in her life, and it had become more and more difficult to her to leave the House even for a day; but the dread of entrusting her document to a strange hand made her decide to carry it herself to the publisher. On the way to Boston she had a sudden vision of the loneliness to which this last parting condemned her. All her youth, all her dreams, all her renunciations lay in that neat bundle on her knee. It was not so much her grandfather's life as her own that she had written; and the knowledge that it would come back to her in all the glorification of print was of no more help than, to a mother's grief, the assurance that the lad she must part with will return with epaulets.

She had naturally addressed herself to the firm which had published her grandfather's works. Its founder, a personal friend of the philosopher's, had survived the Olympian group of which he had been a subordinate member, long enough to bestow his octogenarian approval on Paulina's pious undertaking. But he had died soon afterward; and Miss Anson found herself confronted by his grandson, a person with a brisk commercial view of his trade, who was said to have put "new blood" into the firm.

This gentleman listened attentively, fingering her manuscript as though literature were a tactile substance; then, with a confidential twist of his revolving chair, he emitted the verdict: "We ought to have had this ten years sooner."

Miss Anson took the words as an allusion to the repressed avidity of her readers. "It has been a long time for the public to wait," she solemnly assented.

The publisher smiled. "They haven't waited," he said.

She looked at him strangely. "Haven't waited?"

"No—they've gone off; taken another train. Literature's like a big railway-station now, you know: there's a train starting every minute. People are not going to hang round the waiting-room. If they can't get to a place when they want to they go somewhere else."

The application of this parable cost Miss Anson several minutes of throbbing silence. At length she said: "Then I am to understand that the public is no longer interested in—in my grandfather?" She felt as though heaven must blast the lips that risked such a conjecture.

"Well, it's this way. He's a name still, of course. People don't exactly want to be caught not knowing who he is; but they don't want to spend two dollars finding out, when they can look him up for nothing in any biographical dictionary."

Miss Anson's world reeled. She felt herself adrift among mysterious forces, and no more thought of prolonging the discussion than of opposing an earthquake with argument. She went home carrying the manuscript like a wounded thing. On the return journey she found herself travelling straight toward a fact that had lurked for months in the background of her life, and that now seemed to await her on the very threshold: the fact that fewer visitors came to the House. She owned to herself that for the last four or five years the number had steadily diminished. Engrossed in her work, she had noted the change only to feel thankful that she had fewer interruptions. There had been a time when, at the travelling season, the bell rang continuously, and the ladies of the House lived in a chronic state of "best silks" and expectancy. It

would have been impossible then to carry on any consecutive work; and
she now saw that the silence which had gathered round her task had
been the hush of death.

Not of *his* death! The very walls cried out against the implication. It
was the world's enthusiasm, the world's faith, the world's loyalty that had
died. A corrupt generation that had turned aside to worship the brazen
serpent. Her heart yearned with a prophetic passion over the lost sheep
straying in the wilderness. But all great glories had their interlunar
period; and in due time her grandfather would once more flash full-
orbed upon a darkling world.

The few friends to whom she confided her adventure reminded her
with tender indignation that there were other publishers less subject to
the fluctuations of the market; but much as she had braved for her
grandfather she could not again brave that particular probation. She
found herself, in fact, incapable of any immediate effort. She had lost
her way in a labyrinth of conjecture where her worst dread was that she
might put her hand upon the clue.

She locked up the manuscript and sat down to wait. If a pilgrim had
come just then the priestess would have fallen on his neck; but she continued to celebrate her rites alone. It was a double solitude; for she had
always thought a great deal more of the people who came to see the House
than of the people who came to see her. She fancied that the neighbors
kept a keen eye on the path to the House; and there were days when the
figure of a stranger strolling past the gate seemed to focus upon her the
scorching sympathies of the village. For a time she thought of travelling; of
going to Europe, or even to Boston; but to leave the House now would
have seemed like deserting her post. Gradually her scattered energies
centred themselves in the fierce resolve to understand what had happened. She was not the woman to live long in an unmapped country or to
accept as final her private interpretation of phenomena. Like a traveller in
unfamiliar regions she began to store for future guidance the minutest
natural signs. Unflinchingly she noted the accumulating symptoms of
indifference that marked her grandfather's descent toward posterity. She
passed from the heights on which he had been grouped with the sages of
his day to the lower level where he had come to be "the friend of Emerson," "the correspondent of Hawthorne," or (later still) "the Dr. Anson"
mentioned in their letters. The change had taken place as slowly and
imperceptibly as a natural process. She could not say that any ruthless
hand had stripped the leaves from the tree: it was simply that, among the
evergreen glories of his group, her grandfather's had proved deciduous.

She had still to ask herself why. If the decay had been a natural process, was it not the very pledge of renewal? It was easier to find such arguments than to be convinced by them. Again and again she tried to drug her solicitude with analogies; but at last she saw that such expedients were but the expression of a growing incredulity. The best way of proving her faith in her grandfather was not to be afraid of his critics. She had no notion where these shadowy antagonists lurked; for she had never heard of the great man's doctrine being directly combated. Oblique assaults there must have been, however, Parthian shots at the giant that none dared face; and she thirsted to close with such assailants. The difficulty was to find them. She began by re-reading the *Works*; thence she passed to the writers of the same school, those whose rhetoric bloomed perennial in *First Readers* from which her grandfather's prose had long since faded. Amid that clamor of far-off enthusiasms she detected no controversial note. The little knot of Olympians held their views in common with an early-Christian promiscuity. They were continually proclaiming their admiration for each other, the public joining as chorus in this guileless antiphon of praise; and she discovered no traitor in their midst.

What then had happened? Was it simply that the main current of thought had set another way? Then why did the others survive? Why were they still marked down as tributaries to the philosophic stream? This question carried her still farther afield, and she pressed on with the passion of a champion whose reluctance to know the worst might be construed into a doubt of his cause. At length — slowly but inevitably — an explanation shaped itself. Death had overtaken the doctrines about which her grandfather had draped his cloudy rhetoric. They had disintegrated and been re-absorbed, adding their little pile to the dust drifted about the mute lips of the Sphinx. The great man's contemporaries had survived not by reason of what they taught, but of what they were; and he, who had been the mere mask through which they mouthed their lesson, the instrument on which their tune was played, lay buried deep among the obsolete tools of thought.

The discovery came to Paulina suddenly. She looked up one evening from her reading and it stood before her like a ghost. It had entered her life with stealthy steps, creeping close before she was aware of it. She sat in the library, among the carefully-tended books and portraits; and it seemed to her that she had been walled alive into a tomb hung with the effigies of dead ideas. She felt a desperate longing to escape into the outer air, where people toiled and loved, and living sympathies went hand in hand. It was the sense of wasted labor that oppressed her; of two lives consumed in that ruthless process that uses generations of effort to build a single cell. There was a dreary parallel between her grandfather's fruitless toil and her own unprofitable sacrifice. Each in turn had kept vigil by a corpse.

III

The bell rang—she remembered it afterward—with a loud thrilling note. It was what they used to call the "visitor's ring"; not the tentative tinkle of a neighbor dropping in to borrow a sauce-pan or discuss parochial incidents, but a decisive summons from the outer world.

Miss Anson put down her knitting and listened. She sat up-stairs now, making her rheumatism an excuse for avoiding the rooms below. Her interests had insensibly adjusted themselves to the perspective of her neighbors' lives, and she wondered—as the bell re-echoed—if it could mean that Mrs. Heminway's baby had come. Conjecture had time to ripen into certainty, and she was limping toward the closet where her cloak and bonnet hung, when her little maid fluttered in with the announcement: "A gentleman to see the house."

"The *House?*"

"Yes, m'm. I don't know what he means," faltered the messenger, whose memory did not embrace the period when such announcements were a daily part of the domestic routine.

Miss Anson glanced at the proffered card. The name it bore—*Mr. George Corby*—was unknown to her, but the blood rose to her languid cheek. "Hand me my Mechlin cap, Katy," she said, trembling a little, as she laid aside her walking stick. She put her cap on before the mirror, with rapid unsteady touches. "Did you draw up the library blinds?" she breathlessly asked.

She had gradually built up a wall of commonplace between herself and her illusions, but at the first summons of the past filial passion swept away the frail barriers of expediency.

She walked down-stairs so hurriedly that her stick clicked like a girlish heel; but in the hall she paused, wondering nervously if Katy had put a match to the fire. The autumn air was cold and she had the reproachful vision of a visitor with elderly ailments shivering by her inhospitable hearth. She thought instinctively of the stranger as a survivor of the days when such a visit was a part of the young enthusiast's itinerary.

The fire was unlit and the room forbiddingly cold; but the figure which, as Miss Anson entered, turned from a lingering scrutiny of the book-shelves, was that of a fresh-eyed sanguine youth clearly independent of any artificial caloric. She stood still a moment, feeling herself the victim of some anterior impression that made this robust presence an insubstantial thing; but the young man advanced with an air of genial assurance which rendered him at once more real and more reminiscent.

"Why this, you know," he exclaimed, "is simply immense!"

The words, which did not immediately present themselves as slang to Miss Anson's unaccustomed ear, echoed with an odd familiarity through the academic silence.

"The room, you know, I mean," he explained with a comprehensive gesture. "These jolly portraits, and the books — that's the old gentleman himself over the mantelpiece, I suppose? — and the elms outside, and — and the whole business. I do like a congruous background — don't you?"

His hostess was silent. No one but Hewlett Winsloe had ever spoken of her grandfather as "the old gentleman."

"It's a hundred times better than I could have hoped," her visitor continued, with a cheerful disregard of her silence. "The seclusion, the remoteness, the philosophic atmosphere — there's so little of that kind of flavor left! I should have simply hated to find that he lived over a grocery, you know. — I had the deuce of a time finding out where he *did* live," he began again, after another glance of parenthetical enjoyment. "But finally I got on the trail through some old book on Brook Farm. I was bound I'd get the environment right before I did my article."

Miss Anson, by this time, had recovered sufficient self-possession to seat herself and assign a chair to her visitor.

"Do I understand," she asked slowly, following his rapid eye about the room, "that you intend to write an article about my grandfather?"

"That's what I'm here for," Mr. Corby genially responded; "that is, if you're willing to help me; for I can't get on without your help," he added with a confident smile.

There was another pause, during which Miss Anson noticed a fleck of dust on the faded leather of the writing-table and a fresh spot of discoloration in the right-hand upper corner of Raphael Morghen's "Parnassus."

"Then you believe in him?" she said, looking up. She could not tell what had prompted her; the words rushed out irresistibly.

"Believe in him?" Corby cried, springing to his feet. "Believe in

Orestes Anson? Why, I believe he's simply the greatest—the most stupendous—the most phenomenal figure we've got!"

The color rose to Miss Anson's brow. Her heart was beating passionately. She kept her eyes fixed on the young man's face, as though it might vanish if she looked away.

"You—you mean to say this in your article?" she asked.

"Say it? Why, the facts will say it," he exulted. "The baldest kind of a statement would make it clear. When a man is as big as that he doesn't need a pedestal!"

Miss Anson sighed. "People used to say that when I was young," she murmured. "But now—"

Her visitor stared. "When you were young? But how did they know—when the thing hung fire as it did? When the whole edition was thrown back on his hands?"

"The whole edition—what edition?" It was Miss Anson's turn to stare.

"Why, of his pamphlet—*the* pamphlet—the one thing that counts, that survives, that makes him what he is! For heaven's sake," he tragically adjured her, "don't tell me there isn't a copy of it left!"

Miss Anson was trembling slightly. "I don't think I understand what you mean," she faltered, less bewildered by his vehemence than by the strange sense of coming on an unexplored region in the very heart of her dominion.

"Why, his account of the *amphioxus*, of course! You can't mean that his family didn't know about it—that *you* don't know about it? I came across it by the merest accident myself, in a letter of vindication that he wrote in 1830 to an old scientific paper; but I understood there were journals—early journals; there must be references to it somewhere in the 'twenties. He must have been at least ten or twelve years ahead of Yarrell; and he saw the whole significance of it, too—he saw where it led to. As I understand it, he actually anticipated in his pamphlet Saint Hilaire's theory of the universal type, and supported the hypothesis by describing the notochord of the *amphioxus* as a cartilaginous vertebral column. The specialists of the day jeered at him, of course, as the specialists in Goethe's time jeered at the plant-metamorphosis. As far as I can make out, the anatomists and zoologists were down on Dr. Anson to a man; that was why his cowardly publishers went back on their bargain. But the pamphlet must be here somewhere—he writes as though, in his first disappointment, he had destroyed the whole edition; but surely there must be at least one copy left?"

His scientific jargon was as bewildering as his slang; and there were even moments in his discourse when Miss Anson ceased to distinguish between them; but the suspense with which he continued to gaze on her acted as a challenge to her scattered thoughts.

"The *amphioxus*," she murmured, half-rising. "It's an animal, isn't it — a fish? Yes, I think I remember." She sank back with the inward look of one who retraces some lost line of association.

Gradually the distance cleared, the details started into life. In her researches for the biography she had patiently followed every ramification of her subject, and one of these overgrown paths now led her back to the episode in question. The great Orestes's title of "Doctor" had in fact not been merely the spontaneous tribute of a national admiration; he had actually studied medicine in his youth, and his diaries, as his granddaughter now recalled, showed that he had passed through a brief phase of anatomical ardor before his attention was diverted to supersensual problems. It had indeed seemed to Paulina, as she scanned those early pages, that they revealed a spontaneity, a freshness of feeling somehow absent from his later lucubrations — as though this one emotion had reached him directly, the others through some intervening medium. In the excess of her commemorative zeal she had even struggled through the unintelligible pamphlet to which a few lines in the journal had bitterly directed her. But the subject and the phraseology were alien to her and unconnected with her conception of the great man's genius; and after a hurried perusal she had averted her thoughts from the episode as from a revelation of failure. At length she rose a little unsteadily, supporting herself against the writing-table. She looked hesitatingly about the room; then she drew a key from her old-fashioned reticule and unlocked a drawer beneath one of the book-cases. Young Corby watched her breathlessly. With a tremulous hand she turned over the dusty documents that seemed to fill the drawer. "Is this it?" she said, holding out a thin discolored volume.

He seized it with a gasp. "Oh, by George," he said, dropping into the nearest chair.

She stood observing him strangely as his eye devoured the mouldy pages.

"Is this the only copy left?" he asked at length, looking up for a moment as a thirsty man lifts his head from his glass.

"I think it must be. I found it long ago, among some old papers that my aunts were burning up after my grandmother's death. They said it was of no use — that he'd always meant to destroy the whole edition and that I ought to respect his wishes. But it was something *he* had written; to burn it was like shutting the door against his voice — against something he had once wished to say, and that nobody had listened to. I wanted him to feel that I was always here, ready to listen, even when others hadn't thought it worth while; and so I kept the pamphlet, meaning to carry out his wish and destroy it before my death."

Her visitor gave a groan of retrospective anguish. "And but for me — but for to-day — you would have?"

"I should have thought it my duty."

"Oh, by George — by George," he repeated, subdued afresh by the inadequacy of speech.

She continued to watch him in silence. At length he jumped up and impulsively caught her by both hands.

"He's bigger and bigger!" he almost shouted. "He simply leads the field! You'll help me go to the bottom of this, won't you? We must turn out all the papers — letters, journals, memoranda. He must have made notes. He must have left some record of what led up to this. We must leave nothing unexplored. By Jove," he cried, looking up at her with his bright convincing smile, "do you know you're the granddaughter of a Great Man?"

Her color flickered like a girl's. "Are you — sure of him?" she whispered, as though putting him on his guard against a possible betrayal of trust.

"Sure! Sure! My dear lady — " he measured her again with his quick confident glance. "Don't *you* believe in him?"

She drew back with a confused murmur. "I — used to." She had left her hands in his: their pressure seemed to send a warm current to her heart. "It ruined my life!" she cried with sudden passion. He looked at her perplexedly.

"I gave up everything," she went on wildly, "to keep *him* alive. I sacrificed myself — others — I nursed his glory in my bosom and it died — and left me — left me here alone." She paused and gathered her courage with a gasp. "Don't make the same mistake!" she warned him.

He shook his head, still smiling. "No danger of that! You're not alone, my dear lady. He's here with you — he's come back to you to-day. Don't you see what's happened? Don't you see that it's your love that has kept him alive? If you'd abandoned your post for an instant — let things pass into other hands — if your wonderful tenderness hadn't perpetually kept guard — this might have been — must have been — irretrievably lost." He laid his hand on the pamphlet. "And then — then he *would* have been dead!"

"Oh," she said, "don't tell me too suddenly!" And she turned away and sank into a chair.

The young man stood watching her in an awed silence. For a long time she sat motionless, with her face hidden, and he thought she must be weeping.

At length he said, almost shyly: "You'll let me come back, then? You'll help me work this thing out?"

She rose calmly and held out her hand. "I'll help you," she declared.

"I'll come to-morrow, then. Can we get to work early?"

"As early as you please."

"At eight o'clock, then," he said briskly. "You'll have the papers ready?"

"I'll have everything ready." She added with a half-playful hesitancy: "And the fire shall be lit for you."

He went out with his bright nod. She walked to the window and watched his buoyant figure hastening down the elm-shaded street. When she turned back into the empty room she looked as though youth had touched her on the lips.

Willa Cather

(1873–1947)

WILLA CATHER'S PARENTS moved west ten years after she was born in West Virginia. The family eventually settled in the town of Red Cloud, Nebraska, and there Cather and her six brothers and sisters became familiar with the "pioneer" spirit evoked in much of her fiction. Surrounded by Swedish, Russian, Bohemian and French immigrants, Cather discovered these people's sense of isolation as well as the determination that survival in the sometimes harsh environment required. Like Jewett, Freeman and Chopin, Cather was a realist. Her best-known works, including *O Pioneers!* (1913) and *My Ántonia* (1918), are set in the vast expanses and pioneer towns of the prairie states of her childhood, and portray a disappearing way of life.

"Paul's Case: A Study in Temperament" was published in Cather's first short-story collection, *The Troll Garden*, in 1905, and in many ways it anticipates the modernist movement. Cather portrays a young protagonist whose search for romance alienates him from everyone around him. Paul's deep yearning to escape "the flavourless, colourless mass of every-day existence" provokes the reader's sympathy, yet there is something disconcerting about his desires. His passion for opera and theater does not arise from a desire to participate, nor is Paul "stagestruck." He wants only "to see, to be in the atmosphere, float on the wave of it, to be carried out, blue league after blue league, away from everything."

Cather emphasizes Paul's isolation by her refusal to gloss over his faults, or to contrive a happy ending. The tragedy of Paul's case lies in its inevitability as part of what Cather calls "the immense design of things."

Paul's Case

A Study in Temperament

IT WAS PAUL'S afternoon to appear before the faculty of the Pittsburgh High School to account for his various misdemeanours. He had been suspended a week ago, and his father had called at the Principal's office and confessed his perplexity about his son. Paul entered the faculty room suave and smiling. His clothes were a trifle outgrown and the tan velvet on the collar of his open overcoat was frayed and worn; but for all that there was something of the dandy about him, and he wore an opal pin in his neatly knotted black four-in-hand, and a red carnation in his button-hole. This latter adornment the faculty somehow felt was not properly significant of the contrite spirit befitting a boy under the ban of suspension.

Paul was tall for his age and very thin, with high, cramped shoulders and a narrow chest. His eyes were remarkable for a certain hysterical brilliancy, and he continually used them in a conscious, theatrical sort of way, peculiarly offensive in a boy. The pupils were abnormally large, as though he were addicted to belladonna, but there was a glassy glitter about them which that drug does not produce.

When questioned by the Principal as to why he was there, Paul stated, politely enough, that he wanted to come back to school. This was a lie, but Paul was quite accustomed to lying; found it, indeed, indispensable for overcoming friction. His teachers were asked to state their respective charges against him, which they did with such a rancour and aggrievedness as evinced that this was not a usual case. Disorder and impertinence were among the offences named, yet each of his instructors felt that it was scarcely possible to put into words the real cause of the trouble, which lay in a sort of hysterically defiant manner of the boy's; in the contempt which they all knew he felt for them, and which he seemingly made not the least effort to conceal. Once, when he had been making a synopsis of a paragraph at the blackboard, his English teacher had stepped to his side and attempted to guide his hand. Paul had started back with a shudder and thrust his hands violently behind him. The astonished woman could scarcely have been more hurt and embarrassed had he struck at her. The insult was so involuntary and definitely personal as to be unforgettable. In one way and another, he had made all his teachers, men and women alike, conscious of the same feeling of physical aversion. In one class he habitually sat with his hand shading his eyes; in another he always looked out of the window during the recitation; in another he made a running commentary on the lecture, with humorous intention.

His teachers felt this afternoon that his whole attitude was symbolized by his shrug and his flippantly red carnation flower, and they fell upon him without mercy, his English teacher leading the pack. He stood through it smiling, his pale lips parted over his white teeth. (His lips were continually twitching, and he had a habit of raising his eyebrows that was contemptuous and irritating to the last degree.) Older boys than Paul had broken down and shed tears under that baptism of fire, but his set smile did not once desert him, and his only sign of discomfort was the nervous trembling of the fingers that toyed with the buttons of his overcoat, and an occasional jerking of the other hand that held his hat. Paul was always smiling, always glancing about him, seeming to feel that people might be watching him and trying to detect something. This conscious expression, since it was as far as possible from boyish mirthfulness, was usually attributed to insolence or "smartness."

As the inquisition proceeded, one of his instructors repeated an impertinent remark of the boy's, and the Principal asked him whether he thought that a courteous speech to have made a woman. Paul shrugged his shoulders slightly and his eyebrows twitched.

"I don't know," he replied. "I didn't mean to be polite or impolite, either. I guess it's a sort of way I have of saying things regardless."

The Principal, who was a sympathetic man, asked him whether he didn't think that a way it would be well to get rid of. Paul grinned and said he guessed so. When he was told that he could go, he bowed gracefully and went out. His bow was but a repetition of the scandalous red carnation.

His teachers were in despair, and his drawing master voiced the feeling of them all when he declared there was something about the boy which none of them understood. He added: "I don't really believe that smile of his comes altogether from insolence; there's something sort of haunted about it. The boy is not strong, for one thing. I happen to know that he was born in Colorado, only a few months before his mother died out there of a long illness. There is something wrong about the fellow."

The drawing master had come to realize that, in looking at Paul, one saw only his white teeth and the forced animation of his eyes. One warm afternoon the boy had gone to sleep at his drawing-board, and his master had noted with amazement what a white, blue-veined face it was; drawn and wrinkled like an old man's about the eyes, the lips twitching even in his sleep, and stiff with a nervous tension that drew them back from his teeth.

His teachers left the building dissatisfied and unhappy; humiliated to have felt so vindictive toward a mere boy, to have uttered this feeling in cutting terms, and to have set each other on, as it were, in the grewsome game of intemperate reproach. Some of them remembered having seen a miserable street cat set at bay by a ring of tormentors.

As for Paul, he ran down the hill whistling the Soldiers' Chorus from *Faust* looking wildly behind him now and then to see whether some of his teachers were not there to writhe under his light-heartedness. As it was now late in the afternoon and Paul was on duty that evening as usher at Carnegie Hall, he decided that he would not go home to supper. When he reached the concert hall the doors were not yet open and, as it was chilly outside, he decided to go up into the picture gallery — always deserted at this hour — where there were some of Raffelli's gay studies of Paris streets and an airy blue Venetian scene or two that always exhilarated him. He was delighted to find no one in the gallery but the old guard, who sat in one corner, a newspaper on his knee, a black patch over one eye and the other closed. Paul possessed himself of the place and walked confidently up and down, whistling under his breath. After a while he sat down before a blue Rico and lost himself. When he bethought him to look at his watch, it was after seven o'clock, and he rose with a start and ran downstairs, making a face at Augustus, peering out from the cast-room, and an evil gesture at the Venus of Milo as he passed her on the stairway.

When Paul reached the ushers' dressing-room half-a-dozen boys were there already, and he began excitedly to tumble into his uniform. It was one of the few that at all approached fitting, and Paul thought it very becoming — though he knew that the tight, straight coat accentuated his narrow chest, about which he was exceedingly sensitive. He was always considerably excited while he dressed, twanging all over to the tuning of the strings and the preliminary flourishes of the horns in the music-room; but to-night he seemed quite beside himself, and he teased and plagued the boys until, telling him that he was crazy, they put him down on the floor and sat on him.

Somewhat calmed by his suppression, Paul dashed out to the front of the house to seat the early comers. He was a model usher; gracious and smiling he ran up and down the aisles; nothing was too much trouble for him; he carried messages and brought programmes as though it were his greatest pleasure in life, and all the people in his section thought him a charming boy, feeling that he remembered and admired them. As the house filled, he grew more and more vivacious and animated, and the colour came to his cheeks and lips. It was very much as though this were a great reception and Paul were the host. Just as the musicians came out to take their places, his English teacher arrived with checks for the seats which a prominent manufacturer had taken for the season. She betrayed some embarrassment when she handed Paul the tickets, and a *hauteur* which subsequently made her feel very foolish. Paul was startled for a moment, and had the feeling of wanting to put her out; what business had she here among all these fine people and gay colours? He looked her over and decided that she was not appropriately dressed and must be a fool to sit downstairs in such togs. The tickets had probably been sent her out of kindness, he reflected as he put down a seat for her, and she had about as much right to sit there as he had.

When the symphony began Paul sank into one of the rear seats with a long sigh of relief, and lost himself as he had done before the Rico. It was not that symphonies, as such, meant anything in particular to Paul, but the first sigh of the instruments seemed to free some hilarious and potent spirit within him; something that struggled there like the Genius in the bottle found by the Arab fisherman. He felt a sudden zest of life; the lights danced before his eyes and the concert hall blazed into unimaginable splendour. When the soprano soloist came on, Paul forgot even the nastiness of his teacher's being there and gave himself up to the peculiar stimulus such personages always had for him. The soloist chanced to be a German woman, by no means in her first youth, and the mother of many children; but she wore an elaborate gown and a tiara, and above all she had that indefinable air of achievement, that world-shine upon her, which, in Paul's eyes, made her a veritable queen of Romance.

After a concert was over, Paul was always irritable and wretched until he got to sleep, and to-night he was even more than usually restless. He had the feeling of not being able to let down, of its being impossible to give up this delicious excitement which was the only thing that could be called living at all. During the last number he withdrew and, after hastily changing his clothes in the dressing-room, slipped out to the side door where the soprano's carriage stood. Here he began pacing rapidly up and down the walk, waiting to see her come out.

Over yonder the Schenley, in its vacant stretch, loomed big and square through the fine rain, the windows of its twelve stories glowing like those of a lighted card-board house under a Christmas tree. All the actors and singers of the better class stayed there when they were in the city, and a number of the big manufacturers of the place lived there in the winter. Paul had often hung about the hotel, watching the people go in and out, longing to enter and leave school-masters and dull care behind him forever.

At last the singer came out, accompanied by the conductor, who helped her into her carriage and closed the door with a cordial *auf wiedersehen* which set Paul to wondering whether she were not an old sweetheart of his. Paul followed the carriage over to the hotel, walking so rapidly as not to be far from the entrance when the singer alighted and disappeared behind the swinging glass doors that were opened by a negro in a tall hat and a long coat. In the moment that the door was ajar, it seemed to Paul that he, too, entered. He seemed to feel himself go after her up the steps, into the warm, lighted building, into an exotic, a tropical world of shiny, glistening surfaces and basking ease. He reflected upon the mysterious dishes that were brought into the dining-room, the green bottles in buckets of ice, as he had seen them in the supper party pictures of the *Sunday World* supplement. A quick gust of wind brought the rain down with sudden vehemence, and Paul was startled to find that he was still outside in the slush of the gravel driveway; that his boots were letting in the water and his scanty overcoat was clinging wet about him; that the lights in front of the concert hall were out, and that the rain was driving in sheets between him and the orange glow of the windows above him. There it was, what he wanted — tangibly before him, like the fairy world of a Christmas pantomime, but mocking spirits stood guard at the doors, and, as the rain beat in his face, Paul wondered whether he were destined always to shiver in the black night outside, looking up at it.

He turned and walked reluctantly toward the car tracks. The end had to come sometime; his father in his night-clothes at the top of the stairs, explanations that did not explain, hastily improvised fictions that were forever tripping him up, his upstairs room and its horrible yellow wall-paper, the creaking bureau with the greasy plush collar-box, and over his painted wooden bed the pictures of George Washington and John

Calvin, and the framed motto, "Feed my Lambs," which had been worked in red worsted by his mother.

Half an hour later, Paul alighted from his car and went slowly down one of the side streets off the main thoroughfare. It was a highly respectable street, where all the houses were exactly alike, and where business men of moderate means begot and reared large families of children, all of whom went to Sabbath-school and learned the shorter catechism, and were interested in arithmetic; all of whom were as exactly alike as their homes, and of a piece with the monotony in which they lived. Paul never went up Cordelia Street without a shudder of loathing. His home was next the house of the Cumberland minister. He approached it to-night with the nerveless sense of defeat, the hopeless feeling of sinking back forever into ugliness and commonness that he had always had when he came home. The moment he turned into Cordelia Street he felt the waters close above his head. After each of these orgies of living, he experienced all the physical depression which follows a debauch; the loathing of respectable beds, of common food, of a house penetrated by kitchen odours; a shuddering repulsion for the flavourless, colourless mass of every-day existence; a morbid desire for cool things and soft lights and fresh flowers.

The nearer he approached the house, the more absolutely unequal Paul felt to the sight of it all; his ugly sleeping chamber; the cold bathroom with the grimy zinc tub, the cracked mirror, the dripping spiggots; his father, at the top of the stairs, his hairy legs sticking out from his nightshirt, his feet thrust into carpet slippers. He was so much later than usual that there would certainly be inquiries and reproaches. Paul stopped short before the door. He felt that he could not be accosted by his father to-night; that he could not toss again on that miserable bed. He would not go in. He would tell his father that he had no car fare, and it was raining so hard he had gone home with one of the boys and stayed all night.

Meanwhile, he was wet and cold. He went around to the back of the house and tried one of the basement windows, found it open, raised it cautiously, and scrambled down the cellar wall to the floor. There he stood, holding his breath, terrified by the noise he had made, but the floor above him was silent, and there was no creak on the stairs. He found a soap-box, and carried it over to the soft ring of light that streamed from the furnace door, and sat down. He was horribly afraid of rats, so he did not try to sleep, but sat looking distrustfully at the dark, still terrified lest he might have awakened his father. In such reactions, after one of the experiences which made days and nights out of the dreary blanks of the calendar, when his senses were deadened, Paul's head was always singularly clear. Suppose his father had heard him getting in at the window and had come down and shot him for a burglar? Then, again, suppose his father had come down, pistol in hand, and he had cried out in time to save himself, and his father had been horrified to think how nearly he had killed him? Then, again, suppose a day should come when his father would remember that night, and wish there had been no warning cry to stay his hand? With this last supposition Paul entertained himself until daybreak.

The following Sunday was fine; the sodden November chill was broken by the last flash of autumnal summer. In the morning Paul had to go to church and Sabbath-school, as always. On seasonable Sunday afternoons the burghers of Cordelia Street always sat out on their front "stoops," and talked to their neighbours on the next stoop, or called to those across the street in neighbourly fashion. The men usually sat on gay cushions placed upon the steps that led down to the sidewalk, while the women, in their Sunday "waists," sat in rockers on the cramped porches, pretending to be greatly at their ease. The children played in the streets; there were so many of them that the place resembled the recreation grounds of a kindergarten. The men on the steps — all in their shirt sleeves, their vests unbuttoned — sat with their legs well apart, their stomachs comfortably protruding, and talked of the prices of things, or told anecdotes of the sagacity of their various chiefs and overlords. They occasionally looked over the multitude of squabbling children, listened affectionately to their high-pitched, nasal voices, smiling to see their own proclivities reproduced in their offspring, and interspersed their legends of the iron kings with remarks about their sons' progress at school, their grades in arithmetic, and the amounts they had saved in their toy banks.

On this last Sunday of November, Paul sat all the afternoon on the lowest step of his "stoop," staring into the street, while his sisters, in their rockers, were talking to the minister's daughters next door about how many shirt-waists they had made in the last week, and how many waffles some one had eaten at the last church supper. When the weather was warm, and his father was in a particularly jovial frame of mind, the girls made lemonade, which was always brought out in a red-glass pitcher, ornamented with forget-me-nots in blue enamel. This the girls thought very fine, and the neighbours always joked about the suspicious colour of the pitcher.

To-day Paul's father sat on the top step, talking to a young man who shifted a restless baby from knee to knee. He happened to be the young man who was daily held up to Paul as a model, and after whom it was his father's dearest hope that he would pattern. This young man was of a ruddy complexion, with a compressed, red mouth, and faded, near-sighted eyes, over which he wore thick spectacles, with gold bows that curved about his ears. He was clerk to one of the magnates of a great steel corporation, and was looked upon in Cordelia Street as a young man with a future. There was a story that, some five years ago — he was now barely twenty-six — he had been a trifle dissipated but in order to curb his appetites and save the loss of time and strength that a sowing of wild oats might have entailed, he had taken his chief's advice, oft reiterated to his employees, and at twenty-one had married the first woman whom he could persuade to share his fortunes. She happened to be an angular school-mistress, much older than he, who also wore thick glasses, and who had now borne him four children, all near-sighted, like herself.

The young man was relating how his chief, now cruising in the Mediterranean, kept in touch with all the details of the business, arranging his office hours on his yacht just as though he were at home, and "knocking off work enough to keep two stenographers busy." His father told, in turn, the plan his corporation was considering, of putting in an electric railway plant at Cairo. Paul snapped his teeth; he had an awful apprehension that they might spoil it all before he got there. Yet he rather liked to hear these legends of the iron kings, that were told and retold on Sundays and holidays; these stories of palaces in Venice, yachts on the Mediterranean, and high play at Monte Carlo appealed to his fancy, and he was interested in the triumphs of these cash boys who had become famous, though he had no mind for the cash-boy stage.

After supper was over, and he had helped to dry the dishes, Paul nervously asked his father whether he could go to George's to get some help in his geometry, and still more nervously asked for car fare. This latter request he had to repeat, as his father, on principle, did not like to hear requests for money, whether much or little. He asked Paul whether he could not go to some boy who lived nearer, and told him that he ought not to leave his school work until Sunday; but he gave him the dime. He was not a poor man, but he had a worthy ambition to come up in the world. His only reason for allowing Paul to usher was, that he thought a boy ought to be earning a little.

Paul bounded upstairs, scrubbed the greasy odour of the dish-water from his hands with the ill-smelling soap he hated, and then shook over his fingers a few drops of violet water from the bottle he kept hidden in his drawer. He left the house with his geometry conspicuously under his arm, and the moment he got out of Cordelia Street and boarded a downtown car, he shook off the lethargy of two deadening days, and began to live again.

The leading juvenile of the permanent stock company which played at one of the downtown theatres was an acquaintance of Paul's, and the boy had been invited to drop in at the Sunday-night rehearsals whenever he could. For more than a year Paul had spent every available moment loitering about Charley Edwards's dressing-room. He had won a place among Edwards's following not only because the young actor, who could not afford to employ a dresser, often found him useful, but because he recognized in Paul something akin to what churchmen term "vocation."

It was at the theatre and at Carnegie Hall that Paul really lived; the rest was but a sleep and a forgetting. This was Paul's fairy tale, and it had for him all the allurement of a secret love. The moment he inhaled the gassy, painty, dusty odour behind the scenes, he breathed like a prisoner set free, and felt within him the possibility of doing or saying splendid, brilliant, poetic things. The moment the cracked orchestra beat out the overture from *Martha*, or jerked at the serenade from *Rigoletto*, all stupid and ugly things slid from him, and his senses were deliciously, yet delicately fired.

Perhaps it was because, in Paul's world, the natural nearly always wore the guise of ugliness, that a certain element of artificiality seemed to him necessary in beauty. Perhaps it was because his experience of life elsewhere was so full of Sabbath-school picnics, petty economies, wholesome advice as to how to succeed in life, and the unescapable odours of cooking, that he found this existence so alluring, these smartly-clad men and women so attractive, that he was so moved by these starry apple orchards that bloomed perennially under the lime-light.

It would be difficult to put it strongly enough how convincingly the stage entrance of that theatre was for Paul the actual portal of Romance. Certainly none of the company ever suspected it, least of all Charley Edwards. It was very like the old stories that used to float about London of fabulously rich Jews, who had subterranean halls there, with palms, and fountains, and soft lamps and richly apparelled women who never saw the disenchanting light of London day. So, in the midst of that smoke-palled city, enamoured of figures and grimy toil, Paul had his secret temple, his wishing carpet, his bit of blue-and-white Mediterranean shore bathed in perpetual sunshine.

Several of Paul's teachers had a theory that his imagination had been perverted by garish fiction, but the truth was that he scarcely ever read at all. The books at home were not such as would either tempt or corrupt a youthful mind, and as for reading the novels that some of his friends urged upon him — well, he got what he wanted much more quickly from music; any sort of music, from an orchestra to a barrel organ. He needed only the spark, the indescribable thrill that made his imagination master of his senses, and he could make plots and pictures enough of his own. It was equally true that he was not stage struck — not, at any rate, in the usual acceptation of that expression. He had no desire to become an actor, any more than he had to become a musician. He felt no necessity to do any of these things; what he wanted was to see, to be in the atmosphere, float on the wave of it, to be carried out, blue league after blue league, away from everything.

After a night behind the scenes, Paul found the school-room more than ever repulsive; the bare floors and naked walls; the prosy men who never wore frock coats, or violets in their button-holes; the women with their dull gowns, shrill voices, and pitiful seriousness about prepositions that govern the dative. He could not bear to have the other pupils think, for a moment, that he took these people seriously; he must convey to them that he considered it all trivial, and was there only by way of a jest, anyway. He had autograph pictures of all the members of the stock company which he showed his classmates, telling them the most incredible stories of his familiarity with these people, of his acquaintance with the soloists who came to Carnegie Hall, his suppers with them and the flowers he sent them. When these stories lost their effect, and his audience grew listless, he became desperate and would bid all the boys good-bye, announcing that he was going to travel for awhile; going to Naples, to Venice, to Egypt. Then, next Monday, he would slip back, conscious and nervously smiling; his sister was ill, and he should have to defer his voyage until spring.

Matters went steadily worse with Paul at school. In the itch to let his instructors know how heartily he despised them and their homilies, and how thoroughly he was appreciated elsewhere, he mentioned once or twice that he had no time to fool with theorems; adding — with a twitch of the eyebrows and a touch of that nervous bravado which so perplexed them — that he was helping the people down at the stock company; they were old friends of his.

The upshot of the matter was, that the Principal went to Paul's father, and Paul was taken out of school and put to work. The manager at Carnegie Hall was told to get another usher in his stead; the doorkeeper at the theatre was warned not to admit him to the house; and Charley Edwards remorsefully promised the boy's father not to see him again.

The members of the stock company were vastly amused when some of Paul's stories reached them — especially the women. They were hard-working women, most of them supporting indigent husbands or brothers, and they laughed rather bitterly at having stirred the boy to such fervid and florid inventions. They agreed with the faculty and with his father that Paul's was a bad case.

The east-bound train was ploughing through a January snow-storm; the dull dawn was beginning to show grey when the engine whistled a mile out of Newark. Paul started up from the seat where he had lain curled in uneasy slumber, rubbed the breath-misted window glass with his hand, and peered out. The snow was whirling in curling eddies above the white bottom lands, and the drifts lay already deep in the fields and along the fences, while here and there the long dead grass and dried weed stalks protruded black above it. Lights shone from the scattered houses, and a gang of labourers who stood beside the track waved their lanterns.

Paul had slept very little, and he felt grimy and uncomfortable. He had made the all-night journey in a day coach, partly because he was ashamed, dressed as he was, to go into a Pullman, and partly because he was afraid of being seen there by some Pittsburgh business man, who might have noticed him in Denny & Carson's office. When the whistle awoke him, he clutched quickly at his breast pocket, glancing about him with an uncertain smile. But the little, clay-bespattered Italians were still sleeping, the slatternly women across the aisle were in open-mouthed oblivion, and even the crumby, crying babies were for the nonce stilled. Paul settled back to struggle with his impatience as best he could.

When he arrived at the Jersey City station, he hurried through his breakfast, manifestly ill at ease and keeping a sharp eye about him. After he reached the Twenty-third Street station, he consulted a cabman, and had himself driven to a men's furnishing establishment that was just opening for the day. He spent upward of two hours there, buying with endless reconsidering and great care. His new street suit he put on in the fitting-room; the frock coat and dress clothes he had bundled into the cab with his linen. Then he drove to a hatter's and a shoe house. His next errand was at Tiffany's, where he selected his silver and a new scarf-pin. He would not wait to have his silver marked, he said. Lastly, he stopped at a trunk shop on Broadway, and had his purchases packed into various travelling bags.

It was a little after one o'clock when he drove up to the Waldorf, and after settling with the cabman, went into the office. He registered from Washington; said his mother and father had been abroad, and that he had come down to await the arrival of their steamer. He told his story plausibly and had no trouble, since he volunteered to pay for them in advance, in engaging his rooms; a sleeping-room, sitting-room and bath.

Not once, but a hundred times Paul had planned this entry into New York. He had gone over every detail of it with Charley Edwards, and in his scrap book at home there were pages of description about New York hotels, cut from the Sunday papers. When he was shown to his sitting-room on the eighth floor, he saw at a glance that everything was as it should be; there was but one detail in his mental picture that the place did not realize, so he rang for the bell boy and sent him down for flowers. He moved about nervously until the boy returned, putting away his new linen and fingering it delightedly as he did so. When the flowers came, he put them hastily into water, and then tumbled into a hot bath. Presently he came out of his white bath-room, resplendent in his new silk underwear, and playing with the tassels of his red robe. The snow was whirling so fiercely outside his windows that he could scarcely see across the street, but within the air was deliciously soft and fragrant. He put the violets and jonquils on the taboret beside the couch, and threw himself down, with a long sigh, covering himself with a Roman blanket. He was thoroughly tired; he had been in such haste, he had stood up to such a strain, covered so much ground in the last twenty-four hours, that he wanted to think how it had all come about. Lulled by the sound of the wind, the warm air, and the cool fragrance of the flowers, he sank into deep, drowsy retrospection.

It had been wonderfully simple; when they had shut him out of the theatre and concert hall, when they had taken away his bone, the whole thing was virtually determined. The rest was a mere matter of opportunity. The only thing that at all surprised him was his own courage — for he realized well enough that he had always been tormented by fear, a sort of apprehensive dread that, of late years, as the meshes of the lies he had told closed about him, had been pulling the muscles of his body tighter and tighter. Until now, he could not remember the time when he had not been dreading something. Even when he was a little boy, it was always there — behind him, or before, or on either side. There had always been the shadowed corner, the dark place into which he dared not look, but from which something seemed always to be watching him — and Paul had done things that were not pretty to watch, he knew.

But now he had a curious sense of relief, as though he had at last thrown down the gauntlet to the thing in the corner.

Yet it was but a day since he had been sulking in the traces; but yesterday afternoon that he had been sent to the bank with Denny & Carson's deposit, as usual — but this time he was instructed to leave the book to be balanced. There was above two thousand dollars in checks, and nearly a thousand in the bank notes which he had taken from the book and quietly transferred to his pocket. At the bank he had made out a new deposit slip. His nerves had been steady enough to permit of his returning to the office, where he had finished his work and asked for a full day's holiday to-morrow, Saturday, giving a perfectly reasonable pretext. The bank book, he knew, would not be returned before Monday or Tuesday, and his father would be out of town for the next week. From the time he slipped the bank notes into his pocket until he boarded the night train for New York, he had not known a moment's hesitation. It was not the first time Paul had steered through treacherous waters.

How astonishingly easy it had all been; here he was, the thing done; and this time there would be no awakening, no figure at the top of the stairs. He watched the snow flakes whirling by his window until he fell asleep.

When he awoke, it was three o'clock in the afternoon. He bounded up with a start; half of one of his precious days gone already! He spent more than an hour in dressing, watching every stage of his toilet carefully in the mirror. Everything was quite perfect; he was exactly the kind of boy he had always wanted to be.

When he went downstairs, Paul took a carriage and drove up Fifth Avenue toward the Park. The snow had somewhat abated; carriages and tradesmen's wagons were hurrying soundlessly to and fro in the winter twilight; boys in woollen mufflers were shovelling off the doorsteps; the avenue stages made fine spots of colour against the white street. Here and there on the corners were stands, with whole flower gardens blooming under glass cases, against the sides of which the snow flakes stuck and melted; violets, roses, carnations, lilies of the valley — somehow vastly more lovely and alluring that they blossomed thus unnaturally in the snow. The Park itself was a wonderful stage winter-piece.

When he returned, the pause of the twilight had ceased, and the tune of the streets had changed. The snow was falling faster, lights streamed from the hotels that reared their dozen stories fearlessly up into the storm, defying the raging Atlantic winds. A long, black stream of carriages poured down the avenue, intersected here and there by other streams, tending horizontally. There were a score of cabs about the entrance of his hotel, and his driver had to wait. Boys in livery were running in and out of the awning stretched across the sidewalk, up and down the red velvet carpet laid from the door to the street. Above, about, within it all was the rumble and roar, the hurry and toss of thousands of human beings as hot for pleasure as himself, and on every side of him towered the glaring affirmation of the omnipotence of wealth.

The boy set his teeth and drew his shoulders together in a spasm of realization; the plot of all dramas, the text of all romances, the nerve-stuff of all sensations was whirling about him like the snow flakes. He burnt like a faggot in a tempest.

When Paul went down to dinner, the music of the orchestra came floating up the elevator shaft to greet him. His head whirled as he stepped into the thronged corridor, and he sank back into one of the chairs against the wall to get his breath. The lights, the chatter, the perfumes, the bewildering medley of colour — he had, for a moment, the feeling of not being able to stand it. But only for a moment; these were his own people, he told himself. He went slowly about the corridors, through the writing-rooms, smoking-rooms, reception-rooms, as though he were exploring the chambers of an enchanted palace, built and peopled for him alone.

When he reached the dining-room he sat down at a table near a window. The flowers, the white linen, the many-coloured wine glasses, the gay toilettes of the women, the low popping of corks, the undulating repetitions of the *Blue Danube* from the orchestra, all flooded Paul's dream with bewildering radiance. When the roseate tinge of his champagne was added — that cold, precious, bubbling stuff that creamed and foamed in his glass — Paul wondered that there were honest men in the world at all. This was what all the world was fighting for, he reflected; this was what all the struggle was about. He doubted the reality of his past. Had he ever known a place called Cordelia Street, a place where fagged-looking business men got on the early car; mere rivets in a machine they seemed to Paul, — sickening men, with combings of children's hair always hanging to their coats, and the smell of cooking in their clothes. Cordelia Street — Ah! that belonged to another time and country; had he not always been thus, had he not sat here night after night, from as far back as he could remember, looking pensively over just such shimmering textures, and slowly twirling the stem of a glass like this one between his thumb and middle finger? He rather thought he had.

He was not in the least abashed or lonely. He had no especial desire to meet or to know any of these people; all he demanded was the right to look on and conjecture, to watch the pageant. The mere stage properties were all he contended for. Nor was he lonely later in the evening, in his lodge at the Metropolitan. He was now entirely rid of his nervous misgivings, of his forced aggressiveness, of the imperative desire to show himself different from his surroundings. He felt now that his surroundings explained him. Nobody questioned the purple; he had only to wear it passively. He had only to glance down at his attire to reassure himself that here it would be impossible for any one to humiliate him.

He found it hard to leave his beautiful sitting-room to go to bed that night, and sat long watching the raging storm from his turret window. When he went to sleep it was with the lights turned on in his bedroom; partly because of his old timidity, and partly so that, if he should wake in the night, there would be no wretched moment of doubt, no horrible suspicion of yellow wall-paper, or of Washington and Calvin above his bed.

Sunday morning the city was practically snow-bound. Paul break-fasted late, and in the afternoon he fell in with a wild San Francisco boy, a freshman at Yale, who said he had run down for a "little flyer" over Sunday. The young man offered to show Paul the night side of the town, and the two boys went out together after dinner, not returning to the hotel until seven o'clock the next morning. They had started out in the confiding warmth of a champagne friendship, but their parting in the elevator was singularly cool. The freshman pulled himself together to make his train, and Paul went to bed. He awoke at two o'clock in the afternoon, very thirsty and dizzy, and rang for ice-water, coffee, and the Pittsburgh papers.

On the part of the hotel management, Paul excited no suspicion. There was this to be said for him, that he wore his spoils with dignity and in no way made himself conspicuous. Even under the glow of his wine he was never boisterous, though he found the stuff like a magician's wand for wonder-building. His chief greediness lay in his ears and eyes, and his excesses were not offensive ones. His dearest pleasures were the grey winter twilights in his sitting-room; his quiet enjoyment of his flowers, his clothes, his wide divan, his cigarette and his sense of power. He could not remember a time when he had felt so at peace with himself. The mere release from the necessity of petty lying, lying every day and every day, restored his self-respect. He had never lied for pleasure, even at school; but to be noticed and admired, to assert his difference from other Cordelia Street boys; and he felt a good deal more

manly, more honest, even, now that he had no need for boastful preten-
sions, now that he could, as his actor friends used to say, "dress the part."
It was characteristic that remorse did not occur to him. His golden days
went by without a shadow, and he made each as perfect as he could.

On the eighth day after his arrival in New York, he found the whole
affair exploited in the Pittsburgh papers, exploited with a wealth of detail
which indicated that local news of a sensational nature was at a low ebb.
The firm of Denny & Carson announced that the boy's father had re-
funded the full amount of the theft, and that they had no intention of
prosecuting. The Cumberland minister had been interviewed, and expressed his hope of yet reclaiming the motherless lad, and his Sabbath-
school teacher declared that she would spare no effort to that end. The
rumour had reached Pittsburgh that the boy had been seen in a New York
hotel, and his father had gone East to find him and bring him home.

Paul had just come in to dress for dinner; he sank into a chair, weak to
the knees, and clasped his head in his hands. It was to be worse than jail,
even; the tepid waters of Cordelia Street were to close over him finally
and forever. The grey monotony stretched before him in hopeless,
unrelieved years; Sabbath-school, Young People's Meeting, the yellow-
papered room, the damp dish-towels; it all rushed back upon him with a
sickening vividness. He had the old feeling that the orchestra had
suddenly stopped, the sinking sensation that the play was over. The
sweat broke out on his face, and he sprang to his feet, looked about him
with his white, conscious smile, and winked at himself in the mirror.
With something of the old childish belief in miracles with which he had
so often gone to class, all his lessons unlearned, Paul dressed and dashed
whistling down the corridor to the elevator.

He had no sooner entered the dining-room and caught the measure of
the music than his remembrance was lightened by his old elastic power
of claiming the moment, mounting with it, and finding it all sufficient.
The glare and glitter about him, the mere scenic accessories had again,
and for the last time, their old potency. He would show himself that he
was game, he would finish the thing splendidly. He doubted, more than
ever, the existence of Cordelia Street, and for the first time he drank his
wine recklessly. Was he not, after all, one of those fortunate beings born to
the purple, was he not still himself and in his own place? He drummed a
nervous accompaniment to the Pagliacci music and looked about him,
telling himself over and over that it had paid.

He reflected drowsily, to the swell of the music and the chill sweetness
of his wine, that he might have done it more wisely. He might have

caught an outbound steamer and been well out of their clutches before now. But the other side of the world had seemed too far away and too uncertain then; he could not have waited for it; his need had been too sharp. If he had to choose over again, he would do the same thing to-morrow. He looked affectionately about the dining-room, now gilded with a soft mist. Ah, it had paid indeed!

Paul was awakened next morning by a painful throbbing in his head and feet. He had thrown himself across the bed without undressing, and had slept with his shoes on. His limbs and hands were lead heavy, and his tongue and throat were parched and burnt. There came upon him one of those fateful attacks of clear-headedness that never occurred except when he was physically exhausted and his nerves hung loose. He lay still and closed his eyes and let the tide of things wash over him.

His father was in New York; "stopping at some joint or other," he told himself. The memory of successive summers on the front stoop fell upon him like a weight of black water. He had not a hundred dollars left; and he knew now, more than ever, that money was everything, the wall that stood between all he loathed and all he wanted. The thing was winding itself up; he had thought of that on his first glorious day in New York, and had even provided a way to snap the thread. It lay on his dressing-table now; he had got it out last night when he came blindly up from dinner, but the shiny metal hurt his eyes, and he disliked the looks of it.

He rose and moved about with a painful effort, succumbing now and again to attacks of nausea. It was the old depression exaggerated; all the world had become Cordelia Street. Yet somehow he was not afraid of anything, was absolutely calm; perhaps because he had looked into the dark corner at last and knew. It was bad enough, what he saw there, but somehow not so bad as his long fear of it had been. He saw everything clearly now. He had a feeling that he had made the best of it, that he had lived the sort of life he was meant to live, and for half an hour he sat staring at the revolver. But he told himself that was not the way, so he went downstairs and took a cab to the ferry.

When Paul arrived at Newark, he got off the train and took another cab, directing the driver to follow the Pennsylvania tracks out of the town. The snow lay heavy on the roadways and had drifted deep in the open fields. Only here and there the dead grass or dried weed stalks projected, singularly black, above it. Once well into the country, Paul dismissed the carriage and walked, floundering along the tracks, his mind a medley of irrelevant things. He seemed to hold in his brain an actual picture of everything he had seen that morning. He remembered every feature of both his drivers, of the toothless old woman from whom he had bought the red flowers in his coat, the agent from whom he had got his ticket, and all of his fellow-passengers on the ferry. His mind, unable to cope with vital matters near at hand, worked feverishly and deftly at sorting and grouping these images. They made for him a part of the ugliness of the world, of the ache in his head, and the bitter burning on his tongue. He stooped and put a handful of snow into his mouth as he walked, but that, too, seemed hot. When he reached a little hillside, where the tracks ran through a cut some twenty feet below him, he stopped and sat down.

The carnations in his coat were drooping with the cold, he noticed; their red glory all over. It occurred to him that all the flowers he had seen in the glass cases that first night must have gone the same way, long before this. It was only one splendid breath they had, in spite of their brave mockery at the winter outside the glass; and it was a losing game in the end, it seemed, this revolt against the homilies by which the world is run. Paul took one of the blossoms carefully from his coat and scooped a little hole in the snow, where he covered it up. Then he dozed a while, from his weak condition, seeming insensible to the cold.

The sound of an approaching train awoke him, and he started to his feet, remembering only his resolution, and afraid lest he should be too late. He stood watching the approaching locomotive, his teeth chattering, his lips drawn away from them in a frightened smile; once or twice he glanced nervously sidewise, as though he were being watched. When the right moment came, he jumped. As he fell, the folly of his haste occurred to him with merciless clearness, the vastness of what he had left undone. There flashed through his brain, clearer than ever before, the blue of Adriatic water, the yellow of Algerian sands.

He felt something strike his chest, and that his body was being thrown swiftly through the air, on and on, immeasurably far and fast, while his limbs were gently relaxed. Then, because the picture making mechanism was crushed, the disturbing visions flashed into black, and Paul dropped back into the immense design of things.

Alice Dunbar-Nelson

(1875–1935)

BORN IN NEW ORLEANS, Louisiana, Alice Ruth Moore Dunbar-Nelson was the daughter of a seamstress, Patricia Wright, and Joseph Moore of the merchant marine. In 1892 she graduated from Straight (now Dillard) University in New Orleans. Dunbar-Nelson privately printed her first book, *Violets and Other Tales*, a collection of sketches, essays, poems and stories, in 1895. Two years later she moved north to teach in Brooklyn, New York, and to continue her studies at the University of Pennsylvania, Cornell University and the School of Industrial Art.

Dunbar-Nelson married the poet Paul Laurence Dunbar in 1898, and moved with him to Washington, D.C. Both writers were well-known figures of the Harlem Renaissance, Dunbar-Nelson writing for various newspapers and magazines, such as the *Washington Eagle* and the *Pittsburgh Courier*, *Crisis*, *Opportunity*, the *Messenger* and *Collier's*. Dunbar-Nelson's *The Goodness of St. Rocque* — the first collection of short fiction published by an African-American woman — appeared in 1899.

The Dunbars divorced in 1902, and Dunbar-Nelson moved to Wilmington, Delaware. There she became more heavily involved in teaching, political activities, lecturing, writing and editing. In 1914, she compiled *Masterpieces of Negro Eloquence: The Best Speeches Delivered by the Negro from the Days of Slavery to the Present Time*. Six years later she published another anthology of African-American writings, *The Dunbar Speaker and Entertainer*.

Much of Dunbar-Nelson's fiction depicts the scenes and dialect of her native New Orleans. But whereas her earlier evocations of scenes from Creole and Cajun Louisiana contributed to her reputation as a local colorist, in "The Stones of the Village" Dunbar-Nelson directly confronts questions of race and the trauma suffered by victims of a segregated society.

130

The Stones of the Village

VICTOR GRABERT STRODE down the one wide, tree-shaded street of the village, his heart throbbing with a bitterness and anger that seemed too great to bear. So often had he gone home in the same spirit, however, that it had grown nearly second nature to him — this dull, sullen resentment, flaming out now and then into almost murderous vindictiveness. Behind him there floated derisive laughs and shouts, the taunts of little brutes, boys of his own age.

He reached the tumbledown cottage at the farther end of the street and flung himself on the battered step. Grandmère Grabert sat rocking herself and fro, crooning a bit of song brought over from the West Indies years ago; but when the boy sat silent, his head bowed in his hands, she paused in the midst of a line and regarded him with keen, piercing eyes.

"Eh, Victor?" she asked. That was all, but he understood. He raised his head and waved a hand angrily down the street towards the lighted square that marked the village center.

"Dose boy," he gulped.

Grandmère Grabert laid a sympathetic hand on his black curls, but withdrew it the next instant.

"*Bien,*" she said angrily. "Fo' what you go by dem, eh? W'y not keep to yo'self? Dey don' want you, dey don' care fo' you. H'ain' you got no sense?"

"Oh, but Grandmère," he wailed piteously, "I wan' fo' to play."

The old woman stood up in the doorway, her tall, spare form towering menacingly over him.

"You wan' fo' to play, eh? Fo' w'y? You don' need no play. Dose boy" — she swept a magnificent gesture down the street — "dey fools!"

131

"Eef I could play wid — " began Victor, but his grandmother caught him by the wrist, and held him as in a vise.

"Hush," she cried. "You mus' be goin' crazy," and still holding him by the wrist, she pulled him indoors.

It was a two-room house, bare and poor and miserable, but never had it seemed so meagre before to Victor as it did this night. The supper was frugal almost to the starvation point. They ate in silence, and afterwards Victor threw himself on his cot in the corner of the kitchen and closed his eyes. Grandmère Grabert thought him asleep, and closed the door noiselessly as she went into her own room. But he was awake, and his mind was like a shifting kaleidoscope of miserable incidents and heartaches. He had lived fourteen years and he could remember most of them as years of misery. He had never known a mother's love, for his mother had died, so he was told, when he was but a few months old. No one ever spoke to him of a father, and Grandmère Grabert had been all to him. She was kind, after a stern, unloving fashion, and she provided for him as best she could. He had picked up some sort of an education at the parish school. It was a good one after its way, but his life there had been such a succession of miseries, that he rebelled one day and refused to go any more.

His earliest memories were clustered about this poor little cottage. He could see himself toddling about its broken steps, playing alone with a few broken pieces of china which his fancy magnified into glorious toys. He remembered his first whipping too. Tired one day of the loneliness which even the broken china could not mitigate, he had toddled out the side gate after a merry group of little black and yellow boys of his own age. When Grandmère Grabert, missing him from his accustomed garden corner, came to look for him, she found him sitting contentedly in the center of the group in the dusty street, all of them gravely scooping up handsful of the gravelly dirt and trickling it down their chubby bare legs. Grandmère snatched at him fiercely, and he whimpered, for he was learning for the first time what fear was.

"What you mean?" she hissed at him. "What you mean playin' in de strit wid dose niggers?" And she struck at him wildly with her open hand.

He looked up into her brown face surmounted by a wealth of curly black hair faintly streaked with gray, but he was too frightened to question.

It had been loneliness ever since. For the parents of the little black and yellow boys, resenting the insult Grandmère had offered their offspring, sternly bade them have nothing more to do with Victor. Then when he toddled after some other little boys, whose faces were white like his own, they ran away with derisive hoots of "Nigger! Nigger!" And again, he could not understand.

Hardest of all, though, was when Grandmère sternly bade him cease speaking the soft, Creole patois that they chattered together, and forced him to learn English. The result was a confused jumble which was no language at all; that when he spoke it in the streets or in the school, all the boys, white and black and yellow, hooted at him and called him "White nigger! White nigger!"

He writhed on his cot that night and lived over all the anguish of his years until hot tears scalded their way down a burning face, and he fell into a troubled sleep wherein he sobbed over some dreamland miseries.

The next morning, Grandmère eyed his heavy, swollen eyes sharply, and a momentary thrill of compassion passed over her and found expression in a new tenderness of manner towards him as she served his breakfast. She too, had thought over the matter in the night, and it bore fruit in an unexpected way.

Some few weeks after, Victor found himself timidly ringing the doorbell of a house on Hospital Street in New Orleans. His heart throbbed in painful unison to the jangle of the bell. How was he to know that old Madame Guichard, Grandmère's one friend in the city, to whom she had confided him, would be kind? He had walked from the river landing to the house, timidly inquiring the way of busy pedestrians. He was hungry and frightened. Never in all his life had he seen so many people before, and in all the busy streets there was not one eye which would light up with recognition when it met his own. Moreover, it had been a weary journey down the Red River, thence into the Mississippi, and finally here. Perhaps it had not been devoid of interest, after its fashion, but Victor did not know. He was too heartsick at leaving home.

However, Mme. Guichard was kind. She welcomed him with a volubility and overflow of tenderness that acted like balm to the boy's sore spirit. Thence they were firm friends, even confidants.

Victor must find work to do. Grandmère Grabert's idea in sending him to New Orleans was that he might "mek one man of himse'f" as she phrased it. And Victor, grown suddenly old in the sense that he had a responsibility to bear, set about his search valiantly.

It chanced one day that he saw a sign in an old bookstore on Royal Street that stated in both French and English the need of a boy. Almost before he knew it, he had entered the shop and was gasping out some choked words to the little old man who sat behind the counter.

The old man looked keenly over his glasses at the boy and rubbed his bald head reflectively. In order to do this, he had to take off an old black silk cap which he looked at with apparent regret.

"Eh, what you say?" he asked sharply, when Victor had finished.

"I — I — want a place to work," stammered the boy again.

"Eh, you do? Well, can you read?"

"Yes, sir," replied Victor.

The old man got down from his stool, came from behind the counter, and, putting his finger under the boy's chin, stared hard into his eyes. They met his own unflinchingly, though there was the suspicion of pathos and timidity in their brown depths.

"Do you know where you live, eh?"

"On Hospital Street," said Victor. It did not occur to him to give the number, and the old man did not ask.

"*Trés bien*," grunted the bookseller, and his interest relaxed. He gave a few curt directions about the manner of work Victor was to do, and settled himself again upon his stool, poring into his dingy book with renewed ardor.

Thus began Victor's commercial life. It was an easy one. At seven, he opened the shutters of the little shop and swept and dusted. At eight, the bookseller came downstairs, and passed out to get his coffee at the restaurant across the street. At eight in the evening, the shop was closed again. That was all.

Occasionally, there came a customer, but not often, for there were only odd books and rare ones in the shop, and those who came were usually old, yellow, querulous bookworms, who nosed about for hours, and went away leaving many bank notes behind them. Sometimes there was an errand to do, and sometimes there came a customer when the proprietor was out. It was an easy matter to wait on them. He had but to point to the shelves and say, "Monsieur will be in directly," and all was settled, for those who came here to buy had plenty of leisure and did not mind waiting.

So a year went by, then two and three, and the stream of Victor's life flowed smoothly on its uneventful way. He had grown tall and thin, and often Mme. Guichard would look at him and chuckle to herself, "Ha, he is lak one beanpole, yaas, *mais* —" and there would be a world of unfinished reflection in that last word.

Victor had grown pale from much reading. Like a shadow of the old bookseller, he sat day after day poring into some dusty yellow-paged book, and his mind was a queer jumble of ideas. History and philosophy and old-fashioned social economy were tangled with French romance and classic mythology and astrology and mysticism. He had made few friends, for his experience in the village had made him chary of strangers. Every week, he wrote to Grandmère Grabert and sent her part of his earnings. In his way he was happy, and if he was lonely, he had ceased to care about it, for his world was peopled with images of his own fancying.

Then all at once, the world he had built about him tumbled down, and he was left staring helplessly at its ruins. The little bookseller died one day, and his shop and its books were sold by an unscrupulous nephew who cared not for bindings or precious yellowed pages, but only for the grossly material things that money can buy. Victor ground his teeth as the auctioneer's strident voice sounded through the shop where all once had been hushed quiet, and wept as he saw some of his favorite books carried away by men and women, whom he was sure could not appreciate their value.

He dried his tears, however, the next day when a grave-faced lawyer came to the little house on Hospital Street, and informed him that he had been left a sum of money by the bookseller.

Victor sat staring at him helplessly. Money meant little to him. He never needed it, never used it. After he had sent Grandmère her sum each week, Mme. Guichard kept the rest and doled it out to him as he needed it for carfare and clothes.

"The interest of the money," continued the lawyer, clearing his throat, "is sufficient to keep you very handsomely, without touching the principal. It was my client's wish that you should enter Tulane College, and there fit yourself for your profession. He had great confidence in your ability."

"Tulane College!" cried Victor. "Why — why — why —" Then he stopped suddenly, and the hot blood mounted to his face. He glanced furtively about the room. Mme. Guichard was not near; the lawyer had seen no one but him. Then why tell him? His heart leaped wildly at the thought. Well, Grandmère would have willed it so.

The lawyer was waiting politely for him to finish his sentence.

"Why — why — I should have to study in order to enter there," finished Victor lamely.

"Exactly so," said Mr. Buckley, "and as I have, in a way, been appointed your guardian, I will see to that."

Victor found himself murmuring confused thanks and good-byes to Mr. Buckley. After he had gone, the boy sat down and gazed blankly at the wall. Then he wrote a long letter to Grandmère.

A week later, he changed boarding places at Mr. Buckley's advice, and entered a preparatory school for Tulane. And still, Mme. Guichard and Mr. Buckley had not met.

It was a handsomely furnished office on Carondelet Street in which Lawyer Grabert sat some years later. His day's work done, he was leaning back in his chair and smiling pleasantly out of the window. Within was warmth and light and cheer; without, the wind howled and gusty rains beat against the windowpane. Lawyer Grabert smiled again as he looked about at the comfort, and found himself half pitying those without who were forced to buffet the storm afoot. He rose finally and, donning his overcoat, called a cab and was driven to his rooms in the most fashionable part of the city. There he found his old-time college friend, awaiting him with some impatience.

"Thought you never were coming, old man" was his greeting.

Grabert smiled pleasantly. "Well, I was a bit tired, you know," he answered, "and I have been sitting idle for an hour or more, just relaxing, as it were."

Vannier laid his hand affectionately on the other's shoulder. "That was a mighty effort you made today," he said earnestly. "I, for one, am proud of you."

"Thank you," replied Grabert simply, and the two sat silent for a minute.

"Going to the Charles' dance tonight?" asked Vannier finally.

"I don't believe I am. I am tired and lazy."

"It will do you good. Come on."

"No, I want to read and ruminate."

"Ruminate over your good fortune of today?"

"If you will have it so, yes."

But it was not simply his good fortune of that day over which Grabert pondered. It was over the good fortune of the past fifteen years. From school to college and from college to law school he had gone, and thence into practice, and he was now accredited a successful young lawyer. His small fortune, which Mr. Buckley, with generous kindness, had invested wisely, had almost doubled, and his school career, while not of the brilliant, meteoric kind, had been pleasant and profitable. He had made friends, at first, with the boys he met, and they in turn had taken him into their homes. Now and then, the Buckleys asked him to dinner, and he was seen occasionally in their box at the opera. He was rapidly becoming a social favorite, and girls vied with each other to dance with him. No one had asked any questions, and he had volunteered no information concerning himself. Vannier, who had known him in preparatory school days, had said that he was a young country fellow with some money, no connections, and a ward of Mr. Buckley's, and somehow, contrary to the usual social custom of the South, this meagre account had passed muster. But Vannier's family had been a social arbiter for many years, and Grabert's personality was pleasing, without being aggressive, so he had passed through the portals of the social world and was in the inner circle.

One year, when he and Vannier were in Switzerland, pretending to climb impossible mountains and in reality smoking many cigars a day on hotel porches, a letter came to Grabert from the priest of his old-time town, telling him that Grandmère Grabert had been laid away in the parish churchyard. There was no more to tell. The little old hut had been sold to pay funeral expenses.

"Poor Grandmère," sighed Victor. "She did care for me after her fashion. I'll go take a look at her grave when I go back."

But he did not go, for when he returned to Louisiana, he was too busy, then he decided that it would be useless, sentimental folly. Moreover, he had no love for the old village. Its very name suggested things that made him turn and look about him nervously. He had long since eliminated Mme. Guichard from his list of acquaintances.

And yet, as he sat there in his cosy study that night, and smiled as he went over in his mind triumph after triumph which he had made since the old bookstore days in Royal Street, he was conscious of a subtle undercurrent of annoyance; a sort of mental reservation that placed itself on every pleasant memory.

"I wonder what's the matter with me?" he asked himself as he rose and paced the floor impatiently. Then he tried to recall his other triumph, the one of the day. The case of Tate vs. Tate, a famous will contest, had been dragging through the courts for seven years and his speech had decided it that day. He could hear the applause of the courtroom as he sat down, but it rang hollow in his ears, for he remembered another scene. The day before he had been in another court, and found himself interested in the prisoner before the bar. The offense was a slight one, a mere technicality. Grabert was conscious of something pleasant in the man's face; a scrupulous neatness in his dress, an unostentatious conforming to the prevailing style. The Recorder, however, was short and brusque.

"Wilson — Wilson — " he growled. "Oh, yes, I know you, always kicking up some sort of a row about theatre seats and cars. Hum-um. What do you mean by coming before me with a flower in your buttonhole?"

The prisoner looked down indifferently at the bud on his coat, and made no reply.

"Hey?" growled the Recorder. "You niggers are putting yourselves up too much for me."

At the forbidden word, the blood rushed to Grabert's face, and he started from his seat angrily. The next instant, he had recovered himself and buried his face in a paper. After Wilson had paid his fine, Grabert looked at him furtively as he passed out. His face was perfectly impassive, but his eyes flashed defiantly. The lawyer was tingling with rage and indignation, although the affront had not been given him.

"If Recorder Grant had any reason to think that I was in any way like Wilson, I would stand no better show," he mused bitterly.

However, as he thought it over tonight, he decided that he was a sentimental fool. "What have I to do with them?" he asked himself. "I must be careful."

The next week, he discharged the man who cared for his office. He was a Negro, and Grabert had no fault to find with him generally, but he found himself with a growing sympathy towards the man, and since the episode in the courtroom, he was morbidly nervous lest something in his manner betray him. Thereafter, a round-eyed Irish boy cared for his rooms.

The Vanniers were wont to smile indulgently at his every move. Elise Vannier, particularly, was more than interested in his work. He had a way of dropping in of evenings and talking over his cases and speeches with her in a cosy corner of the library. She had a gracious sympathetic manner that was soothing and a cheery fund of repartee to whet her conversation. Victor found himself drifting into sentimental bits of talk now and then. He found himself carrying around in his pocketbook a faded rose which she had once worn, and when he laughed at it one day and started to throw it in the wastebasket, he suddenly kissed it instead, and replaced it in the pocketbook. That Elise was not indifferent to him he could easily see. She had not learned yet how to veil her eyes and mask her face under a cool assumption of superiority. She would give him her hand when they met with a girlish impulsiveness, and her color came and went under his gaze. Sometimes, when he held her hand a bit longer than necessary, he could feel it flutter in his own, and she would sigh a quick little gasp that made his heart leap and choked his utterance.

They were tucked away in their usual cosy corner one evening, and the conversation had drifted to the problem of where they would spend the summer.

"Papa wants to go to the country house," pouted Elise, "and Mama and I don't want to go. It isn't fair, of course, because when we go so far away, Papa can be with us only for a few weeks when he can get away from his office, while if we go to the country place, he can run up every few days. But it is so dull there, don't you think so?"

Victor recalled some pleasant vacation days at the plantation home and laughed. "Not if you are there."

"Yes, but you see, I can't take myself for a companion. Now if you'll promise to come up sometimes, it will be better."

"If I may, I shall be delighted to come."

Elise laughed intimately. "If you 'may' " she replied, "as if such a word had to enter into our plans. Oh, but Victor, haven't you some sort of plantation somewhere? It seems to me that I heard Steven years ago speak of your home in the country, and I wondered sometimes that you never spoke of it, or ever mentioned having visited it."

The girl's artless words were bringing cold sweat to Victor's brow, his tongue felt heavy and useless, but he managed to answer quietly, "I have no home in the country."

"Well, didn't you ever own one, or your family?"

"It was old quite a good many years ago," he replied, and a vision of the little old hut with its tumbledown steps and weed-grown garden came into his mind.

"Where was it?" pursued Elise innocently.

"Oh, away up in St. Landry parish, too far away from civilization to mention." He tried to laugh, but it was a hollow, forced attempt that rang false. But Elise was too absorbed in her own thoughts of the summer to notice.

"And you haven't a relative living?" she continued.

"Not one."

"How strange. Why it seems to me if I did not have half a hundred cousins and uncles and aunts that I should feel somehow out of touch with the world."

He did not reply, and she chattered away on another topic.

When he was alone in his room that night, he paced the floor again, chewing wildly at a cigar that he had forgotten to light.

"What did she mean? What did she mean?" he asked himself over and over. Could she have heard or suspected anything that she was trying to

find out about? Could any action, any unguarded expression of his have
set the family thinking? But he soon dismissed the thought as unworthy
of him. Elise was too frank and transparent a girl to stoop to subterfuge.
If she wished to know anything, she was wont to ask out at once, and if
she had once thought anyone was sailing under false colors, she would
say so frankly, and dismiss them from her presence.

Well, he must be prepared to answer questions if he were going to
marry her. The family would want to know all about him, and Elise
herself would be curious for more than her brother, Steven Vannier's
meagre account. But was he going to marry Elise? That was the question.

He sat down and buried his head in his hands. Would it be right for
him to take a wife, especially such a woman as Elise, and from such a
family as the Vanniers? Would it be fair? Would it be just? If they knew
and were willing, it would be different. But they did not know, and they
would not consent if they did. In fancy, he saw the dainty girl, whom he
loved, shrinking from him as he told her of Grandmère Grabert and the
village boys. This last thought made him set his teeth hard, and the hot
blood rushed to his face.

Well, why not, after all, why not? What was the difference between
him and the hosts of other suitors who hovered about Elise? They had
money; so had he. They had education, polite training, culture, social
position; so had he. But they had family traditions, and he had none.
Most of them could point to a long line of family portraits with justifi-
able pride; while if he had had a picture of Grandmère Grabert, he
would have destroyed it fearfully, lest it fall into the hands of some too
curious person. This was the subtle barrier that separated them. He
recalled with a sting how often he had had to sit silent and constrained
when the conversation turned to ancestors and family traditions. He
might be one with his companions and friends in everything but this. He
must ever be on the outside, hovering at the gates, as it were. Into the
inner life of his social world, he might never enter. The charming
impoliteness of an intercourse begun by their fathers and grandfathers
was not for him. There must always be a certain formality with him,
even though they were his most intimate friends. He had not fifty
cousins; therefore, as Elise phrased it, he was "out of touch with the
world."

"If ever I have a son or a daughter," he found himself saying unconsciously, "I would try to save him from this."

Then he laughed bitterly as he realized the irony of the thought. Well, anyway, Elise loved him. There was a sweet consolation in that. He had but to look into her frank eyes and read her soul. Perhaps she wondered why he had not spoken. Should he speak? There he was back at the old question again.

"According to the standard of the world," he mused reflectively, "my blood is tainted in two ways. Who knows it? No one but myself, and I shall not tell. Otherwise, I am quite as good as the rest, and Elise loves me."

But even this thought failed of its sweetness in a moment. Elise loved him because she did not know. He found a sickening anger and disgust rising in himself at a people whose prejudices made him live a life of deception. He would cater to their traditions no longer; he would be honest. Then he found himself shrinking from the alternative with a dread that made him wonder. It was the old problem of his life in the village; and the boys, both white and black and yellow, stood as before, with stones in their hands to hurl at him.

He went to bed worn out with the struggle, but still with no definite idea what to do. Sleep was impossible. He rolled and tossed miserably, and cursed the fate that had thrown him in such a position. He had never thought very seriously over the subject before. He had rather drifted with the tide and accepted what came to him as a sort of recompense the world owed him for his unhappy childhood. He had known fear, yes, and qualms now and then, and a hot resentment occasionally when the outsideness of his situation was inborn to him; but that was all. Elise had awakened a disagreeable conscientiousness within him, which he decided was as unpleasant as it was unnecessary.

He could not sleep, so he arose and, dressing, walked out and stood on the banquette. The low hum of the city came to him like the droning of some sleepy insect, and ever and anon the quick flash and fire of the gashouses, like a huge winking fiery eye, lit up the south of the city. It was inexpressibly soothing to Victor — the great unknowing city, teeming with life and with lives whose sadness mocked his own teacup tempest. He smiled and shook himself as a dog shakes off the water from his coat.

"I think a walk will help me out," he said absently, and presently he was striding down St. Charles Avenue, around Lee Circle and down to Canal Street, where the lights and glare absorbed him for a while. He walked out the wide boulevard towards Claiborne Street, hardly thinking, hardly realizing that he was walking. When he was thoroughly worn out, he retraced his steps and dropped wearily into a restaurant near Bourbon Street.

"Hullo!" said a familiar voice from a table as he entered. Victor turned and recognized Frank Ward, a little oculist, whose office was in the same building as his own.

"Another night owl besides myself," laughed Ward, making room for him at his table. "Can't you sleep too, old fellow?"

"Not very well," said Victor, taking the proffered seat. "I believe I'm getting nerves. Think I need toning up."

"Well, you'd have been toned up if you had been in here a few minutes ago. Why — why — " And Ward went off into peals of laughter at the memory of the scene.

"What was it?" asked Victor.

"Why — a fellow came in here, nice sort of fellow, apparently, and wanted to have supper. Well, would you believe it, when they wouldn't serve him, he wanted to fight everything in sight. It was positively exciting for a time."

"Why wouldn't the waiter serve him?" Victor tried to make his tone indifferent, but he felt the quaver in his voice.

"Why? Why, he was a darky, you know."

"Well, what of it?" demanded Grabert fiercely. "Wasn't he quiet, well-dressed, polite? Didn't he have money?"

"My dear fellow," began Ward mockingly. "Upon my word, I believe you are losing your mind. You do need toning up or something. Would you — could you — ?"

"Oh, pshaw," broke in Grabert. "I — I — believe I am losing my mind. Really, Ward, I need something to make me sleep. My head aches."

Ward was at once all sympathy and advice, and chiding to the waiter for his slowness in filling their order. Victor toyed with his food, and made an excuse to leave the restaurant as soon as he could decently.

"Good heavens," he said when he was alone. "What will I do next?" His outburst of indignation at Ward's narrative had come from his lips almost before he knew it, and he was frightened, frightened at his own unguardedness. He did not know what had come over him.

"I must be careful, I must be careful," he muttered to himself. "I must go to the other extreme, if necessary." He was pacing his rooms again, and, suddenly, he faced the mirror.

"You wouldn't fare any better than the rest, if they knew," he told the reflection. "You poor wretch, what are you?"

When he thought of Elise, he smiled. He loved her, but he hated the traditions which she represented. He was conscious of a blind fury which bade him wreak vengeance on those traditions, and of a cowardly fear which cried out to him to retain his position in the world's and Elise's eyes at any cost.

Mrs. Grabert was delighted to have visiting her her old school friend from Virginia, and the two spent hours laughing over their girlish escapades, and comparing notes about their little ones. Each was confident that her darling had said the cutest things, and their polite deference to each other's opinions on the matter was a sham through which each saw without resentment.

"But, Elise," remonstrated Mrs. Allen, "I think it so strange you don't have a mammy for Baby Vannier. He would be so much better cared for than by that harum-scarum young white girl you have."

"I think so too, Adelaide," sighed Mrs. Grabert. "It seems strange for me not to have a darky maid about, but Victor can't bear them. I cried and cried for my old mammy, but he was stern. He doesn't like darkies, you know, and he says old mammies just frighten children, and ruin their childhood. I don't see how he could say that, do you?" She looked wistfully to Mrs. Allen for sympathy.

"I don't know," mused that lady. "We were all looked after by our mammies, and I think they are the best kind of nurses."

"And Victor won't have any kind of darky servant either here or at the office. He says they're shiftless and worthless and generally no-account. Of course, he knows, he's had lots of experience with them in his business."

Mrs. Allen folded her hands behind her head and stared hard at the ceiling. "Oh, well, men don't know everything," she said, "and Victor may come around to our way of thinking after all."

It was late that evening when the lawyer came in for dinner. His eyes had acquired a habit of veiling themselves under their lashes, as if they were constantly concealing something which they feared might be wrenched from them by a stare. He was nervous and restless, with a habit of glancing about him furtively, and a twitching compressing of his lips when he had finished a sentence, which somehow reminded you of a kindhearted judge, who is forced to give a death sentence.

Elise met him at the door as was her wont, and she knew from the first glance into his eyes that something had disturbed him more than usual that day, but she forbore asking questions, for she knew he would tell her when the time had come.

They were in their room that night when the rest of the household lay in slumber. He sat for a long while gazing at the open fire, then he passed his hand over his forehead wearily.

"I have had a rather unpleasant experience today," he began.

"Yes."

"Pavageau, again."

His wife was brushing her hair before the mirror. At the name she turned hastily with the brush in her uplifted hand.

"I can't understand, Victor, why you must have dealings with that man. He is constantly irritating you. I simply wouldn't associate with him."

"I don't," and he laughed at her feminine argument. "It isn't a question of association, cherie, it's a purely business and unsocial relation, if relation it may be called, that throws us together."

She threw down the brush petulantly, and came to his side. "Victor," she began hesitatingly, her arms about his neck, her face close to his, "won't you — won't you give up politics for me? It was ever so much nicer when you were just a lawyer and wanted only to be the best lawyer in the state, without all this worry about corruption and votes and such things. You've changed, oh, Victor, you've changed so. Baby and I won't know you after a while."

He put her gently on his knee. "You mustn't blame the poor politics, darling. Don't you think, perhaps, it's the inevitable hardening and embittering that must come to us all as we grow older?"

"No, I don't," she replied emphatically. "Why do you go into this struggle, anyhow? You have nothing to gain but an empty honor. It won't bring you more money, or make you more loved or respected. Why must you be mixed up with such — such — awful people?"

"I don't know," he said wearily.

And in truth, he did not know. He had gone on after his marriage with Elise making one success after another. It seemed that a beneficent Providence had singled him out as the one man in the state upon whom to heap the most lavish attentions. He was popular after the fashion of those who are high in the esteem of the world; and this very fact made him tremble the more, for he feared that should some disclosure come, he could not stand the shock of public opinion that must overwhelm him.

"What disclosure?" he would say impatiently when such a thought would come to him. "Where could it come from, and then, what is there to disclose?"

Thus he would deceive himself for as much as a month at a time.

He was surprised to find awaiting him in his office one day the man Wilson, whom he remembered in the courtroom before Recorder Grant. He was surprised and annoyed. Why had the man come to his office? Had he seen the telltale flush on his face that day?

But it was soon evident that Wilson did not even remember having seen him before.

"I came to see if I could retain you in a case of mine," he began, after the usual formalities of greeting were over.

"I am afraid, my good man," said Grabert brusquely, "that you have mistaken the office."

Wilson's face flushed at the appellation, but he went on bravely. "I have not mistaken the office. I know you are the best civil lawyer in the city, and I want your services."

"An impossible thing."

"Why? Are you too busy? My case is a simple thing, a mere point in law, but I want the best authority and the best opinion brought to bear on it."

"I could not give you any help — and — I fear, we do not understand each other — I do not wish to." He turned to his desk abruptly.

"What could he have meant by coming to me?" he questioned himself fearfully, as Wilson left the office. "Do I look like a man likely to take up his impossible contentions?"

He did not look like it, nor was he. When it came to a question involving the Negro, Victor Grabert was noted for his stern, unrelenting attitude; it was simply impossible to convince him that there was anything but sheerest incapacity in that race. For him, no good could come out of this Nazareth. He was liked and respected by men of his political belief, because, even when he was a candidate for a judgeship, neither money nor the possible chance of a deluge of votes from the First and Fourth Wards could cause him to swerve one hair's breadth from his opinion of the black inhabitants of those wards.

Pavageau, however, was his *bête noire*.[1] Pavageau was a lawyer, a coolheaded, calculating man with steely eyes set in a grim brown face. They had first met in the courtroom in a case which involved the question whether a man may set aside the will of his father, who, disregarding the legal offspring of another race than himself, chooses to leave his property to educational institutions which would not have

1. *bête noire*] literally "black beast"; a person or thing strongly detested or avoided.

granted admission to that son. Pavageau represented the son. He lost, of course. The judge, the jury, the people and Grabert were against him; but he fought his fight with a grim determination which commanded Victor's admiration and respect.

"Fools," he said between his teeth to himself, when they were crowding about him with congratulations. "Fools, can't they see who is the abler man of the two?"

He wanted to go up to Pavageau and give him his hand; to tell him that he was proud of him and that he had really won the case, but public opinion was against him; but he dared not. Another one of his colleagues might; but he was afraid. Pavageau and the world might misunderstand, or would it be understanding?

Thereafter they met often. Either by some freak of nature, or because there was a shrewd sense of the possibilities in his position, Pavageau was of the same political side of the fence as Grabert. Secretly, Grabert admired the man; he respected him; he liked him; and because of this Grabert was always ready with sneer and invective for him. He fought him bitterly when there was no occasion for fighting, and Pavageau became his enemy, and his name a very synonym of horror to Elise, who learned to trace her husband's fits of moodiness and depression to the one source.

Meanwhile, Vannier Grabert was growing up, a handsome lad, with his father's and mother's physical beauty, and a strength and force of character that belonged to neither. In him, Grabert saw the reparation of all his childhood's wrongs and sufferings. The boy realized all his own longings. He had family traditions, and a social position which was his from birth and an inalienable right to hold up his head without an unknown fear gripping at his heart. Grabert felt that he could forgive all — the village boys of long ago, and the imaginary village boys of today — when he looked at his son. He had bought and paid for Vannier's freedom and happiness. The coins may have been each a drop of his heart's blood, but he had reckoned the cost before he had given it.

It was a source of great pride for Grabert, now that he was a judge, to take the boy to court with him, and one Saturday morning when he was starting out, Vannier asked if he might go.

"There is nothing that would interest you today, *mon fils*,"[2] he said tenderly, "but you may go."

In fact, there was nothing interesting that day; merely a trouble-

2. *mon fils*] my son.

some old woman, who instead of taking her fair-skinned grandchild out of the school where it had been found it did not belong, had preferred to bring the matter to court. She was represented by Pavageau. Of course, there was not the ghost of a show for her. Pavageau had told her that. The law was very explicit about the matter. The only question lay in proving the child's affinity to the Negro race, which was not such a difficult matter to do, so the case was quickly settled, since the child's grandmother accompanied him. The judge, however, was irritated. It was a hot day and he was provoked that such a trivial matter should have taken up his time. He lost his temper as he looked at his watch.

"I don't see why these people want to force their children into the white schools," he declared. "There should be a rigid inspection to prevent it, and all the suspected children put out and made to go where they belong."

Pavageau, too, was irritated that day. He looked up from some papers which he was folding, and his gaze met Grabert's with a keen, cold, penetrating flash.

"Perhaps Your Honor would like to set the example by taking your son from the schools."

There was an instant silence in the courtroom, a hush intense and eager. Every eye turned upon the judge, who sat still, a figure carven in stone with livid face and fear-stricken eyes. After the first flash of his eyes, Pavageau had gone on cooly sorting the papers.

The courtroom waited, waited, for the judge to rise and thunder forth a fine against the daring Negro lawyer for contempt. A minute passed, which seemed like an hour. Why did not Grabert speak? Pavageau's implied accusation was too absurd for denial; but he should be punished. Was His Honor ill, or did he merely hold the man in too much contempt to notice him or his remark?

Finally Grabert spoke; he moistened his lips, for they were dry and parched, and his voice was weak and sounded far away in his own ears. "My son — does — not — attend the public schools."

Someone in the rear of the room laughed, and the atmosphere lightened at once. Plainly Pavageau was an idiot, and His Honor too far above him; too much of a gentleman to notice him. Grabert continued calmly: "The gentleman" — there was an unmistakable sneer in this word, habit if nothing else, and not even fear could restrain him — "the gentleman doubtless intended a little pleasantry, but I shall have to fine him for contempt of court."

"As you will," replied Pavageau, and he flashed another look at Grabert. It was a look of insolent triumph and derision. His Honor's eyes dropped beneath it.

"What did that man mean, Father, by saying you should take me out of school?" asked Vannier on his way home.

"He was provoked, my son, because he had lost his case, and when a man is provoked he is likely to say silly things. By the way, Vannier, I hope you won't say anything to your mother about the incident. It would only annoy her."

For the public, the incident was forgotten as soon as it had closed, but for Grabert, it was indelibly stamped on his memory; a scene that shrieked in his mind and stood out before him at every footstep he took. Again and again as he tossed on a sleepless bed did he see the cold flash of Pavageau's eyes, and hear his quiet accusation. How did he know? Where had he gotten his information? For he spoke, not as one who makes a random shot in anger, but as one who knows, who has known a long while, and who is betrayed by irritation into playing his trump card too early in the game.

He passed a wretched week, wherein it seemed that his every footstep was dogged, his every gesture watched and recorded. He fancied that Elise, even, was suspecting him. When he took his judicial seat each morning, it seemed that every eye in the courtroom was fastened upon him in derision; everyone who spoke, it seemed, was but biding his time to shout the old village street refrain which had haunted him all his life, "Nigger! — Nigger! — White nigger!"

Finally, he could stand it no longer; and with leaden feet and furtive glances to the right and left for fear he might be seen, he went up a flight of dusty stairs in an Exchange Alley building, which led to Pavageau's office.

The latter was frankly surprised to see him. He made a polite attempt to conceal it, however. It was the first time in his legal life that Grabert had ever sought out a Negro; the first time that he had ever voluntarily opened conversation with one.

He mopped his forehead nervously as he took the chair Pavageau offered him; he stared about the room for an instant; then with a sudden, almost brutal directness, he turned on the lawyer.

"See here, what did you mean by that remark you made in court the other day?"

"I meant just what I said" was the cool reply.

Grabert paused. "Why did you say it?" he asked slowly.

"Because I was a fool. I should have kept my mouth shut until another time, should I not?"

"Pavageau," said Grabert softly, "let's not fence. Where did you get your information?"

Pavageau paused for an instant. He put his fingertips together and closed his eyes as one who meditates. Then he said with provoking calmness, "You seem anxious—well, I don't mind letting you know. It doesn't really matter."

"Yes, yes," broke in Grabert impatiently.

"Did you ever hear of a Mme. Guichard of Hospital Street?"

The sweat broke out on the judge's brow as he replied weakly, "Yes."

"Well, I am her nephew."

"And she?"

"Is dead. She told me about you once—with pride, let me say. No one else knows."

Grabert sat dazed. He had forgotten about Mme. Guichard. She had never entered into his calculations at all. Pavageau turned to his desk with a sigh, as if he wished the interview were ended. Grabert rose.

"If—if—this were known—to—to—my—my wife," he said thickly, "it would hurt her very much."

His head was swimming. He had had to appeal to this man, and to appeal to his wife's name. His wife, whose name he scarcely spoke to men whom he considered his social equals.

Pavageau looked up quickly. "It happens that I often have cases in your court," he spoke deliberately. "I am willing, if I lose fairly, to give up; but I do not like to have a decision made against me because my opponent is of a different complexion from mine, or because the decision against me would please a certain class of people. I only ask what I have never had from you—fair play."

"I understand," said Grabert.

He admired Pavageau more than ever as he went out of his office, yet this admiration was tempered by the knowledge that this man was the only person in the whole world who possessed positive knowledge of his secret. He groveled in a self-abasement at his position; and yet he could not but feel a certain relief that the vague, formless fear which had hitherto dogged his life and haunted it had taken on a definite shape. He knew where it was now; he could lay his hands on it, and fight it.

But with what weapons? There were none offered him save a substantial backing down from his position on certain questions; the position that had been his for so long that he was almost known by it. For in the quiet deliberate sentence of Pavageau's, he read that he must cease all the oppression, all the little injustices which he had offered Pavageau's clientele. He must act now as his convictions and secret sympathies and affiliations had bidden him act, not as prudence and fear and cowardice had made him act.

Then what would be the result? he asked himself. Would not the suspicions of the people be aroused by this sudden change in his manner? Would not they begin to question and to wonder? Would not someone remember Pavageau's remark that morning and, putting two and two together, start some rumor flying? His heart sickened again at the thought.

There was a banquet that night. It was in his honor, and he was to speak, and the thought was distasteful to him beyond measure. He knew how it all would be. He would be hailed with shouts and acclamations, as the finest flower of civilization. He would be listened to deferentially, and younger men would go away holding him in their hearts as a truly worthy model. When all the while —

He threw back his head and laughed. Oh, what a glorious revenge he had on those little white village boys! How he had made a race atone for Wilson's insult in the courtroom; for the man in the restaurant at whom Ward had laughed so uproariously; for all the affronts seen and unseen given these people of his own whom he had denied. He had taken a diploma from their most exclusive college; he had broken down the barriers of their social world; he had taken the highest possible position among them and, aping their own ways, had shown them that he, too, could despise this inferior race they despised. Nay, he had taken for his wife the best woman among them all, and she had borne him a son. Ha, ha! What a joke on them all!

And he had not forgotten the black and yellow boys either. They had stoned him too, and he had lived to spurn them; to look down upon them, and to crush them at every possible turn from his seat on the bench. Truly, his life had not been wasted.

He had lived forty-nine years now, and the zenith of his power was not yet reached. There was much more to do, much more, and he was going to do it. He owed it to Elise and the boy. For their sake he must go on and on and keep his tongue still, and truckle to Pavageau and suffer alone. Someday, perhaps, he would have a grandson, who would point with pride to "My grandfather, the famous Judge Grabert!" Ah, that in itself, was a reward. To have founded a dynasty; to bequeath to others that which he had never possessed himself, and the lack of which had made his life a misery.

It was a banquet with a political significance; one that meant a virtual triumph for Judge Grabert in the next contest for the District Judge. He smiled around at the eager faces which were turned up to his as he arose to speak. The tumult of applause which had greeted his rising had died away, and an expectant hush fell on the room.

"What a sensation I could make now," he thought. He had but to open his mouth and cry out, "Fools! Fools! I whom you are honoring, I am one of the despised ones. Yes, I'm a nigger — do you hear, a nigger!" What a temptation it was to end the whole miserable farce. If he were alone in the world, if it were not for Elise and the boy, he would, just to see their horror and wonder. How they would shrink from him! But what could they do? They could take away his office; but his wealth, and his former successes, and his learning, they could not touch. Well, he must speak, and he must remember Elise and the boy.

Every eye was fastened on him in eager expectancy. Judge Grabert's speech was expected to outline the policy of their faction in the coming campaign. He turned to the chairman at the head of the table.

"Mr. Chairman," he began, and paused again. How peculiar it was that in the place of the chairman there sat Grandmère Grabert, as she had been wont to sit on the steps of the tumbledown cottage in the village. She was looking at him sternly and bidding him give an account of his life since she had kissed him good-bye ere he had sailed down the river to New Orleans. He was surprised, and not a little annoyed. He had expected to address the chairman, not Grandmère Grabert. He cleared his throat and frowned.

"Mr. Chairman," he said again. Well, what was the use of addressing her that way? She would not understand him. He would call her Grandmère, of course. Were they not alone again on the cottage steps at twilight with the cries of the little brutish boys ringing derisively from the distant village square?

"Grandmère," he said softly, "you don't understand — " And then he was sitting down in his seat pointing one finger angrily at her because the other words would not come. They stuck in his throat, and he choked and beat the air with his hands. When the men crowded around him with water and hastily improvised fans, he fought them away wildly and desperately with furious curses that came from his blackened lips. For were they not all boys with stones to pelt him because he wanted to play with them? He would run away to Grandmère who would soothe him and comfort him. So he arose and, stumbling, shrieking and beating them back from him, ran the length of the hall, and fell across the threshold of the door.

The secret died with him, for Pavageau's lips were ever sealed.

Susan Glaspell

(1876–1948)

SUSAN GLASPELL was born and raised in Davenport, Iowa. After graduating from Drake University in 1899, she began writing for the *Des Moines Daily News*. Her early short stories appeared in literary magazines such as *Harper's* and the *Ladies' Home Journal*.

In 1911, Glaspell moved to New York City's Greenwich Village and two years later she married George Cram Cook, another native of Davenport. Together the two founded the Provincetown Playhouse, an experimental theater that produced only original plays by American playwrights. The plays produced in Provincetown by Glaspell, Eugene O'Neill, Edna St. Vincent Millay, John Reed and Michael Gold represented the most progressive work in American drama at that time.

"A Jury of Her Peers" was originally produced as a one-act play, *Trifles*, which premiered August 8, 1916 in Provincetown and which Glaspell rewrote in short-story form a year later. Set in her native Midwest, Glaspell's story explores the effect of isolation — physical and mental — on the individual. The protagonist, Minnie Wright, never appears in the story, but for the two women who become the "jury of her peers" her presence is evidenced by the pieces of quilting she has left behind. For Mrs. Hale and Mrs. Peters, the quilted blocks become the text of Minnie Wright's story, a text that remains closed to the male characters. Glaspell's use of sewing imagery is ironic and self-conscious; whereas needlework — in fiction and in real life — represented the sublimation of female desires, in Glaspell's story it quite literally liberates them.

A Jury of Her Peers

WHEN MARTHA HALE opened the storm-door and got a cut of the north wind, she ran back for her big woolen scarf. As she hurriedly wound that round her head her eye made a scandalized sweep of her kitchen. It was no ordinary thing that called her away — it was probably farther from ordinary than anything that had ever happened in Dickson County. But what her eye took in was that her kitchen was in no shape for leaving: her bread all ready for mixing, half the flour sifted and half unsifted.

She hated to see things half done; but she had been at that when the team from town stopped to get Mr. Hale, and then the sheriff came running in to say his wife wished Mrs. Hale would come too — adding, with a grin, that he guessed she was getting scarey and wanted another woman along. So she had dropped everything right where it was.

"Martha!" now came her husband's impatient voice. "Don't keep folks waiting out here in the cold."

She again opened the storm-door, and this time joined the three men and the one woman waiting for her in the big two-seated buggy.

After she had the robes tucked around her she took another look at the woman who sat beside her on the back seat. She had met Mrs. Peters the year before at the county fair, and the thing she remembered about her was that she didn't seem like a sheriff's wife. She was small and thin and didn't have a strong voice. Mrs. Gorman, the sheriff's wife before Gorman went out and Peters came in, had a voice that somehow seemed to be backing up the law with every word. But if Mrs. Peters didn't look like a sheriff's wife, Peters made it up in looking like a sheriff. He was to a dot the kind of man who could get himself elected sheriff — a heavy man with a big voice, who was particularly genial with the law-abiding, as if to make it plain that he knew the difference between criminals and non-criminals. And right there it came into Mrs. Hale's mind, with a stab, that this man who was so pleasant and lively with all of them was going to the Wrights' now as a sheriff.

"The country's not very pleasant this time of year," Mrs. Peters at last ventured, as if she felt they ought to be talking as well as the men.

Mrs. Hale scarcely finished her reply, for they had gone up a little hill and could see the Wright place now, and seeing it did not make her feel like talking. It looked very lonesome this cold March morning. It had always been a lonesome-looking place. It was down in a hollow, and the poplar trees around it were lonesome-looking trees. The men were looking at it and talking about what had happened. The county attorney was bending to one side of the buggy, and kept looking steadily at the place as they drew up to it.

"I'm glad you came with me," Mrs. Peters said nervously, as the two women were about to follow the men in through the kitchen door.

Even after she had her foot on the door-step, her hand on the knob, Martha Hale had a moment of feeling she could not cross that threshold. And the reason it seemed she couldn't cross it now was simply because she hadn't crossed it before. Time and time again it had been in her mind, "I ought to go over and see Minnie Foster"—she still thought of her as Minnie Foster, though for twenty years she had been Mrs. Wright. And then there was always something to do and Minnie Foster would go from her mind. But *now* she could come.

The men went over to the stove. The women stood close together by the door. Young Henderson, the county attorney, turned around and said:

"Come up to the fire, ladies."

Mrs. Peters took a step forward, then stopped. "I'm not—cold," she said.

The men talked for a minute about what a good thing it was the sheriff had sent his deputy out that morning to make a fire for them, and then Sheriff Peters stepped back from the stove, unbuttoned his outer coat, and leaned his hands on the kitchen table in a way that seemed to mark the beginning of official business. "Now, Mr. Hale," he said in a sort of semi-official voice, "before we move things about, you tell Mr. Henderson just what it was you saw when you came here yesterday morning."

The county attorney was looking around the kitchen.

"By the way," he said, "has anything been moved?" He turned to the sheriff. "Are things just as you left them yesterday?"

Peters looked from cupboard to sink; from that to a small worn rocker a little to one side of the kitchen table.

"It's just the same."

"Somebody should have been left here yesterday," said the county attorney.

"Oh — yesterday," returned the sheriff, with a little gesture as of yesterday having been more than he could bear to think of. "When I had to send Frank to Morris Center for that man who went crazy — let me tell you, I had my hands full *yesterday*. I knew you could get back from Omaha by today, George, and as long as I went over everything here myself—"

"Well, Mr. Hale," said the county attorney, in a way of letting what was past and gone go, "tell just what happened when you came here yesterday morning."

Mrs. Hale, still leaning against the door, had that sinking feeling of the mother whose child is about to speak a piece. Lewis often wandered along and got things mixed up in a story. She hoped he would tell this straight and plain, and not say unnecessary things that would just make things harder for Minnie Foster. He didn't begin at once, and she noticed that he looked queer — as if standing in that kitchen and having to tell what he had seen there yesterday morning made him almost sick.

"Harry and I had started to town with a load of potatoes," Mrs. Hale's husband began.

Harry was Mrs. Hale's oldest boy. He wasn't with them now, for the very good reason that those potatoes never got to town yesterday and he was taking them this morning, so he hadn't been home when the sheriff stopped to say he wanted Mr. Hale to come over to the Wright place and tell the county attorney his story there, where he could point it all out.

"We came along this road," Hale was going on, with a motion of his hand to the road over which they had just come, "and as we got in sight of the house I says to Harry, 'I'm goin' to see if I can't get John Wright to take a telephone.' You see," he explained to Henderson, "unless I can get somebody to go in with me they won't come out this branch road except for a price *I* can't pay. I'd spoke to Wright about it once before; but he put me off, saying folks talked too much anyway, and all he asked was peace and quiet — guess you know about how much he talked himself. But I thought maybe if I went to the house and talked about it before his wife, and said all the women-folks liked the telephones, and that in this lonesome stretch of road it would be a good thing—well, I said to Harry that that was what I was going to say—though I said at the same time that I didn't know as what his wife wanted made much difference to John—"

Now, there he was!—saying things he didn't need to say. Mrs. Hale tried to catch her husband's eye, but fortunately the county attorney interrupted with:

"Let's talk about that a little later, Mr. Hale. I do want to talk about that, but I'm anxious now to get along to just exactly what happened when you got here."

When he began this time, it was very deliberately and carefully:

"I didn't see or hear anything. I knocked at the door. And still it was all quiet inside. I knew they must be up—it was past eight o'clock. So I knocked again, louder, and I thought I heard somebody say, 'Come in.' I wasn't sure—I'm not sure yet. But I opened the door—this door," jerking a hand toward the door by which the two women stood, "and there, in that rocker"—pointing to it—"sat Mrs. Wright."

Everyone in the kitchen looked at the rocker. It came into Mrs. Hale's mind that that rocker didn't look in the least like Minnie Foster—the Minnie Foster of twenty years before. It was a dingy red, with wooden rungs up the back, and the middle rung was gone, and the chair sagged to one side.

"How did she—look?" the county attorney was inquiring.

"Well," said Hale, "she looked—queer."

"How do you mean—queer?"

As he asked it he took out a notebook and pencil. Mrs. Hale did not like the sight of that pencil. She kept her eye fixed on her husband, as if to keep him from saying unnecessary things that would go into that notebook and make trouble.

Hale did speak guardedly, as if the pencil had affected him too.

"Well, as if she didn't know what she was going to do next. And kind of—done up."

"How did she seem to feel about your coming?"

"Why, I don't think she minded—one way or other. She didn't pay much attention. I said, 'Ho' do, Mrs. Wright? It's cold, ain't it?' And she said, 'Is it?'—and went on pleatin' at her apron.

"Well, I was surprised. She didn't ask me to come up to the stove, or to sit down, but just set there, not even lookin' at me. And so I said: 'I want to see John.' And then she laughed. I guess you would call it a laugh.

"I thought of Harry and the team outside, so I said, a little sharp, 'Can I see John?' 'No,' says she — kind of dull like. 'Ain't he home?' says I. Then she looked at me. 'Yes,' says she, 'he's home.' 'Then why can't I see him?' I asked her, out of patience with her now. ' 'Cause he's dead,' says she, just as quiet and dull — and fell to pleatin' her apron. 'Dead?' says I, like you do when you can't take in what you've heard.

"She just nodded her head, not getting a bit excited, but rockin' back and forth.

" 'Why — where is he?' says I, not knowing *what* to say.

"She just pointed upstairs — like this" — pointing to the room above.

"I got up, with the idea of going up there myself. By this time I — didn't know what to do. I walked from there to here; then I says: 'Why, what did he die of?'

" 'He died of a rope round his neck,' says she; and just went on pleatin' at her apron."

Hale stopped speaking, and stood staring at the rocker, as if he were still seeing the woman who had sat there the morning before. Nobody spoke; it was as if everyone were seeing the woman who had sat there the morning before.

"And what did you do then?" the county attorney at last broke the silence.

"I went out and called Harry. I thought I might — need help. I got Harry in, and we went upstairs." His voice fell almost to a whisper. "There he was — lying over the —"

"I think I'd rather have you go into that upstairs," the attorney interrupted, "where you can point it all out. Just go on now with the rest of the story."

"Well, my first thought was to get that rope off. It looked —"

He stopped, his face twitching.

"But Harry, he went up to him, and he said, 'No, he's dead all right, and we'd better not touch anything.' So we went downstairs. She was still sitting that same way. 'Has anybody been notified?' I asked. 'No,' said she, unconcerned.

" 'Who did this, Mrs. Wright?' said Harry. He said it business-like, and she stopped pleatin' at her apron. 'I don't know,' she says. 'You don't *know?*' says Harry. 'Weren't you sleepin' in the bed with him?' 'Yes,' says she, 'but I was on the inside.' 'Somebody slipped a rope round his neck and strangled him, and you didn't wake up?' says Harry. 'I didn't wake up,' she said after him.

"We may have looked as if we didn't see how that could be, for after a minute she said, 'I sleep sound.'

"Harry was going to ask her more questions, but I said maybe that weren't our business; maybe we ought to let her tell her story first to the coroner or the sheriff. So Harry went fast as he could over to High Road — the Rivers' place, where there's a telephone."

"And what did she do when she knew you had gone for the coroner?" The attorney got his pencil in his hand all ready for writing.

"She moved from that chair to this one over here" — Hale pointed to a small chair in the corner — "and just sat there with her hands held together and looking down. I got a feeling that I ought to make some conversation, so I said I had come in to see if John wanted to put in a telephone; and at that she started to laugh, and then she stopped and looked at me — scared."

At the sound of a moving pencil the man who was telling the story looked up.

"I dunno — maybe it wasn't scared," he hastened; "I wouldn't like to say it was. Soon Harry got back, and then Dr. Lloyd came, and you, Mr. Peters, and so I guess that's all I know that you don't."

He said that last with relief, and moved a little, as if relaxing. Everyone moved a little. The county attorney walked toward the stair door.

"I guess we'll go upstairs first — then out to the barn and around."

He paused and looked around the kitchen.

"You're convinced there was nothing important here?" he asked the sheriff. "Nothing that would — point to any motive?"

The sheriff too looked all around, as if to re-convince himself.

"Nothing here but kitchen things," he said, with a little laugh for the insignificance of kitchen things.

The county attorney was looking at the cupboard — a peculiar, ungainly structure, half closet and half cupboard, the upper part of it being built in the wall, and the lower part just the old-fashioned kitchen cupboard. As if its queerness attracted him, he got a chair and opened the upper part and looked in. After a moment he drew his hand away sticky.

"Here's a nice mess," he said resentfully.

The two women had drawn nearer, and now the sheriff's wife spoke.

"Oh — her fruit," she said, looking to Mrs. Hale for sympathetic understanding. She turned back to the county attorney and explained: "She worried about that when it turned so cold last night. She said the fire would go out and her jars burst."

Mrs. Peters' husband broke into a laugh.

"Well, can you beat the women! Held for murder, and worrying about her preserves!"

The young attorney set his lips.

"I guess before we're through she may have something more serious than preserves to worry about."

"Oh, well," said Mrs. Hale's husband, with good-natured superiority, "women are used to worrying over trifles."

The two women moved a little closer together. Neither of them spoke. The county attorney seemed suddenly to remember his manners — and think of his future.

"And yet," said he, with the gallantry of a young politician, "for all their worries, what would we do without the ladies?"

The women did not speak, did not unbend. He went to the sink and began washing his hands. He turned to wipe them on the roller towel — whirled it for a cleaner place.

"Dirty towels! Not much of a housekeeper, would you say, ladies?" He kicked his foot against some dirty pans under the sink.

"There's a great deal of work to be done on a farm," said Mrs. Hale stiffly.

"To be sure. And yet" — with a little bow to her — "I know there are some Dickson County farm-houses that do not have such roller towels."

"Those towels get dirty awful quick. Men's hands aren't always as clean as they might be."

"Ah, loyal to your sex, I see," he laughed. He stopped and gave her a keen look. "But you and Mrs. Wright were neighbors. I suppose you were friends, too."

Martha Hale shook her head.

"I've seen little enough of her of late years. I've not been in this house — it's more than a year."

"And why was that? You didn't like her?"

"I liked her well enough," she replied with spirit. "Farmers' wives have their hands full, Mr. Henderson. And then — " She looked around the kitchen.

"Yes?" he encouraged.

"It never seemed a very cheerful place," said she, more to herself than to him.

"No," he agreed; "I don't think anyone would call it cheerful. I shouldn't say she had the home-making instinct."

"Well, I don't know as Wright had, either," she muttered.

"You mean they didn't get on very well?" he was quick to ask.

"No; I don't mean anything," she answered, with decision. As she turned a little away from him, she added: "But I don't think a place would be any the cheerfuller for John Wright's bein' in it."

"I'd like to talk to you about that a little later, Mrs. Hale," he said. "I'm anxious to get the lay of things upstairs now."

He moved toward the stair door, followed by the two men.

"I suppose anything Mrs. Peters does'll be all right?" the sheriff inquired. "She was to take in some clothes for her, you know — and a few little things. We left in such a hurry yesterday."

The county attorney looked at the two women whom they were leaving alone there among the kitchen things.

"Yes — Mrs. Peters," he said, his glance resting on the woman who was not Mrs. Peters, the big farmer woman who stood behind the sheriff's wife. "Of course Mrs. Peters is one of us," he said, in a manner of entrusting responsibility. "And keep your eye out, Mrs. Peters, for anything that might be of use. No telling; you women might come upon a clue to the motive — and that's the thing we need."

Mr. Hale rubbed his face after the fashion of a showman getting ready for a pleasantry.

"But would the women know a clue if they did come upon it?" he said; and, having delivered himself of this, he followed the others through the stair door.

The women stood motionless and silent, listening to the footsteps, first upon the stairs, then in the room above.

Then, as if releasing herself from something strange, Mrs. Hale began to arrange the dirty pans under the sink, which the county attorney's disdainful push of the foot had deranged.

"I'd hate to have men comin' into my kitchen," she said testily — "snoopin' round and criticizin'."

"Of course it's no more than their duty," said the sheriff's wife, in her manner of timid acquiescence.

"Duty's all right," replied Mrs. Hale bluffly; "but I guess that deputy sheriff that come out to make the fire might have got a little of this on." She gave the roller towel a pull. "Wish I'd thought of that sooner! Seems mean to talk about her for not having things slicked up, when she had to come away in such a hurry."

She looked around the kitchen. Certainly it was not "slicked up." Her eye was held by a bucket of sugar on a low shelf. The cover was off the wooden bucket, and beside it was a paper bag — half full.

Mrs. Hale moved toward it.

"She was putting this in there," she said to herself—slowly.

She thought of the flour in her kitchen at home — half sifted. She had been interrupted, and had left things half done. What had interrupted Minnie Foster? Why had that work been left half done? She made a move as if to finish it — unfinished things always bothered her — and then she glanced around and saw that Mrs. Peters was watching her — and she didn't want Mrs. Peters to get that feeling she had got of work begun and then — for some reason — not finished.

"It's a shame about her fruit," she said, and walked toward the cupboard that the county attorney had opened, and got on the chair, murmuring: "I wonder if it's all gone."

It was a sorry enough looking sight, but "Here's one that's all right," she said at last. She held it toward the light. "This is cherries, too." She looked again. "I declare I believe that's the only one."

With a sigh, she got down from the chair, went to the sink, and wiped off the bottle.

"She'll feel awful bad, after all her hard work in the hot weather. I remember the afternoon I put up my cherries last summer."

She set the bottle on the table, and, with another sigh, started to sit down in the rocker. But she did not sit down. Something kept her from sitting down in that chair. She straightened — stepped back, and, half turned away, stood looking at it, seeing the woman who had sat there "pleatin' at her apron."

The thin voice of the sheriff's wife broke in upon her: "I must be getting those things from the front room closet." She opened the door into the other room, started in, stepped back. "You coming with me, Mrs. Hale?" she asked nervously. "You — you could help me get them."

They were soon back — the stark coldness of that shut-up room was not a thing to linger in.

"My!" said Mrs. Peters, dropping the things on the table and hurrying to the stove.

Mrs. Hale stood examining the clothes the woman who was being detained in town had said she wanted.

"Wright was close!" she exclaimed, holding up a shabby black skirt that bore the marks of much making over. "I think maybe that's why she kept so much to herself. I s'pose she felt she couldn't do her part; and then, you don't enjoy things when you feel shabby. She used to wear pretty clothes and be lively — when she was Minnie Foster, one of the town girls, singing in the choir. But that — oh, that was twenty years ago."

With a carefulness in which there was something tender, she folded the shabby clothes and piled them at one corner of the table. She looked up at Mrs. Peters, and there was something in the other woman's look that irritated her.

"She don't care," she said to herself. "Much difference it makes to her whether Minnie Foster had pretty clothes when she was a girl."

Then she looked again, and she wasn't so sure; in fact, she hadn't at any time been perfectly sure about Mrs. Peters. She had that shrinking manner, and yet her eyes looked as if they could see a long way into things.

"This all you was to take in?" asked Mrs. Hale.

"No," said the sheriff's wife; "she said she wanted an apron. Funny thing to want," she ventured in her nervous little way, "for there's not much to get you dirty in jail, goodness knows. But I suppose just to make her feel more natural. If you're used to wearing an apron —. She said they were in the bottom drawer of this cupboard. Yes — here they are. And then her little shawl that always hung on the stair door."

She took the small gray shawl from behind the door leading upstairs.

Suddenly Mrs. Hale took a quick step toward the other woman.

"Mrs. Peters!"

"Yes, Mrs. Hale?"

"Do you think she — did it?"

A frightened look blurred the other thing in Mrs. Peters' eyes.

"Oh, I don't know," she said, in a voice that seemed to shrink away from the subject.

"Well, I don't think she did," affirmed Mrs. Hale stoutly. "Asking for an apron, and her little shawl. Worryin' about her fruit."

"Mr. Peters says —." Footsteps were heard in the room above; she stopped, looked up, then went on in a lowered voice: "Mr. Peters says — it looks bad for her. Mr. Henderson is awful sarcastic in a speech, and he's going to make fun of her saying she didn't — wake up."

For a moment Mrs. Hale had no answer. Then, "Well, I guess John Wright didn't wake up — when they was slippin' that rope under his neck," she muttered.

"No, it's *strange*," breathed Mrs. Peters. "They think it was such a — funny way to kill a man."

"That's just what Mr. Hale said," said Mrs. Hale, in a resolutely natural voice. "There was a gun in the house. He says that's what he can't understand."

"Mr. Henderson said, coming out, that what was needed for the case was a motive. Something to show anger — or sudden feeling."

"Well, I don't see any signs of anger around here," said Mrs. Hale. "I don't — "

She stopped. It was as if her mind tripped on something. Her eye was caught by a dish-towel in the middle of the kitchen table. Slowly she moved toward the table. One half of it was wiped clean, the other half messy. Her eyes made a slow, almost unwilling turn to the bucket of sugar and the half empty bag beside it. Things begun — and not finished.

After a moment she stepped back, and said, in that manner of releasing herself: "Wonder how they're finding things upstairs? I hope she had it a little more red up there. You know" — she paused, and feeling gathered — "it seems kind of *sneaking*: locking her up in town and coming out here to get her own house to turn against her!"

"But, Mrs. Hale," said the sheriff's wife, "the law is the law."

"I s'pose 'tis," answered Mrs. Hale shortly.

She turned to the stove, worked with it a minute, and when she straightened up she said aggressively:

"The law is the law — and a bad stove is a bad stove. How'd you like to cook on this?" — pointing with the poker to the broken lining. She opened the oven door and started to express her opinion of the oven; but she was swept into her own thoughts, thinking of what it would mean, year after year, to have that stove to wrestle with. The thought of Minnie Foster trying to bake in that oven — and the thought of her never going over to see Minnie Foster —

She was startled by hearing Mrs. Peters say:

"A person gets discouraged — and loses heart."

The sheriff's wife had looked from the stove to the pail of water which had been carried in from outside. The two women stood there silent, above them the footsteps of the men who were looking for evidence against the woman who had worked in that kitchen. That look of seeing into things, of seeing through a thing to something else, was in the eyes of the sheriff's wife now. When Mrs. Hale next spoke to her, it was gently:

"Better loosen up your things, Mrs. Peters. We'll not feel them when we go out."

Mrs. Peters went to the back of the room to hang up the fur tippet she was wearing. A moment later she exclaimed, "Why, she was piecing a quilt," and held up a large sewing basket piled high with quilt pieces.

Mrs. Hale spread some of the blocks out on the table.

"It's log-cabin pattern," she said, putting several of them together. "Pretty, isn't it?"

They were so engaged with the quilt that they did not hear the footsteps on the stairs. Just as the stair door opened Mrs. Hale was saying:

"Do you suppose she was going to quilt it or just knot it?"

The sheriff threw up his hands.

"They wonder whether she was going to quilt it or just knot it!" he cried.

There was a laugh for the ways of women, a warming of hands over the stove, and then the county attorney said briskly:

"Well, let's go right out to the barn and get that cleared up."

"I don't see as there's anything so strange," Mrs. Hale said resentfully, after the outside door had closed on the three men — "our taking up our time with little things while we're waiting for them to get the evidence. I don't see as it's anything to laugh about."

"Of course they've got awful important things on their minds," said the sheriff's wife apologetically.

They returned to an inspection of the block for the quilt. Mrs. Hale was looking at the fine, even sewing, and preoccupied with thoughts of the woman who had done that sewing, when she heard the sheriff's wife say, in a queer tone:

"Why, look at this one."

She turned to take the block held out to her.

"The sewing," said Mrs. Peters, in a troubled way. "All the rest of them have been so nice and even — but — this one. Why, it looks as if she didn't know what she was about!"

Their eyes met — something flashed to life, passed between them; then, as if with an effort, they seemed to pull away from each other. A moment Mrs. Hale sat there, her hands folded over that sewing which was so unlike all the rest of the sewing. Then she had pulled a knot and drawn the threads.

"Oh, what are you doing, Mrs. Hale?" asked the sheriff's wife.

"Just pulling out a stitch or two that's not sewed very good," said Mrs. Hale mildly.

"I don't think we ought to touch things," Mrs. Peters said, a little helplessly.

"I'll just finish up this end," answered Mrs. Hale, still in that mild, matter-of-fact fashion.

She threaded a needle and started to replace bad sewing with good. For a little while she sewed in silence. Then, in that thin, timid voice, she heard:

"Mrs. Hale!"

"Yes, Mrs. Peters?"

"What do you suppose she was so — nervous about?"

"Oh, I don't know," said Mrs. Hale, as if dismissing a thing not important enough to spend much time on. "I don't know as she was — nervous. I sew awful queer sometimes when I'm just tired."

She cut a thread, and out of the corner of her eye looked up at Mrs. Peters. The small, lean face of the sheriff's wife seemed to have tightened up. Her eyes had that look of peering into something. But next moment she moved, and said in her indecisive way:

"Well, I must get those clothes wrapped. They may be through sooner than we think. I wonder where I could find a piece of paper — and string."

"In that cupboard, maybe," suggested Mrs. Hale, after a glance around.

One piece of the crazy sewing remained unripped. Mrs. Peter's back turned, Martha Hale now scrutinized that piece, compared it with the dainty, accurate sewing of the other blocks. The difference was startling. Holding this block made her feel queer, as if the distracted thoughts of the woman who had perhaps turned to it to try and quiet herself were communicating themselves to her.

Mrs. Peters' voice roused her.

"Here's a bird-cage," she said. "Did she have a bird, Mrs. Hale?"

"Why, I don't know whether she did or not." She turned to look at the cage Mrs. Peters was holding up. "I've not been here in so long." She sighed. "There was a man last year selling canaries cheap — but I don't know as she took one. Maybe she did. She used to sing real pretty herself."

"Seems kind of funny to think of a bird here." She half laughed — an attempt to put up a barrier. "But she must have had one — or why would she have a cage? I wonder what happened to it."

"I suppose maybe the cat got it," suggested Mrs. Hale, resuming her sewing.

"No; she didn't have a cat. She's got that feeling some people have about cats — being afraid of them. When they brought her to our house yesterday, my cat got in the room, and she was real upset and asked me to take it out."

"My sister Bessie was like that," laughed Mrs. Hale.

The sheriff's wife did not reply. The silence made Mrs. Hale turn around. Mrs. Peters was examining the bird-cage.

"Look at this door," she said slowly. "It's broke. One hinge has been pulled apart."

Mrs. Hale came nearer.

"Looks as if someone must have been — rough with it."

Again their eyes met — startled, questioning, apprehensive. For a moment neither spoke nor stirred. Then Mrs. Hale, turning away, said brusquely:

"If they're going to find any evidence, I wish they'd be about it. I don't like this place."

"But I'm awful glad you came with me, Mrs. Hale." Mrs. Peters put the bird-cage on the table and sat down. "It would be lonesome for me — sitting here alone."

"Yes, it would, wouldn't it?" agreed Mrs. Hale, a certain very determined naturalness in her voice. She had picked up the sewing, but now it dropped in her lap, and she murmured in a different voice: "But I tell you what I *do* wish, Mrs. Peters. I wish I had come over sometimes when she was here. I wish — I had."

"But of course you were awful busy, Mrs. Hale. Your house — and your children."

"I could've come," retorted Mrs. Hale shortly. "I stayed away because it weren't cheerful — and that's why I ought to have come. I" — she looked around — "I've never liked this place. Maybe because it's down in a hollow and you don't see the road. I don't know what it is, but it's a lonesome place, and always was. I wish I had come over to see Minnie Foster sometimes. I can see now — " She did not put it into words.

"Well, you mustn't reproach yourself," counseled Mrs. Peters. "Somehow, we just don't see how it is with other folks till — something comes up."

"Not having children makes less work," mused Mrs. Hale, after a silence, "but it makes a quiet house — and Wright out to work all day — and no company when he did come in. Did you know John Wright, Mrs. Peters?"

"Not to know him. I've seen him in town. They say he was a good man."

"Yes — good," conceded John Wright's neighbor grimly. "He didn't drink, and kept his word as well as most, I guess, and paid his debts. But he was a hard man, Mrs. Peters. Just to pass the time of day with him — " She stopped, shivered a little. "Like a raw wind that gets to the bone." Her eyes fell upon the cage on the table before her, and she added, almost bitterly: "I should think she would've wanted a bird!"

Suddenly she leaned forward, looking intently at the cage. "But what do you s'pose went wrong with it?"

"I don't know," returned Mrs. Peters; "unless it got sick and died."

But after she said it she reached over and swung the broken door. Both women watched it as if somehow held by it.

"You didn't know — her?" Mrs. Hale asked, a gentler note in her voice.

"Not till they brought her yesterday," said the sheriff's wife.

"She — come to think of it, she was kind of like a bird herself. Real sweet and pretty, but kind of timid and — fluttery. How — she — did — change."

That held her for a long time. Finally, as if struck with a happy thought and relieved to get back to everyday things, she exclaimed:

"Tell you what, Mrs. Peters, why don't you take the quilt in with you? It might take up her mind."

"Why, I think that's a real nice idea, Mrs. Hale," agreed the sheriff's wife, as if she too were glad to come into the atmosphere of a simple kindness. "There couldn't possibly be any objection to that, could there? Now, just what will I take? I wonder if her patches are in here — and her things."

They turned to the sewing basket.

"Here's some red," said Mrs. Hale, bringing out a roll of cloth. Underneath that was a box. "Here, maybe her scissors are in here — and her things." She held it up. "What a pretty box! I'll warrant that was something she had a long time ago — when she was a girl."

She held it in her hand a moment; then, with a little sigh, opened it.

Instantly her hand went to her nose.

"Why — !"

Mrs. Peters drew nearer — then turned away.

"There's something wrapped up in this piece of silk," faltered Mrs. Hale.

Her hand not steady, Mrs. Hale raised the piece of silk. "Oh, Mrs. Peters!" she cried, "it's — "

Mrs. Peters bent closer.

"It's the bird," she whispered.

"But, Mrs. Peters!" cried Mrs. Hale. "*Look* at it! Its *neck* — look at its neck! It's all — other side *to*."

The sheriff's wife again bent closer.

"Somebody wrung its neck," said she, in a voice that was slow and deep.

And then again the eyes of the two women met — this time clung together in a look of dawning comprehension, of growing horror. Mrs. Peters looked from the dead bird to the broken door of the cage. Again their eyes met. And just then there was a sound at the outside door.

Mrs. Hale slipped the box under the quilt pieces in the basket, and sank into the chair before it. Mrs. Peters stood holding to the table. The county attorney and the sheriff came in.

"Well, ladies," said the county attorney, as one turning from serious things to little pleasantries, "have you decided whether she was going to quilt it or knot it?"

"We think," began the sheriff's wife in a flurried voice, "that she was going to — knot it."

He was too preoccupied to notice the change that came in her voice on that last.

"Well, that's very interesting, I'm sure," he said tolerantly. He caught sight of the cage. "Has the bird flown?"

"We think the cat got it," said Mrs. Hale in a voice curiously even.

He was walking up and down, as if thinking something out.

"Is there a cat?" he asked absently.

Mrs. Hale shot a look up at the sheriff's wife.

"Well, not *now*," said Mrs. Peters. "They're superstitious, you know; they leave."

The county attorney did not heed her. "No sign at all of anyone having come in from the outside," he said to Peters, in the manner of continuing an interrupted conversation. "Their own rope. Now let's go upstairs again and go over it, piece by piece. It would have to have been someone who knew just the — "

The stair door closed behind them and their voices were lost.

The two women sat motionless, not looking at each other, but as if peering into something and at the same time holding back. When they spoke now it was as if they were afraid of what they were saying, but as if they could not help saying it.

"She liked the bird," said Martha Hale, low and slowly. "She was going to bury it in that pretty box."

"When I was a girl," said Mrs. Peters, under her breath, "my kitten — there was a boy took a hatchet, and before my eyes — before I could get there — " She covered her face an instant. "If they hadn't held me back I would have" — she caught herself, looked upstairs where footsteps were heard, and finished weakly — "hurt him."

Then they sat without speaking or moving.

"I wonder how it would seem," Mrs. Hale at last began, as if feeling her way over strange ground — "never to have had any children around." Her eyes made a slow sweep of the kitchen, as if seeing what that kitchen had meant through all the years. "No, Wright wouldn't like the bird," she said after that — "a thing that sang. She used to sing. He killed that too." Her voice tightened.

Mrs. Peters moved easily.

"Of course we don't know who killed the bird."

"I knew John Wright," was Mrs. Hale's answer.

"It was an awful thing was done in this house that night, Mrs. Hale," said the sheriff's wife. "Killing a man while he slept — slipping a thing round his neck that choked the life out of him."

Mrs. Hale's hand went out to the bird-cage.

"His neck. Choked the life out of him."

"We don't *know* who killed him," whispered Mrs. Peters wildly. "We don't *know*."

Mrs. Hale had not moved. "If there had been years and years of — nothing, then a bird to sing to you, it would be awful — still — after the bird was still."

It was as if something within her not herself had spoken, and it found in Mrs. Peters something she did not know as herself.

"I know what stillness is," she said, in a queer, monotonous voice. "When we homesteaded in Dakota, and my first baby died — after he was two years old — and me with no other then — "

Mrs. Hale stirred.

"How soon do you suppose they'll be through looking for the evidence?"

"I know what stillness is," repeated Mrs. Peters, in just that same way. Then she too pulled back. "The law has got to punish crime, Mrs. Hale," she said in her tight little way.

"I wish you'd seen Minnie Foster," was the answer, "when she wore a white dress with blue ribbons, and stood up there in the choir and sang."

The picture of that girl, the fact that she had lived neighbor to that girl for twenty years, and had let her die for lack of life, was suddenly more than she could bear.

"Oh, I *wish* I'd come over here once in a while!" she cried. "That was a crime! That was a crime! Who's going to punish that?"

"We mustn't take on," said Mrs. Peters, with a frightened look toward the stairs.

"I might 'a' *known* she needed help! I tell you, it's *queer*, Mrs. Peters. We live close together, and we live far apart. We all go through the same things — it's all just a different kind of the same thing! If it weren't — why do you and I *understand*? Why do we *know* — what we know this minute?"

She dashed her hand across her eyes. Then, seeing the jar of fruit on the table, she reached for it and choked out:

"If I was you I wouldn't *tell* her her fruit was gone! Tell her it *ain't*. Tell her it's all right — all of it. Here — take this in to prove it to her! She — she may never know whether it was broke or not."

Mrs. Peters reached out for the bottle of fruit as if she were glad to take it — as if touching a familiar thing, having something to do, could keep her from something else. She got up, looked about for something to wrap the fruit in, took a petticoat from the pile of clothes she had brought from the front room, and nervously started winding that round the bottle.

"My!" she began, in a high, false voice, "it's a good thing the men couldn't hear us! Getting all stirred up over a little thing like a — dead canary." She hurried over that. "As if that could have anything to do with — with — My, wouldn't they *laugh*?"

Footsteps were heard on the stairs.

"Maybe they would," muttered Mrs. Hale — "maybe they wouldn't."

"No, Peters," said the county attorney incisively; "it's all perfectly clear, except the reason for doing it. But you know juries when it comes to women. If there was some definite thing — something to show. Something to make a story about. A thing that would connect up with this clumsy way of doing it."

In a covert way Mrs. Hale looked at Mrs. Peters. Mrs. Peters was looking at her. Quickly they looked away from each other. The outer door opened and Mr. Hale came in.

"I've got the team round now," he said. "Pretty cold out there."

"I'm going to stay here awhile by myself," the county attorney suddenly announced. "You can send Frank out for me, can't you?" he asked the sheriff. "I want to go over everything. I'm not satisfied we can't do better."

Again, for one brief moment, the two women's eyes found one another.

The sheriff came up to the table.

"Did you want to see what Mrs. Peters was going to take in?"

The county attorney picked up the apron. He laughed. "Oh, I guess they're not very dangerous things the ladies have picked out."

Mrs. Hale's hand was on the sewing basket in which the box was concealed. She felt that she ought to take her hand off the basket. She did not seem able to. He picked up one of the quilt blocks which she had piled on to cover the box. Her eyes felt like fire. She had a feeling that if he took up the basket she would snatch it from him.

But he did not take it up. With another little laugh, he turned away.

"No; Mrs. Peters doesn't need supervising. For that matter, a sheriff's wife is married to the law. Ever think of it that way, Mrs. Peters?"

Mrs. Peters was standing beside the table. Mrs. Hale shot a look up at her; but she could not see her face. Mrs. Peters had turned away. When she spoke, her voice was muffled.

"Not — just that way," she said.

"Married to the law!" chuckled Mrs. Peters' husband. He moved toward the door into the front room, and said to the county attorney:

"I just want you to come in here a minute, George. We ought to take a look at these windows."

"Oh — windows," said the county attorney scoffingly.

"We'll be right out, Mr. Hale," said the sheriff to the farmer.

Hale went to look after the horses. The sheriff followed the county attorney into the other room. Again — for one final moment — the two women were alone in that kitchen.

Martha Hale sprang up, her hands tight together, looking at that other woman, with whom it rested. At first she could not see her eyes, for the sheriff's wife had not turned back since she turned away at that suggestion of being married to the law. But now Mrs. Hale made her turn back. Her eyes made her turn back. Slowly, unwillingly, Mrs. Peters turned her head until her eyes met the eyes of the other woman. There was a moment when they held each other in a steady, burning look in which there was no evasion nor flinching.

Then Martha Hale's eyes pointed the way to the basket in which was hidden the thing that would make certain the conviction of the other woman — that woman who was not there and yet who had been there with them all through that hour.

For a moment Mrs. Peters did not move. And then she did it. With a rush forward, she threw back the quilt pieces, got the box, tried to put it in her handbag. It was too big. Desperately she opened it, started to take the bird out. But there she broke — she could not touch the bird. She stood there helpless, foolish.

There was the sound of a knob turning in the inner door. Martha Hale snatched the box from the sheriff's wife, and got it in the pocket of her big coat just as the sheriff and the county attorney came back.

"Well, Henry," said the county attorney facetiously, "at least we found out that she was not going to quilt it. She was going to — what is it you call it, ladies?"

Mrs. Hale's hand was against the pocket of her coat.

"We call it — knot it, Mr. Henderson."

Djuna Barnes

(1892–1982)

BORN IN CORNWALL-ON-HUDSON, New York, Djuna Barnes was the product of what would today be called a dysfunctional family. Barnes's father was artistic and eccentric; her paternal grandmother, Zadel, was a dominant figure in her life, and biographers have noted their close, possibly sexual, relationship. Whatever the nature of the relationship, Barnes's writings reflect the unconventionality of her childhood.

From 1913 to 1919, Barnes earned her living as a writer for various New York newspapers. In addition to celebrity interviews and feature articles, Barnes's newspaper writings included drama and short fiction, often accompanied by her own illustrations. In 1920, she moved to Europe and stayed there until 1941. Leading the life of an expatriate at the height of the modernist movement, Barnes assumed a respected place in avant-garde circles. A multidimensional artist herself (journalist, playwright, novelist and short-story writer), she counted James Joyce, T. S. Eliot, Mina Loy and Samuel Beckett among her friends. She also frequented the bohemian and lesbian salons of Natalie Barney and Gertrude Stein. Barnes's long affair with sculptor Thelma Wood was the subject of her most famous novel, *Nightwood* (1936), considered by many her finest work.

"Smoke" explores the effect of traditional family structures on the individual. The Fenkens, Zelka, her father and her husband Swart, are all fine specimens of strength and vitality. But the demands of living up to such strength — injunctions to keep "a little iron in the blood" — prove too much for Zelka's son and his daughter, Little Lief. The Fenkens, as one character notes, "live themselves thin," and eventually go "out like a puff of smoke." Barnes's story is full of such striking imagery, and her experimental prose style, evident even in the early newspaper pieces, marks her as one of this century's most innovative writers.

Smoke

THERE WAS SWART with his bushy head and Fenken with the half shut eyes and the grayish beard, and there also was Zelka with her big earrings and her closely bound inky hair, who had often been told that "she was very beautiful in a black way."

Ah, what a fine strong creature she had been and what a fine strong creature her father Fenken had been before her, and what a specimen was her husband Swart, with his gentle melancholy mouth and his strange strong eyes and his brown neck.

Fenken in his youth had loaded the cattle boats, and in his twilight of age he would sit in the round-backed chair by the open fireplace, his two trembling hands folded, and would talk of what he had been.

"A bony man I was, Zelka — my two knees as hard as a pavement, so that I clapped them with great discomfort to my own hands; sometimes," he would add, with a twinkle in his old eyes, "I'd put you between them and my hand; it hurt less."

Zelka would turn her eyes on him slowly — they moved around into sight from under her eyebrows like the barrel of a well-kept gun; they were hard like metal and strong, and she was always conscious of them even in sleep. When she would close her eyes before saying her prayers she would remark to Swart, "I draw the hood over the artillery." And Swart would smile, nodding his large head.

In the town these three were called the "Bullets" — when they came down the street little children sprang aside, not because they were afraid, but because they came so fast and brought with them something so healthy, something so potent, something unconquerable. Fenken could make his fingers snap against his palm like the crack of a cabby's whip just by shutting his hand abruptly, and he did this often, watching the gamin and smiling.

175

*   *   *

Swart, too, had his power, but there was a hint at something softer in him, something that made the lips kind when they were sternest, something that gave him a sad expression when he was thinking — something that had drawn Zelka to him in their first days of courting. "We Fenkens," she would say, "have iron in our veins — in yours I fear there's a little blood."

Zelka was cleanly; she washed her linen clean as though she were punishing the dirt. Had the linen been less durable there would have been holes in it from her knuckles in a six months'. Everything Zelka cooked was tender — she had bruised it with her preparations.

And then Zelka's baby had come. A healthy, fat, little crying thing, with eyes like its father's and with its father's mouth. In vain did Zelka look for something about it that would give it away as one of the Fenken blood — it had a maddeningly tender way of stroking her face, its hair was finer than blown gold, and it squinted up its pale blue eyes when it fell over its nose. Sometimes Zelka would turn the baby around in bed, placing its little feet against her side waiting for it to kick. And when it finally did, it was gently and without great strength and with much good humor. "Swart," Zelka would say, "your child is entirely human. I'm afraid all his veins run blood," and she would add to her father, "Sonny will never load the cattle ships."

When it was old enough to crawl Zelka would get down on hands and knees and chase it about the little ash-littered room. The baby would crawl ahead of her, giggling and driving Zelka mad with a desire to stop and hug him; but when she roared behind him like a lion to make him hurry, the baby would roll over slowly, struggle into a sitting posture, and putting his hand up would sit staring at her as though he would like to study out something that made this difference between them.

When it was seven it would escape from the house and wander down to the shore, and stand for hours watching the boats coming in, being loaded and unloaded. Once one of the men put the cattle belt about him and lowered him into the boat. He went down sadly, his little golden head drooping and his feet hanging down. When they brought him back on shore again and dusted him off they were puzzled at him — he had neither cried nor laughed. They said, "Didn't you like that?" And he had only answered by looking at them fixedly.

And when he grew up he was very tender to his mother, who had taken to shaking her head over him. Fenken had died the Summer of his grandchild's thirtieth year, so that after the funeral Swart had taken the round-backed chair for his own. And now he sat there with folded hands, but he never said what a strong lad he had been. Sometimes he would say, "Do you remember how Fenken used to snap his fingers together like a whip?" and Zelka would answer, "I do."

And finally when her son married, Zelka was seen at the feast dressed in a short blue skirt leaning upon Swart's arm, both of them still strong and handsome and capable of lifting the buckets of cider.

Zelka's son had chosen a strange woman for a wife. A thin little thing, with a tiny waistline and a narrow chest and a small, very lovely throat. She was the daughter of a ship owner and had a good deal of money in her own name. When she married Zelka's son she brought him some ten thousand a year, and so he stopped the shipping of cattle and went in for exports and imports of Oriental silks and perfumes.

When his mother and father died he moved a little inland away from the sea and hired clerks to do his bidding. Still, he never forgot what his mother had said to him:

"There must always be a little iron in the blood, sonny."

He reflected on this when he looked at Lief, his wife. He was a silent, taciturn man as he grew older, and Lief had grown afraid of him, because of his very kindness and his melancholy.

There was only one person to whom he was a bit stern, and this was his daughter, "Little Lief." Toward her he showed a strange hostility, a touch even of that fierceness that had been his mother's — once she had rushed shrieking from his room because he had suddenly roared behind her as his mother had done behind him. When she was gone he sat for a long time by his table, his hands stretched out in front of him, thinking.

He had succeeded well; he had multiplied his wife's money now into the many thousands — they had a house in the country and servants. They were spoken of in the town as a couple who had an existence that might be termed as "pretty soft," and when the carriage drove by of a Sunday with baby Lief up front on her mother's lap and Lief's husband beside her in his gray cloth coat, they stood aside not to be trampled on by the swift legged, slender ankled "pacer" that Lief had bought that day when she had visited the "old home" — the beach that had known her and her husband when they were children. This horse was the very one that she had asked for when she saw how beautiful it was as they fastened the belt to it preparatory to lowering it over the side. It was then that she

remembered how when her husband had been a little boy they had
lowered him over into the boat with this same belting.

During the Winter that followed, which was a very hard one, Lief took
cold and resorted to hot water bottles and thin tea. She became very
fretful, and annoyed at her husband's constant questionings as to her
health; even Little Lief was a nuisance because she was so noisy. She
would steal into the room, and crawling under her mother's bed would
begin to sing in a high, thin treble, pushing the ticking with her patent
leather boots to see them crinkle. Then the mother would cry out, the
nurse would run in and take her away and Lief would spend a half hour
in tears. Finally they would not allow Little Lief in the room, so she
would steal by the door many times, walking noiselessly up and down
the hall; but finally, her youth overcoming her, she would stretch her
legs out into a straight goose step, and for this she was whipped because
on the day that she had been caught her mother had died.

And so the time passed and the years rolled on, taking their toll. It was
now many Summers since that day that Zelka had walked into town
with Swart — now many years since Fenken had snapped his fingers like
a cabby's whip. Little Lief had never even heard that her grandmother
had been called a "beautiful woman in a black sort of way," and she had
only vaguely heard of the nickname that had once been given the
family, the "Bullets." She came to know that great strength had once
been in the family, to such an extent indeed that somehow a phrase was
known to her, "Remember always to keep a little iron in the blood." And
one night she had pricked her arm to see if there were iron in it, and she
had cried because it hurt, and so she knew that there was none.

With her this phrase ended. She never repeated it because of that
night when she had made that discovery.

Her father had taken to solitude and the study of sociology. Sometimes he would turn her about by the shoulder and look at her, breathing in a thick way he had with him of late, and once he told her she was a
good girl but foolish, and left her alone.

They had begun to lose money, and some of Little Lief's tapestries,
given her by her mother, were sold. Her heart broke, but she opened the
windows oftener because she needed some kind of beauty. She made
the mistake of loving tapestries best and nature second best. Somehow
she had gotten the two things mixed — of course it was due to her
bringing up. "If you are poor you live out of doors — but if you are rich

you live in a lovely house." So to her the greatest of calamities had befallen the house; it was beginning to go away by those imperceptible means, that at first leave a house looking unfamiliar and then bare.

Finally she could stand it no longer and she married a thin, wiry man with a long thin nose and a nasty trick of rubbing it with a finger equally long and thin — a man with a fair income and very refined sisters.

This man Misha wanted to be a lawyer. He studied half the night and never seemed happy unless his head was in his palm. His sisters were like this also, only for another reason: they enjoyed weeping. If they could find nothing to cry about they cried for the annoyance of this dearth of destitution and worry. They held daily councils for future domestic trouble — one the gesture of emotional and one of mental desire.

Sometimes Little Lief's father would come to the big iron gate and ask to see her. He would never come in — why? He never explained. So Little Lief and he would talk over the gate top, and sometimes he was gentle and sometimes he was not. When he was harsh to her Little Lief wept, and when she wept he would look at her steadily from under his eyebrows and say nothing. Sometimes he asked her to take a walk with him. This would set Little Lief into a terrible flutter; the corners of her mouth would twitch and her nostrils tremble, but she always went.

Misha worried little about his wife. He was a very selfish man, with that greatest capacity of a selfish nature, the ability to labor untiringly for some one thing that he wanted and that nature had placed beyond his reach. Some people called this quality excellent, pointing out what a great scholar Misha was, holding him up as an example in their own households, looking after him when he went hurriedly down the street with that show of nervous expectancy that a man always betrays when he knows within himself that he is deficient — a sort of peering in the face of life to see if it has discovered the flaw.

Little Lief felt that her father was trying to be something that was not natural to him. What was it? As she grew older, she tried to puzzle it out. Now it happened more often that she would catch him looking at her in a strange way, and once she asked him half playfully if he wished she had been a boy — and he had answered abruptly, "Yes, I do."

Little Lief would stand for hours at the casement and, leaning her head against the glass, try to solve this thing about her father — and then she discovered it when he had said, "Yes, I do." He was trying to be strong — what was it that was in the family? — oh, yes — iron in the blood — he feared there was no longer any iron left — well, perhaps there wasn't — was that the reason he looked at her like this? No, he was worried about himself. Why? — wasn't he satisfied with his own strength? He had been cruel enough very often. This shouldn't have worried him.

She asked him, and he answered, "Yes, but cruelty isn't strength." That was an admission — she was less afraid of him since that day when he had made that answer, but now she kept peering into his face as he had done into hers and he seemed not to notice it. Well, he was getting to be a very old man.

Then one day her two sisters-in-law pounced upon her so that her golden head shook on its thin, delicate neck.

"Your father has come into the garden," cried one.

"Yes, yes," pursued the elder. "He's even sat himself upon the bench."

She hurried out to him. "What's the matter, father?" Her head was aching.

"Nothing." He did not look up.

She sat down beside him, stroking his hand, at first timidly, then with more courage.

"Have you looked at the garden?"

He nodded.

She burst into tears.

He took his hand away from her and began to laugh.

"What's the matter, child? A good dose of hog-killing would do you good."

"You have no right to speak to me in this way — take yourself off!" she cried sharply, holding her side, and her father rocked with laughter.

She stretched her long, thin arms out, clenching her thin fingers together. The lace on her short sleeves trembled, her knuckles grew white.

"A good pig-killing," he repeated, watching her, and she grew sullen.

"Eh?" He pinched her flesh a little and dropped it. She was passive; she made no murmur. He got up, walked to the gate, opened it and went out, closing it after him. He turned back a step and waved to her. She did not answer for a moment, then she waved back slowly with one of her thin, white hands.

She would have liked to refuse to see him again, but she lacked the courage. She would say to herself, "If I am unkind to him now, perhaps later I shall regret it." In this way she tried to excuse herself. The very next time he had sent word that he wished speech with her she had come.

"Little fool!" he said, in a terrible rage, and walked off. She was quite sure that he was slowly losing his mind — a second childhood, she called it, still trying to make things as pleasant as possible.

She had been ill a good deal that Spring, and in the Fall she had terrible headaches. In the Winter months she took to her bed, and early in May the doctor was summoned.

Misha talked to the physician in the drawing-room before he sent him up to his wife.

"You must be gentle with her; she is nervous and frail." The doctor laughed outright. Misha's sisters were weeping, of course, and perfectly happy.

"It will be such a splendid thing for her," they said. Meaning the beef, iron and wine that they expected the doctor to prescribe.

Toward evening Little Lief closed her eyes.

Her child was still-born.

The physician came downstairs and entered the parlor where Misha's sisters stood together, still shedding tears.

He rubbed his hands.

"Send Misha upstairs."

"He has gone."

"Isn't it dreadful? I never could bear corpses, especially little ones."

"A baby isn't a corpse," answered the physician, smiling at his own impending humor. "It's an interrupted plan."

He felt that the baby, not having drawn a breath in this world, could not feel hurt at such a remark, because it has gathered no feminine pride and, also, as it has passed out quicker than the time it took to make the observation, it really could be called nothing more than the background for medical jocularity.

Misha came into the room with red eyes.

"Out like a puff of smoke," he said.

One of his sisters remarked: "Well, the Fenkens lived themselves thin."

The next Summer Misha married into a healthy Swedish family. His second wife had a broad face, with eyes set wide apart, and with broad, flat, healthy, yellow teeth, and she played the piano surprisingly well, though she looked a little heavy as she sat upon the piano stool.

Zora Neale Hurston

(c. 1891–1960)

ZORA NEALE HURSTON was the most famous woman writer of the Harlem Renaissance; when she died in poverty in 1960, her literary reputation was forgotten, and she was buried in an unmarked grave in Ft. Pierce, Florida. Today Hurston's reputation is restored, thanks largely to the work of Alice Walker, whose 1979 anthology of Hurston's writing, *I Love Myself When I Am Laughing . . . and Then Again When I Am Looking Mean and Impressive*, introduced new generations to Hurston's work.

Hurston was born in Eatonville, Florida, the first incorporated all-black town in the United States, where she spent much of her childhood and which would figure prominently in her work. In 1925 Hurston arrived in New York City, where she quickly made a name for herself in the literary circles that flourished during the Harlem Renaissance. She graduated from Barnard College in 1928, after studying anthropology with Franz Boas. During this time, Hurston published articles, essays, stories and plays. She contributed a piece to Alain Locke's landmark volume, *The New Negro*, and her work appeared in the leading periodicals of the day, such as *Crisis*, *Opportunity* and the controversial *Fire!* One of the most prolific writers of her period, Hurston wrote four novels (*Jonah's Vine Gourd*, 1934; *Their Eyes Were Watching God*, 1937; *Moses, Man of the Mountain*, 1939; and *Seraph on the Suwanee*, 1948), two books of folklore (*Mules and Men*, 1935; and *Tell My Horse*, 1938) and an autobiography (*Dust Tracks on the Road*, 1942).

"Sweat" is a showpiece of Hurston's virtuosity as storyteller, anthropologist and stylist. The story features a heroine trying to achieve a sense of her own protagonism within the black community. As in many of Hurston's stories and novels, the relationship between the sexes is fraught with tension. As Delia struggles to shake off the hold of her adulterous husband, the story ends with an ironic twist that sets her free.

Sweat

I

IT WAS ELEVEN o'clock of a Spring night in Florida. It was Sunday. Any other night, Delia Jones would have been in bed for two hours by this time. But she was a washwoman, and Monday morning meant a great deal to her. So she collected the soiled clothes on Saturday when she returned the clean things. Sunday night after church, she sorted and put the white things to soak. It saved her almost a half-day's start. A great hamper in the bedroom held the clothes that she brought home. It was so much neater than a number of bundles lying around.

She squatted on the kitchen floor beside the great pile of clothes, sorting them into small heaps according to color, and humming a song in a mournful key, but wondering through it all where Sykes, her husband, had gone with her horse and buckboard.

Just then something long, round, limp and black fell upon her shoulders and slithered to the floor beside her. A great terror took hold of her. It softened her knees and dried her mouth so that it was a full minute before she could cry out or move. Then she saw that it was the big bull whip her husband liked to carry when he drove.

She lifted her eyes to the door and saw him standing there bent over with laughter at her fright. She screamed at him.

"Sykes, what you throw dat whip on me like dat? You know it would skeer me — looks just like a snake, an' you knows how skeered Ah is of snakes."

"Course Ah knowed it! That's how come Ah done it." He slapped his leg with his hand and almost rolled on the ground in his mirth. "If you such a big fool dat you got to have a fit over a earth worm or a string, Ah don't keer how bad Ah skeer you."

"You ain't got no business doing it. Gawd knows it's a sin. Some day

183

Ah'm gointuh drop dead from some of yo' foolishness. 'Nother thing, where you been wid mah rig? Ah feeds dat pony. He ain't fuh you to be drivin' wid no bull whip."

"You sho' is one aggravatin' nigger woman!" he declared and stepped into the room. She resumed her work and did not answer him at once. "Ah done tole you time and again to keep them white folks' clothes outa dis house."

He picked up the whip and glared at her. Delia went on with her work. She went out into the yard and returned with a galvanized tub and set it on the washbench. She saw that Sykes had kicked all of the clothes together again, and now stood in her way truculently, his whole manner hoping, *praying*, for an argument. But she walked calmly around him and commenced to re-sort the things.

"Next time, Ah'm gointer kick 'em outdoors," he threatened as he struck a match along the leg of his corduroy breeches.

Delia never looked up from her work, and her thin, stooped shoulders sagged further.

"Ah ain't for no fuss t'night Sykes. Ah just come from taking sacrament at the church house."

He snorted scornfully. "Yeah, you just come from de church house on a Sunday night, but heah you is gone to work on them clothes. You ain't nothing but a hypocrite. One of them amen-corner Christians — sing, whoop, and shout, then come home and wash white folks' clothes on the Sabbath."

He stepped roughly upon the whitest pile of things, kicking them helter-skelter as he crossed the room. His wife gave a little scream of dismay, and quickly gathered them together again.

"Sykes, you quit grindin' dirt into these clothes! How can Ah git through by Sat'day if Ah don't start on Sunday?"

"Ah don't keer if you never git through. Anyhow, Ah done promised Gawd and a couple of other men, Ah ain't gointer have it in mah house. Don't gimme no lip neither, else Ah'll throw 'em out and put mah fist up side yo' head to boot."

Delia's habitual meekness seemed to slip from her shoulders like a blown scarf. She was on her feet; her poor little body, her bare knuckly hands bravely defying the strapping hulk before her.

"Looka heah, Sykes, you done gone too fur. Ah been married to you fur fifteen years, and Ah been takin' in washin' fur fifteen years. Sweat, sweat, sweat! Work and sweat, cry and sweat, pray and sweat!"

"What's that got to do with me?" he asked brutally.

"What's it got to do with you, Sykes? Mah tub of suds is filled yo' belly with vittles more times than yo' hands is filled it. Mah sweat is done paid for this house and Ah reckon Ah kin keep on sweatin' in it."

She seized the iron skillet from the stove and struck a defensive pose, which act surprised him greatly, coming from her. It cowed him and he did not strike her as he usually did.

"Naw you won't," she panted, "that ole snaggle-toothed black woman you runnin' with ain't comin' heah to pile up on *mah* sweat and blood. You ain't paid for nothin' on this place, and Ah'm gointer stay right heah till Ah'm toted out foot foremost."

"Well, you better quit gittin' me riled up, else they'll be totin' you out sooner than you expect. Ah'm so tired of you Ah don't know whut to do. Gawd! How Ah hates skinny wimmen!"

A little awed by this new Delia, he sidled out of the door and slammed the back gate after him. He did not say where he had gone, but she knew too well. She knew very well that he would not return until nearly daybreak also. Her work over, she went on to bed but not to sleep at once. Things had come to a pretty pass!

She lay awake, gazing upon the debris that cluttered their matrimonial trail. Not an image left standing along the way. Anything like flowers had long ago been drowned in the salty stream that had been pressed from her heart. Her tears, her sweat, her blood. She had brought love to the union and he had brought a longing after the flesh. Two months after the wedding, he had given her the first brutal beating. She had the memory of his numerous trips to Orlando with all of his wages when he had returned to her penniless, even before the first year had passed. She was young and soft then, but now she thought of her knotty, muscled limbs, her harsh knuckly hands, and drew herself up into an unhappy little ball in the middle of the big feather bed. Too late now to hope for love, even if it were not Bertha it would be someone else. This case differed from the others only in that she was bolder than the others. Too late for everything except her little home. She had built it for her old days, and planted one by one the trees and flowers there. It was lovely to her, lovely.

Somehow, before sleep came, she found herself saying aloud: "Oh well, whatever goes over the Devil's back, is got to come under his belly. Sometime or ruther, Sykes, like everybody else, is gointer reap his sowing." After that she was able to build a spiritual earthworks against her husband. His shells could no longer reach her. AMEN. She went to sleep and slept until he announced his presence in bed by kicking her feet and rudely snatching the covers away.

"Gimme some kivah heah, an' git yo' damn foots over on yo' own side! Ah oughter mash you in yo' mouf fuh drawing dat skillet on me."

Delia went clear to the rail without answering him. A triumphant indifference to all that he was or did.

II

The week was as full of work for Delia as all other weeks, and Saturday found her behind her little pony, collecting and delivering clothes.

It was a hot, hot day near the end of July. The village men on Joe Clarke's porch even chewed cane listlessly. They did not hurl the cane-knots as usual. They let them dribble over the edge of the porch. Even conversation had collapsed under the heat.

"Heah come Delia Jones," Jim Merchant said, as the shaggy pony came 'round the bend of the road toward them. The rusty buckboard was heaped with baskets of crisp, clean laundry.

"Yep," Joe Lindsay agreed. "Hot or col', rain or shine, jes' ez reg'lar ez de weeks roll roun' Delia carries 'em an' fetches 'em on Sat'day."

"She better if she wanter eat," said Moss. "Syke Jones ain't wuth de shot an' powder hit would tek tuh kill 'em. Not to *huh* he ain't."

"He sho' ain't," Walter Thomas chimed in. "It's too bad, too, cause she wuz a right pretty li'l trick when he got huh. Ah'd uh mah'ied huh mahself if he hadnter beat me to it."

Delia nodded briefly at the men as she drove past.

"Too much knockin' will ruin *any* 'oman. He done beat huh 'nough tuh kill three women, let 'lone change they looks," said Elijah Moseley. "How Syke kin stommuck dat big black greasy Mogul he's layin' roun' wid, gits me. Ah swear dat eight-rock couldn't kiss a sardine can Ah done thowed out de back do' 'way las' yeah."

"Aw, she's fat, thass how come. He's allus been crazy 'bout fat women," put in Merchant. "He'd a' been tied up wid one long time ago if he could a' found one tuh have him. Did Ah tell yuh 'bout him come sidlin' roun' *mah* wife — bringin' her a basket uh peecans outa his yard fuh a present? Yessir, mah wife! She tol' him tuh take 'em right straight back home, 'cause Delia works so hard ovah dat washtub she reckon everything on de place taste lak sweat an' soapsuds. Ah jus' wisht Ah'd a' caught 'im 'roun' dere! Ah'd a' made his hips ketch on fiah down dat shell road."

"Ah know he done it, too. Ah sees 'im grinnin' at every 'oman dat passes," Walter Thomas said. "But even so, he useter eat some mighty big hunks uh humble pie tuh git dat li'l 'oman he got. She wuz ez pritty ez a speckled pup! Dat wuz fifteen years ago. He useter be so skeered uh losin' huh, she could make him do some parts of a husband's duty. Dey never wuz de same in de mind."

"There oughter be a law about him," said Lindsay. "He ain't fit tuh carry guts tuh a bear."

Clarke spoke for the first time. "'Tain't no law on earth dat kin make a man be decent if it ain't in 'im. There's plenty men dat takes a wife lak dey do a joint uh sugar-cane. It's round, juicy an' sweet when dey gits it. But dey squeeze an' grind, squeeze an' grind an' wring tell dey wring every drop uh pleasure dat's in 'em out. When dey's satisfied dat dey is wrung dry, dey treats 'em jes' lak dey do a cane-chew. Dey thows 'em away. Dey knows whut dey is doin' while dey is at it, an' hates theirselves fuh it but they keeps on hangin' after huh tell she's empty. Den dey hates huh fuh bein' a cane-chew an' in de way."

"We oughter take Syke an' dat stray 'oman uh his'n down in Lake Howell swamp an' lay on de rawhide till they cain't say Lawd a' mussy. He allus wuz uh ovahbearin' niggah, but since dat white 'oman from up north done teached 'im how to run a automobile, he done got too beggety to live — an' we oughter kill 'im," Old Man Anderson advised.

A grunt of approval went around the porch. But the heat was melting their civic virtue and Elijah Moseley began to bait Joe Clarke.

"Come on, Joe, git a melon outa dere an' slice it up for yo' customers. We'se all sufferin' wid de heat. De bear's done got *me!*"

"Thass right, Joe, a watermelon is jes' whut Ah needs tuh cure de eppizudicks," Walter Thomas joined forces with Moseley. "Come on dere, Joe. We all is steady customers an' you ain't set us up in a long time. Ah chooses dat long, bowlegged Floridy favorite."

"A god, an' be dough. You all gimme twenty cents and slice away," Clarke retorted. "Ah needs a col' slice m'self. Heah, everybody chip in. Ah'll lend y'all mah meat knife."

The money was all quickly subscribed and the huge melon brought forth. At that moment, Sykes and Bertha arrived. A determined silence fell on the porch and the melon was put away again.

Merchant snapped down the blade of his jackknife and moved toward the store door.

"Come on in, Joe, an' gimme a slab uh sow belly an' uh pound uh coffee — almost fuhgot 'twas Sat'day. Got to git on home." Most of the men left also.

Just then Delia drove past on her way home, as Sykes was ordering magnificently for Bertha. It pleased him for Delia to see.

"Git whutsoever yo' heart desires, Honey. Wait a minute, Joe. Give huh two bottles uh strawberry soda-water, uh quart parched ground-peas, an' a block uh chewin' gum."

With all this they left the store, with Sykes reminding Bertha that this was his town and she could have it if she wanted it.

The men returned soon after they left, and held their watermelon feast.

"Where did Syke Jones git da 'oman from nohow?" Lindsay asked.

"Ovah Apopka. Guess dey musta been cleanin' out de town when she lef'. She don't look lak a thing but a hunk uh liver wid hair on it."

"Well, she sho' kin squall," Dave Carter contributed. "When she gits ready tuh laff, she jes' opens huh mouf an' latches it back tuh de las' notch. No ole granpa alligator down in Lake Bell ain't got nothin' on huh."

III

Bertha had been in town three months now. Sykes was still paying her room-rent at Della Lewis'—the only house in town that would have taken her in. Sykes took her frequently to Winter Park to 'stomps'. He still assured her that he was the swellest man in the state.

"Sho' you kin have dat li'l ole house soon's Ah git dat 'oman outa dere. Everything b'longs tuh me an' you sho' kin have it. Ah sho' 'bominates uh skinny 'oman. Lawdy, you sho' is got one portly shape on you! You kin git *anything* you wants. Dis is *mah* town an' you sho' kin have it."

Delia's work-worn knees crawled over the earth in Gethsemane and up the rocks of Calvary many, many times during these months. She avoided the villagers and meeting places in her efforts to be blind and deaf. But Bertha nullified this to a degree, by coming to Delia's house to call Sykes out to her at the gate.

Delia and Sykes fought all the time now with no peaceful interludes. They slept and ate in silence. Two or three times Delia had attempted a timid friendliness, but she was repulsed each time. It was plain that the breaches must remain agape.

The sun had burned July to August. The heat streamed down like a million hot arrows, smiting all things living upon the earth. Grass withered, leaves browned, snakes went blind in shedding and men and dogs went mad. Dog days!

Delia came home one day and found Sykes there before her. She wondered, but started to go on into the house without speaking, even though he was standing in the kitchen door and she must either stoop under his arm or ask him to move. He made no room for her. She noticed a soap box beside the steps, but paid no particular attention to it, knowing that he must have brought it there. As she was stooping to pass under his outstretched arm, he suddenly pushed her backward, laughingly.

"Look in de box dere Delia, Ah done brung yuh somethin'!"

She nearly fell upon the box in her stumbling, and when she saw what it held, she all but fainted outright.

"Syke! Syke, mah Gawd! You take dat rattlesnake 'way from heah! You *gottuh*. Oh, Jesus, have mussy!"

"Ah ain't got tuh do nuthin' uh de kin'—fact is Ah ain't got tuh do nothin' but die. Tain't no use uh you puttin' on airs makin' out lak you skeered uh dat snake—he's gointer stay right heah tell he die. He wouldn't bite me cause Ah knows how tuh handle 'im. Nohow he wouldn't risk breakin' out his fangs 'gin yo skinny laigs."

"Naw, now Syke, don't keep dat thing 'round tryin' tuh skeer me tuh death. You knows Ah'm even feared uh earth worms. Thass de biggest snake Ah evah did see. Kill 'im Syke, please."

"Doan ast me tuh do nothin' fuh yuh. Goin' 'round tryin' tuh be so damn asterperious. Naw, Ah ain't gonna kill it. Ah think uh damn sight mo' uh him dan you! Dat's a nice snake an' anybody doan lak 'im kin jes' hit de grit."

The village soon heard that Sykes had the snake, and came to see and ask questions.

"How de hen-fire did you ketch dat six-foot rattler, Syke?" Thomas asked.

"He's full uh frogs so he cain't hardly move, thass how Ah eased up on 'm. But Ah'm a snake charmer an' knows how tuh handle 'em. Shux, dat ain't nothin'. Ah could ketch one eve'y day if Ah so wanted tuh."

"Whut he needs is a heavy hick'ry club leaned real heavy on his head. Dat's de bes' way tuh charm a rattlesnake."

"Naw, Walt, y'all jes' don't understand dese diamon' backs lak Ah do," said Sykes in a superior tone of voice.

The village agreed with Walter, but the snake stayed on. His box remained by the kitchen door with its screen wire covering. Two or three days later it had digested its meal of frogs and literally came to life. It rattled at every movement in the kitchen or the yard. One day as Delia came down the kitchen steps she saw his chalky-white fangs curved like scimitars hung in the wire meshes. This time she did not run away with averted eyes as usual. She stood for a long time in the doorway in a red fury that grew bloodier for every second that she regarded the creature that was her torment.

That night she broached the subject as soon as Sykes sat down to the table.

"Syke, Ah wants you tuh take dat snake 'way fum heah. You done starved me an' Ah put up widcher, you done beat me and Ah took dat, but you done kilt all mah insides bringin' dat varmint heah."

Sykes poured out a saucer full of coffee and drank it deliberately before he answered her.

"A whole lot Ah keer 'bout how you feels inside uh out. Dat snake ain't goin' no damn wheah till Ah gits ready fuh 'im tuh go. So fur as beatin' is concerned, yuh ain't took near all dat you gointer take ef yuh stay 'round *me*."

Delia pushed back her plate and got up from the table. "Ah hates you, Syke," she said calmly. "Ah hates you tuh de same degree dat Ah useter love yuh. Ah done took an' took till mah belly is full up tuh mah neck. Dat's de reason Ah got mah letter fum de church an' moved mah membership tuh Woodbridge — so Ah don't haftuh take no sacrament wid yuh. Ah don't wantuh see yuh 'round me atall. Lay 'round wid dat 'oman all yuh wants tuh, but gwan 'way fum me an' mah house. Ah hates yuh lak uh suck-egg dog."

Sykes almost let the huge wad of corn bread and collard greens he was chewing fall out of his mouth in amazement. He had a hard time whipping himself up to the proper fury to try to answer Delia.

"Well, Ah'm glad you does hate me. Ah'm sho' tiahed uh you hangin' ontuh me. Ah don't want yuh. Look at yuh stringey ole neck! Yo' rawbony laigs an' arms is enough tuh cut uh man tuh death. You looks jes' lak de devvul's doll-baby tuh *me*. You cain't hate me no worse dan Ah hates you. Ah been hatin' *you* fuh years."

"Yo' ole black hide don't look lak nothin' tuh me, but uh passle uh wrinkled up rubber, wid yo' big ole yeahs flappin' on each side lak uh paih uh buzzard wings. Don't think Ah'm gointuh be run 'way fum mah house neither. Ah'm goin' tuh de white folks 'bout *you*, mah young man, de very nex' time you lay yo' han's on me. Mah cup is done run ovah."

Delia said this with no signs of fear and Sykes departed from the house, threatening her, but made not the slightest move to carry out any of them.

That night he did not return at all, and the next day being Sunday, Delia was glad she did not have to quarrel before she hitched up her pony and drove the four miles to Woodbridge.

She stayed to the night service — 'love feast' — which was very warm and full of spirit. In the emotional winds her domestic trials were borne far and wide so that she sang as she drove homeward,

> Jurden water, black an' col
> Chills de body, not de soul
> An' Ah wantah cross Jurden in uh calm time.

She came from the barn to the kitchen door and stopped.

"Whut's de mattah, ol' Satan, you ain't kickin' up yo' racket?" She addressed the snake's box. Complete silence. She went on into the house with a new hope in its birth struggles. Perhaps her threat to go to the white folks had frightened Sykes! Perhaps he was sorry! Fifteen years of misery and suppression had brought Delia to the place where she would hope *anything* that looked toward a way over or through her wall of inhibitions.

She felt in the match-safe behind the stove at once for a match. There was only one there.

"Dat niggah wouldn't fetch nothin' heah tuh save his rotten neck, but he kin run thew whut Ah brings quick enough. Now he done toted off nigh on tuh haff uh box uh matches. He done had dat 'oman heah in mah house, too."

Nobody but a woman could tell how she knew this even before she struck the match. But she did and it put her into a new fury.

Presently she brought in the tubs to put the white things to soak. This time she decided she need not bring the hamper out of the bedroom; she would go in there and do the sorting. She picked up the pot-bellied lamp and went in. The room was small and the hamper stood hard by the foot of the white iron bed. She could sit and reach through the bedposts — resting as she worked.

"*Ah wantah cross Jurden in uh calm time.*" She was singing again. The mood of the 'love feast' had returned. She threw back the lid of the basket almost gaily. Then, moved by both horror and terror, she sprang back toward the door. *There lay the snake in the basket!* He moved sluggishly at first, but even as she turned round and round, jumped up and down in an insanity of fear, he began to stir vigorously. She saw him pouring his awful beauty from the basket upon the bed, then she seized the lamp and ran as fast as she could to the kitchen. The wind from the open door blew out the light and the darkness added to her terror. She sped to the darkness of the yard, slamming the door after her before she thought to set down the lamp. She did not feel safe even on the ground, so she climbed up in the hay barn.

There for an hour or more she lay sprawled upon the hay a gibbering wreck.

Finally she grew quiet, and after that came coherent thought. With this stalked through her a cold, bloody rage. Hours of this. A period of introspection, a space of retrospection, then a mixture of both. Out of this an awful calm.

"Well, Ah done de bes' Ah could. If things ain't right, Gawd knows tain't mah fault."

She went to sleep—a twitch sleep—and woke up to a faint gray sky. There was a loud hollow sound below. She peered out. Sykes was at the wood-pile, demolishing a wire-covered box.

He hurried to the kitchen door, but hung outside there some minutes before he entered, and stood some minutes more inside before he closed it after him.

The gray in the sky was spreading. Delia descended without fear now, and crouched beneath the low bedroom window. The drawn shade shut out the dawn, shut in the night. But the thin walls held back no sound.

"Dat ol' scratch is woke up now!" She mused at the tremendous whirr inside, which every woodsman knows, is one of the sound illusions. The rattler is a ventriloquist. His whirr sounds to the right, to the left, straight ahead, behind, close under foot—everywhere but where it is. Woe to him who guesses wrong unless he is prepared to hold up his end of the argument! Sometimes he strikes without rattling at all.

Inside, Sykes heard nothing until he knocked a pot lid off the stove while trying to reach the match-safe in the dark. He had emptied his pockets at Bertha's.

The snake seemed to wake up under the stove and Sykes made a quick leap into the bedroom. In spite of the gin he had had, his head was clearing now.

"Mah Gawd!" he chattered, "ef Ah could on'y strack uh light!"

The rattling ceased for a moment as he stood paralyzed. He waited. It seemed that the snake waited also.

"Oh, fuh de light! Ah thought he'd be too sick"—Sykes was muttering to himself when the whirr began again, closer, right underfoot this time. Long before this, Sykes' ability to think had been flattened down to primitive instinct and he leaped — onto the bed.

Outside Delia heard a cry that might have come from a maddened chimpanzee, a stricken gorilla. All the terror, all the horror, all the rage that man possibly could express, without a recognizable human sound.

A tremendous stir inside there, another series of animal screams, the intermittent whirr of the reptile. The shade torn violently down from the window, letting in the red dawn, a huge brown hand seizing the window stick, great dull blows upon the wooden floor punctuating the gibberish of sound long after the rattle of the snake had abruptly subsided. All this Delia could see and hear from her place beneath the window, and it made her ill. She crept over to the four-o'clocks and stretched herself on the cool earth to recover.

She lay there. "Delia, Delia!" She could hear Sykes calling in a most despairing tone as one who expected no answer. The sun crept on up, and he called. Delia could not move — her legs had gone flabby. She never moved, he called, and the sun kept rising.

"Mah Gawd!" She heard him moan, "Mah Gawd fum Heben!" She heard him stumbling about and got up from her flower-bed. The sun was growing warm. As she approached the door she heard him call out hopefully, "Delia, is dat you Ah heah?"

She saw him on his hands and knees as soon as she reached the door. He crept an inch or two toward her — all that he was able, and she saw his horribly swollen neck and his one open eye shining with hope. A surge of pity too strong to support bore her away from that eye that must, could not, fail to see the tubs. He would see the lamp. Orlando with its doctors was too far. She could scarcely reach the chinaberry tree, where she waited in the growing heat while inside she knew the cold river was creeping up and up to extinguish that eye which must know by now that she knew.

Nella Larsen

(c. 1893–1964)

NELLA LARSEN was born in Chicago. Her mother was Danish, her father West Indian. After her father's death, Larsen's mother remarried; with her half-sister, Larsen attended a private school with other students of Scandinavian and German descent. Larsen later attended Fisk University and the University of Copenhagen. From 1912 to 1915, she studied nursing at the Lincoln School for Nurses in New York. After graduating she worked in a teaching hospital in Tuskegee, Alabama, but returned north after one year. In 1919 Larsen married Elmer Samuel Imes, a promising young physicist. Two years later, Larsen left nursing to work for the New York Public Library system.

Larsen began writing while recuperating from an illness that resulted in early retirement. *Quicksand* (1928), her first novel, won immediate acclaim, and Larsen was hailed as one of the most promising writers of the Harlem Renaissance. A second novel, *Passing*, came out in 1929. The following year Larsen was awarded a Guggenheim Fellowship — the first awarded to a black woman writer. Her marriage was failing, and she used the fellowship money to travel to Europe to research a third novel. By the time she returned to the United States, the Harlem Renaissance was in decline, and Larsen did not publish any more work.

"Sanctuary" was published in 1930 in *Forum* magazine. Because of its similarity to a story published in 1922, Larsen was accused of plagiarism. She produced manuscript drafts of her work and attributed the story to an elderly woman who told Larsen the tale when she was studying nursing. The plagiarism charges were never substantiated, but they contributed to the end of Larsen's literary career.

Sanctuary

I

ON THE SOUTHERN coast, between Merton and Shawboro, there is a strip of desolation some half a mile wide and nearly ten miles long between the sea and old fields of ruined plantations. Skirting the edge of this narrow jungle is a partly grown-over road, which still shows traces of furrows made by the wheels of wagons that have long since rotted away or been cut into firewood. This road is little used, now that the state has built its new highway a bit to the west and wagons are less numerous than automobiles.

In the forsaken road a man was walking swiftly. But in spite of his hurry, at every step he set down his feet with infinite care, for the night was windless and the heavy silence intensified each sound; even the breaking of a twig could be plainly heard. And the man had need of caution as well as haste.

Before a lonely cottage that shrank timidly back from the road the man hesitated a moment, then struck out across the patch of green in front of it. Stepping behind a clump of bushes close to the house, he looked in through the lighted window at Annie Poole, standing at her kitchen table mixing the supper biscuits.

He was a big black man with pale brown eyes in which there was an odd mixture of fear and amazement. The light showed streaks of gray soil on his heavy, sweating face and great hands, and on his torn clothes. In his woolly hair clung bits of dried leaves and dead grass.

He made a gesture as if to tap on the window, but turned away to the door instead. Without knocking he opened it and went in.

II

The woman's brown gaze was immediately on him, though she did not move. She said, "You ain't in no hurry, is you, Jim Hammer?" It wasn't, however, entirely a question.

"Ah's in trubble, Mis' Poole," the man explained, his voice shaking, his fingers twitching.

"W'at you done done now?"

"Shot a man, Mis' Poole."

"Trufe?" The woman seemed calm. But the word was spat out.

"Yas'm. Shot 'im." In the man's tone was something of wonder, as if he himself could not quite believe that he had really done this thing which he affirmed.

"Daid?"

"Dunno, Mis' Poole. Dunno."

"White man o' niggah?"

"Cain't say, Mis' Poole. White man, Ah reckons."

Annie Poole looked at him with cold contempt. She was a tiny, withered woman — fifty, perhaps — with a wrinkled face the color of old copper, framed by a crinkly mass of white hair. But about her small figure was some quality of hardness that belied her appearance of frailty. At last she spoke, boring her sharp little eyes into those of the anxious creature before her.

"An' w'at am you lookin' foh me to do 'bout et?"

"Jes' lemme stop till dey's gone by. Hide me till dey passes. Reckon dey ain't fur off now." His begging voice changed to a frightened whimper. "Foh de Lawd's sake, Mis' Poole, lemme stop."

And why, the woman inquired caustically, should she run the dangerous risk of hiding him?

"Obadiah, he'd lemme stop ef he was to home," the man whined.

Annie Poole sighed. "Yas," she admitted slowly, reluctantly, "Ah spec' he would. Obadiah, he's too good to youall no 'count trash." Her slight shoulders lifted in a hopeless shrug. "Yas, Ah reckon he'd do et. Emspecial' seein' how he allus set such a heap o' store by you. Cain't see w'at foh, mahse'f. Ah shuah don' see nuffin' in you but a heap o' dirt."

But a look of irony, of cunning, of complicity passed over her face. She went on, "Still, 'siderin' all an' all, how Obadiah's right fon' o' you, an' how white folks is white folks, Ah'm a-gwine hide you dis one time."

Crossing the kitchen, she opened a door leading into a small bedroom, saying, "Git yo'se'f in dat dere feather baid an' Ah'm a-gwine put de clo's on de top. Don' reckon dey'll fin' you ef dey does look foh you in mah house. An Ah don' spec' dey'll go foh to do dat. Not lessen you been keerless an' let 'em smell you out gittin' hyah." She turned on him a withering look. "But you allus been triflin'. Cain't do nuffin' propah. An' Ah'm a-tellin' you ef dey warn't white folks an' you a po' niggah, Ah shuah wouldn't be lettin' you mess up mah feather baid dis ebenin', 'cose Ah jes' plain don' want you hyah. Ah done kep' mahse'f outen trubble all mah life. So's Obadiah."

"Ah's powahful 'bliged to you, Mis' Poole. You shuah am one good 'oman. De Lawd'll mos' suttinly — "

Annie Poole cut him off. "Dis ain't no time foh all dat kin' o' fiddle-de-roll. Ah does mah duty as Ah sees et 'thout no thanks from you. Ef de Lawd had gib you a white face 'stead o' dat dere black one, Ah shuah would turn you out. Now hush yo' mouf an' git yo'se'f in. An' don' git movin' and scrunchin' undah dose covahs and git yo'se'f kotched in mah house."

Without further comment the man did as he was told. After he had laid his soiled body and grimy garments between her snowy sheets, Annie Poole carefully rearranged the covering and placed piles of freshly laundered linen on top. Then she gave a pat here and there, eyed the result, and, finding it satisfactory, went back to her cooking.

III

Jim Hammer settled down to the racking business of waiting until the approaching danger should have passed him by. Soon savory odors seeped in to him and he realized that he was hungry. He wished that Annie Poole would bring him something to eat. Just one biscuit. But she wouldn't, he knew. Not she. She was a hard one, Obadiah's mother.

By and by he fell into a sleep from which he was dragged back by the rumbling sound of wheels in the road outside. For a second, fear clutched so tightly at him that he almost leaped from the suffocating shelter of the bed in order to make some active attempt to escape the horror that his capture meant. There was a spasm at his heart, a pain so sharp, so slashing that he had to suppress an impulse to cry out. He felt himself falling. Down, down, down ... Everything grew dim and very distant in his memory ... Vanished ... Came rushing back.

Outside there was silence. He strained his ears. Nothing. No foot-steps. No voices. They had gone on then. Gone without even stopping to ask Annie Poole if she had seen him pass that way. A sigh of relief slipped from him. His thick lips curled in an ugly, cunning smile. It had been smart of him to think of coming to Obadiah's mother's to hide. She was an old demon, but he was safe in her house.

He lay a short while longer, listening intently, and, hearing nothing, started to get up. But immediately he stopped, his yellow eyes glowing like pale flames. He had heard the unmistakable sound of men coming toward the house. Swiftly he slid back into the heavy, hot stuffiness of the bed and lay listening fearfully.

The terrifying sounds drew nearer. Slowly. Heavily. Just for a moment he thought they were not coming in — they took so long. But there was a light knock and the noise of a door being opened. His whole body went taut. His feet felt frozen, his hands clammy, his tongue like a weighted, dying thing. His pounding heart made it hard for his straining ears to hear what they were saying out there.

"Ebenin', Mistah Lowndes." Annie Poole's voice sounded as it always did, sharp and dry.

There was no answer. Or had he missed it? With slow care he shifted his position, bringing his head nearer the edge of the bed. Still he heard nothing. What were they waiting for? Why didn't they ask about him?

Annie Poole, it seemed, was of the same mind. "Ah don' reckon youall done traipsed 'way out hyah jes' foh yo' healf," she hinted.

"There's bad news for you, Annie, I'm 'fraid." The sheriff's voice was low and queer.

Jim Hammer visualized him standing out there — a tall, stooped man, his white tobacco-stained mustache drooping limply at the ends, his nose hooked and sharp, his eyes blue and cold. Bill Lowndes was a hard one too. And white.

"W'atall bad news, Mistah Lowndes?" The woman put the question quietly, directly.

"Obadiah —" the sheriff began — hesitated — began again. "Oba-diah — ah — er, he's outside, Annie. I'm 'fraid — "

"Shucks! You done missed. Obadiah, he ain't done nuffin', Mistah Lowndes. Obadiah!" she called stridently. "Obadiah! git hyah an' splain yo'se'f."

But Obadiah didn't answer, didn't come in. Other men came in. Came in with steps that dragged and halted. No one spoke. Not even Annie Poole. Something was laid carefully upon the floor.

"Obadiah, chile," his mother said softly, "Obadiah, chile." Then, with sudden alarm, "He ain't daid, is he? Mistah Lowndes! Obadiah, he ain't daid?"

Jim Hammer didn't catch the answer to that pleading question. A new fear was stealing over him.

"There was a to-do, Annie," Bill Lowndes explained gently, "at the garage back o' the factory. Fellow tryin' to steal tires. Obadiah heerd a noise an' run out with two or three others. Scared the rascal, all right. Fired off his gun an' run. We allow et to be Jim Hammer. Picked up his cap back there. Never was no 'count. Thievin' an' sly. But we'll git 'im, Annie. We'll git 'im."

The man huddled in the feather bed prayed silently. "Oh, Lawd! Ah didn't go to do et. Not Obadiah, Lawd. You knows dat. You knows et." And into his frenzied brain came the thought that it would be better for him to get up and go out to them before Annie Poole gave him away. For he was lost now. With all his great strength he tried to get himself out of the bed. But he couldn't.

"Oh, Lawd!" he moaned. "Oh, Lawd!" His thoughts were bitter and they ran through his mind like panic. He knew that it had come to pass as it said somewhere in the Bible about the wicked. The Lord had stretched out his hand and smitten him. He was paralyzed. He couldn't move hand or foot. He moaned again. It was all there was left for him to do. For in the terror of this new calamity that had come upon him, he had forgotten the waiting danger which was so near out there in the kitchen.

His hunters, however, didn't hear him. Bill Lowndes was saying, "We been a-lookin' for Jim out along the old road. Figured he'd make tracks for Shawboro. You ain't noticed anybody pass this evenin', Annie?"

The reply came promptly, unwaveringly. "No, Ah ain't sees nobody pass. Not yet."

IV

Jim Hammer caught his breath.

"Well," the sheriff concluded, "we'll be gittin' along. Obadiah was a mighty fine boy. Ef they was all like him — I'm sorry, Annie. Anything I c'n do, let me know."

"Thank you, Mistah Lowndes."

With the sound of the door closing on the departing men, power to move came back to the man in the bedroom. He pushed his dirt-caked feet out from the covers and rose up, but crouched down again. He wasn't cold now, but hot all over and burning. Almost he wished that Bill Lowndes and his men had taken him with them.

Annie Poole had come into the room.

It seemed a long time before Obadiah's mother spoke. When she did there were no tears, no reproaches; but there was a raging fury in her voice as she lashed out. "Git outen mah feather baid, Jim Hammer, an' outen mah house, an' don' nevah stop thankin' you' Jesus he done gib you dat black face."